PENGUIN MODERN CLASSICS

DAISY MILLER AND OTHER STORIES

Henry James was born in 1843 in Washington Place, New York, of Scottish and Irish ancestry. His father was a prominent theologian and philosopher and his elder brother, William, was also famous as a philosopher. He attended schools in New York and later in London, Paris and Geneva, entering the Law School at Harvard in 1862. In 1865 he began to contribute reviews and short stories to American journals. In 1875, after two prior visits to Europe, he settled for a year in Paris, where he met Flaubert, Turgenev, and other literary figures. However the next year he moved to London, where he became such an inveterate diner-out that in the winter of 1878–9 he confessed to accepting 107 invitations. In 1898 he left London and went to live at Lamb House, Rye, Sussex. Henry James became naturalized in 1915, was awarded the O.M., and died early in 1916.

In addition to many short stories, plays, books of criticism, autobiography and travel, he wrote some twenty novels, the first published being *Roderick Hudson* (1875). They include *The Europeans*, *Washington Square*, *The Portrait of a Lady*, *The Bostonians*, *The Princess Casamassima*, *The Spoils of Poynton*, *The Awkward Age*, *The Wings of a Dove*, *The Ambassadors* and *The Golden Bowl*.

Ante Đilić
05·06·1986.

HENRY JAMES

Daisy Miller and Other Stories

Edited with an Introduction by
MICHAEL SWAN

PENGUIN BOOKS

Penguin Books Ltd, Harmondsworth, Middlesex, England
Viking Penguin Inc., 40 West 23rd Street, New York, New York 10010, U.S.A.
Penguin Books Australia Ltd, Ringwood, Victoria, Australia
Penguin Books Canada Ltd, 2801 John Street, Markham, Ontario, Canada L3R 1B4
Penguin Books (N.Z.) Ltd, 182–190 Wairau Road, Auckland 10, New Zealand

—

The Last of the Valerii first published 1874
The Real Thing first published 1893
The Lesson of the Master first published 1888
Daisy Miller first published 1878

Published in Penguin Books as *Selected Short Stories* 1963
Reprinted 1964, 1965, 1967, 1969, 1971, 1973, 1975 (twice),
1977, 1978, 1979, 1981
Reissued as *Daisy Miller and Other Stories* 1983
Reprinted 1984, 1985

—

This selection and Introduction copyright © Michael Swan, 1963
All rights reserved

—

Set, printed and bound in Great Britain by
Cox & Wyman Ltd, Reading
Set in Monotype Times

Contents

Introduction

HENRY JAMES was born at 2 Washington Place, New York, on 15 April 1843. His father was an original and remarkable writer on questions of Swedenborgian theology. Henry James the younger was the second son, the eldest being the philosopher, William James. They received a very desultory education, at first in New York, afterwards in London, Paris, and Geneva. Henry James entered the law school at Harvard in 1862. From 1865 onwards he was a regular contributor of reviews and short tales. James's first major piece of fiction was his work *Watch and Ward* (1871).

It was during the years spent in Europe as a boy that James had absorbed once for all what he afterwards called the 'Europe virus', the nostalgia for the old world which made it impossible for him to live permanently elsewhere. In 1869, and again in 1872, he came to Europe as a tourist, lingering chiefly in Rome, Florence, and Paris. He proposed at first to settle in Paris, but after a year there he began to see that London was the place where he could best feel at home. He lived constantly in London, in lodgings off Ficcadilly or in a flat in Kensington. In 1898 he moved to Lamb House, Rye, where he mainly lived for the rest of his life, and where all his later work was written. He never married. He died in London in 1916.

The four short stories of Henry James which have been selected for this volume, reveal the genius which puts him among the finest of the world's short-story writers. From the whimsical to the profound, from the horrific to the romantic, from the brilliant to the light-hearted, these stories have been chosen not only to entertain the devotee of Henry James, but also to help those who are approaching this brilliant writer for the first time.

Nearly half of Henry James's fiction is composed of stories of varying length; the long short story was a form he loved – 'the dear, the blessed *nouvelle*' he called it – and the best of his stories rank among his finest work. They are the best introduction to his work. Often they would be like a sculptor's maquettes; new techniques or themes would first be tried out in his stories and later receive full treatment in his novels. They suited his temperament specially well because he was always interested in 'the particular case' and the unique circumstances; one subject would be studied intimately. His difficulty always seems to have been not to overload his fragile anecdote with complicated developments and yet to make it alive with 'vivid values', knowing all the time that all that is of greatest value in the story 'will have been preponderantly drawn from the depths of the designer's own mind'. He aimed always to make 'chemical reductions and condensations' so that they would be as hard and as shining and as indestructible as a sonnet.

James set out to be a naturalist – Flaubert and Turgenev were his masters and his early travel letters are those of a young man enjoying things seen, the exuberance of contemplating the Colosseum, or the difference between London and Boston tea-parties. These letters are as vital a part of James's writings as are his *Notebooks*, where every observation, every chance conversation is noted down and worked on, and where we find the germ of his stories and novels. Nothing escaped his eye and in the *Notebooks* what he once called the deep well of unconscious cerebration is constantly formulating ideas into stories or novels. He plays with situations, gives them the ironic twist or the missing symmetry which the best *raconteurs* offer their listeners. He mastered the technique of naturalism, making real, intelligent people of the material he had observed, rather than mere characters – 'a certain character', he told his brother William, 'was evolved entirely from my moral consciousness, like every other person I have ever drawn.' I gather he meant that he never drew entirely from *one* particular person. In his early period, when the plots and ideas of his novels were as naturalistic as their treatment, James, in his stories, found a certain freedom in which he could expand his imagination, with the result that later the naturalistic treatment was often at war with the content. His development can be seen in the gradual resolution of this split.

The Last of the Valerii (*Atlantic Monthly*, 1874) is a good example of this first important period in his story writing and shows the unusually intense interest the author had in the super-natural. The Count Valerio discovers a Juno of such beauty in his garden that he neglects his wife and falls in love with the statue. Only when the Juno is buried again does he return to his wife. The Greeks believed that there is poetry in writing of something which is impossible and yet saying nothing but what is true, and though James here suspends our disbelief almost enough to convince us that he has a particle of truth to offer, though there is a straining towards symbolism, the story is ulti-mately nothing more than an exquisite ghost story. The idea of a living creature falling in love with an image of beauty seems to have fascinated James, and with courage it could be said that it symbolizes his retreat from reality. It may have been the result of the close contact with Swedenborgian mysticism which he had experienced through his father which made him become the most subtle and complicated imagist ever to write fiction. His ideas, even his conversation, was conveyed with a plurality of images – everything is capable of being an image of something else.

The Real Thing, for instance, is an ironic playing with the old theme of reality, or retreat from reality. An artist discovers that he can draw his scenes of high life better with a servant girl and an ice-cream vendor as models than with Major and Mrs Monarch, who are the real thing. The texture of the writing is simpler, and the idea, which is an obvious allegory of James's own ideas about art, need not be taken too literally in its par-ticular instance. It was the truth of the situation which concerned him most.

James has been called the master of the situation, but it is inevitably a tragic situation. Frustration, unachieved love, loss of some kind, the tragedy of ignorance – all these 'situations' appear constantly throughout his stories, even in the lightest. Think of Paul Overt's loss of the girl he loves to the man who advised him never to marry in order to preserve himself for his art. *The Lesson of the Master* (*Universal Review*, 1888) is one of the finest examples of the master–disciple theme ever expounded by a writer. Henry St George, a mature, married novelist, has never had 'that sense of having drawn from his intellectual instrument the finest music that nature has hidden in it', and believes that his failure is due to his marriage, happy though it is. He therefore advises young Overt, who is in love with a girl they both know, not to marry her. So far, one would say, this shows James's satisfaction with the bachelor state, but when St George himself on his wife's death marries the girl, a new element arrives. James questions himself as to the possibilities of marriage and the happiness it can bring. And yet James's tragic view is made so charmingly light and deceptive that it is easy to be unconscious of it. In fact his tragedies are rarely big ones.

The 'international situation' is yet another famous Jamesian situation. James was the first novelist to see the possibilities of drama in the Europe–America relationship. In his early thirties, when still wandering round Europe in search of something he couldn't quite comprehend, he became anxious to discover what lay behind the glorious façades of Europe, to know the meaning of the European thought and tradition, how it differed from that of America, and what were the effects of the one on the other. He found it to be a matter of age and experience. This alone sounds like the basis of a story about the innocent abroad, the image of *Daisy Miller* (*Cornhill Magazine*, 1878), who represented the all-American girl, brash, even vulgar, yet still appealing. A girl who finds herself unable to conform to the code of behaviour in Roman society. Because she is innocent she can see no wrong in her behaviour; experience comes to her, but she is unable to profit by it. Daisy flirts in the Colosseum by moonlight, catches malaria, and dies. Again the issues are ambivalent: Europe stands for the outward propriety which its wisdom would demand; America for a naturalness which does not take into account the possibility of immorality. Through her death, James poetically sacrifices Daisy to Europe, just as he sacrificed Roderick, Newman, and Isabel. Europe is master and has eaten well the forbidden fruit.

It is not easy in a one-volume selection to show James's development from his middle twenties to his late sixties, and so show him as a writer of great variety. This is due to his inability to economize on the length of his 'short' stories. I believe that his best stories are among the finest ever written and are the only way in which one can begin to approach James. They are all blessedly readable. He tried hard to be interesting all the time, to hold the attention and plant his surprises; he constructed excellent plots with the classical requirements of a beginning, a middle, and an end. The 'figure in the carpet', the ultimate meaning of his work, may be an obscure one, but the stories can be understood and enjoyed simply as very good short stories.

MICHAEL SWAN

Notes on the Texts

The Last of the Valerii was first published in the *Atlantic Monthly* in 1874, and in book form in *A Passionate Pilgrim* (Osgood, Boston, 1875), which is the text used in this edition. It was not reprinted in the New York Edition of *The Novels and Tales* (Charles Scribner's Sons, New York, 1907–17), but appears in volume XXVI of *The Novels and Stories of Henry James*, the new and complete edition in thirty-five volumes (Macmillan, London, 1921–3) which was edited, with prefatory notes, by Percy Lubbock.

The Real Thing was first published in *The Real Thing and Other Tales* (Macmillan, New York and London, 1893) which is the text used in this edition. It appears in a revised version in volume XVIII of the New York Edition.

The Lesson of the Master was first published in the *Universal Review* in 1888, and in book form in *The Lesson of the Master* (Macmillan, New York and London, 1892), which is the text used in this edition. It appears in a revised version in volume XV of the New York Edition.

Daisy Miller was first published in the *Cornhill Magazine* in 1878, and in book form in *Daisy Miller. A Study* (Harper, New York, and Macmillan, London, 1879), which is the text used in this edition. It appears with other new and revised tales in volume XVIII of the New York Edition.

The Last of the Valerii

I HAD had occasion to declare more than once that if my god-daughter married a foreigner I should refuse to give her away. And yet when the young Conte Valerio was presented to me, in Rome, as her accepted and plighted lover, I found myself looking at the happy fellow, after a momentary stare of amazement, with a certain paternal benevolence; thinking, indeed, that from the pictorial point of view (she with her yellow locks and he with his dusky ones) they were a strikingly well-assorted pair. She brought him up to me half proudly, half timidly, pushing him before her and begging me with one of her dove-like glances to be very polite. I don't know that I usually miss that effect, but she was so deeply impressed with his grandeur that she thought it impossible to do him honour enough. The Conte Valerio's grandeur was doubtless nothing for a young American girl who had the air and almost the habits of a princess, to sound her trumpet about; but she was desperately in love with him, and not only her heart, but her imagination, was touched. He was extremely handsome, and with a beauty which was less a matter of mere fortunate surface than usually happens in the handsome Roman race. There was a latent tenderness in his admirable mask, and his grave, slow smile, if it suggested no great nimble-ness of wit, spoke of a manly constancy which promised well for Martha's happiness. He had little of the light, inexpensive urban-ity of his countrymen, and there was a kind of stupid sincerity in his gaze; it seemed to suspend response until he was sure he understood you. He was certainly a little dense, and I fancied that to a political or aesthetic question the response would be particularly slow. 'He is good and strong and brave,' the young girl however assured me; and I easily believed her. Strong the Conte Valerio certainly was; he had a head and throat like some of the busts in the Vatican. To my eye, which has looked at things now so long with the painter's purpose, it was a real annoyance to see such a throat rising out of the white cravat

of the period. It sustained a head as massively round as that of
the familiar bust of the Emperor Caracalla, and covered with
the same dense sculptural crop of curls. The young man's hair
grew superbly; it was such hair as the old Romans must have
had when they walked bareheaded and bronzed about the world.
It made a perfect arch over his low, clear forehead, and prolonged
itself on cheek and chin in a close, crisp beard, strong with its
own strength and unstiffened by the razor. Neither his nose nor
his mouth was delicate; but they were powerful, shapely, masculine. His complexion was of a deep glowing brown, which no
emotion would alter, and his large, lucid eyes seemed to stare at
you like a pair of polished agates. He was of middle stature, and
his chest was of so generous a girth that you half expected to
hear his linen crack with its even respirations. And yet, with his
simple human smile, he looked neither like a young bullock
nor a gladiator. His powerful voice was the least bit harsh, and
his large, ceremonious reply to my compliment had the massive
sonority with which civil speeches must have been uttered in the
age of Augustus. I had always considered my goddaughter a
very American little person, in all honourable meanings of the
word, and I doubted if this sturdy young Latin would understand
the transatlantic element in her nature; but, evidently, he would
make her a loyal and ardent lover. She seemed to me, in her
tinted prettiness, so tender, so appealing, so bewitching, that it
was impossible to believe he had more thoughts for all this than
for the equally pretty fortune which it yet bothered me to believe
that he must, like a good Italian, have taken the exact measure of.
His own worldly goods consisted of the paternal estate, a villa
within the walls of Rome, which his scanty funds had suffered
to fall into sombre disrepair. 'It's the Villa she's in love with,
quite as much as the Count,' said her mother. 'She dreams of
converting the Count; that's all very well. But she dreams of
refurnishing the Villa!'

The upholsterers were turned into it, I believe, before the wedding, and there was a great scrubbing and sweeping of saloons
and raking and weeding of alleys and avenues. Martha made
frequent visits of inspection while these ceremonies were taking
place; but one day, on her return, she came into my little studio

with an air of amusing horror. She had found them *scraping* the sarcophagus in the great ilex-walk; divesting it of its mossy coat, disincrusting it of the sacred green mould of the ages! This was their idea of making the Villa comfortable. She had made them transport it to the dampest place they could find; for, next after that slow-coming, slow-going smile of her lover, it was the rusty complexion of his patrimonial marbles that she most prized. The young Count's conversion proceeded less rapidly, and indeed I believe that his betrothed brought little zeal to the affair. She loved him so devoutly that she believed no change of faith could better him, and she would have been willing for his sake to say her prayers to the sacred Bambino at the feast of the Epiphany. But he had the good taste to demand no such sacrifice, and I was struck with the happy significance of a scene of which I was an accidental observer. It was at St. Peter's, one Friday afternoon, during the vesper-service which takes place in the chapel of the choir. I met my goddaughter wandering serenely on her lover's arm, her mother being established on her camp-stool, near the entrance of the place. The crowd was collected thereabouts, and the body of the church was empty. Now and then the high voices of the singers escaped into the outer vastness and melted slowly away in the incense-thickened air. Something in the young girl's step and the clasp of her arm in her lover's told me that her contentment was perfect. As she threw back her head and gazed into the magnificent immensity of vault and dome, I felt that she was in that enviable mood in which all consciousness revolves on a single centre, and that her sense of the splendours around her was one with the ecstasy of her trust. They stopped before that sombre group of polyglot confessionals which proclaims so portentously the sinfulness of the world, and Martha seemed to make some almost passionate protestation. A few minutes later I overtook them.

'Don't you agree with me, dear friend,' said the Count, who always addressed me with the most affectionate deference, 'that before I marry so pure and sweet a creature as this, I ought to go into one of those places and confess every sin I ever was guilty of – every evil thought and impulse and desire of my grossly evil nature?'

Martha looked at him, half in deprecation, half in homage, with an eye which seemed at once to insist that her lover could have no vices and to plead that if he had there would be something magnificent in them. 'Listen to him!' she said, smiling. 'The list would be long, and if you waited to finish it, you would be late for the wedding. But if you confess your sins for me, it's only fair I should confess mine for you. Do you know what I have been saying to Marco?' she added, turning to me with the half-filial confidence she had always shown me and with a rosy glow in her cheeks; 'that I want to do something more for him than girls commonly do for their intended – to take some great step, to run some risk, to break some law, even! I am quite willing to change my religion, if he bids me. There are moments when I am terribly tired of simply staring at Catholicism; it will be a relief to come into a church to kneel. That, after all, is what they are meant for! Therefore, Marco *mio*, if it casts a shade across your heart to think that I'm a heretic, I will go and kneel down to that good old priest who has just entered the confessional yonder, and say to him, "My father, I repent, I abjure, I believe. Baptize me in the only faith."'

'If it's as a compliment to the Count,' I said, 'it seems to me he ought to anticipate it by giving up, for you, something equally important.'

She had spoken lightly and with a smile, and yet with an undertone of girlish ardour. The young man looked at her with a solemn, puzzled face, and shook his head. 'Keep your religion,' he said. 'Everyone his own. If you should attempt to embrace mine, I am afraid you would close your arms about a shadow. I am not a good Catholic, a good Christian! I don't understand all these chants and ceremonies and splendours. When I was a child I never could learn my catechism. My poor old confessor long ago gave me up; he told me I was a good boy, but a *pagan*! You must not be more devout than your husband. I don't understand your religion any better, but I beg you not to change it for mine. If it has helped to make you what you are, it must be good.' And taking the young girl's hand, he was about to raise it affectionately to his lips; but suddenly remembering that they were in a place unaccordant with profane passions, he lowered it with a comical smile. 'Let us go,' he murmured, passing his hand over his forehead. 'This heavy atmosphere of St Peter's always stupefies me.'

They were married in the month of May, and we separated for the summer, the Contessa's mamma going to illuminate the domestic circle, beyond the sea, with her reflected dignity. When I returned to Rome in the autumn I found the young couple established at the Villa Valerio, which was now partly reclaimed from its antique decay. I begged that the hand of improvement might be lightly laid on it, for as an unscrupulous old painter of ruins and relics, with an eye to 'subjects', I preferred that crumbling things should be allowed to crumble at their ease. My goddaughter was quite of my way of thinking; she had a high appreciation of antiquity. Advising with me, often, as to projected changes, she was sometimes more conservative even than I, and I more than once smiled at her archaeological zeal, declaring that I believed she had married the Count because he was like a statue of the Decadence. I had a constant invitation to spend my days at the Villa, and my easel was always planted in one of the garden-walks. I grew to have a painter's passion for the place, and to be intimate with every tangled shrub and twisted tree, every moss-coated vase and mouldy sarcophagus and sad, disfeatured bust of those grim old Romans who could so ill afford to become more meagre-visaged. The place was of small extent; but though there were many other villas more pretentious and splendid, none seemed to me more exquisitely romantic, more haunted by the ghosts of the past. There were memories in the fragrance of the untended flowers, in the hum of the insects. It contained, among other idle, untrimmed departments, an old ilex-walk, in which I used religiously to spend half an hour every day – half an hour being, I confess, just as long as I could stay without beginning to sneeze. The trees arched and intertwisted over the dusky vista in the most perfect symmetry; and as it was exposed uninterruptedly to the west, the low evening sun used to transfuse it with a sort of golden mist and play through it – over leaves and knotty boughs and mossy marbles – with a thousand crimson fingers. It was filled with disinterred fragments of sculpture – nameless statues and noseless heads and rough-hewn sarcophagi, which made it deliciously solemn. The statues used to stand in the perpetual twilight like conscious things, brooding on their long observations. I used to linger near them, half expecting they would speak and tell me their stony secrets – whisper hoarsely the whereabouts of their mouldering fellows, still unrecovered from the soil.

My goddaughter was idyllically happy and absolutely in love. I was obliged to confess that even rigid rules have their exceptions, and that now and then an Italian count is as genuine as possible. Marco was a perfect original (not a copy), and seemed quite content to be appreciated. Their life was a childlike interchange of caresses, as candid and natural as those of a shepherd and shepherdess in a bucolic poem. To stroll in the ilex-walk and feel her husband's arm about her waist and his shoulder against her cheek; to roll cigarettes for him while he puffed them in the great marble-paved rotunda in the centre of the house; to fill his glass from an old rusty red amphora – these graceful occupations satisfied the young Countess.

She rode with him sometimes in the grassy shadow of aqueducts and tombs, and sometimes suffered him to show his beautiful wife at Roman dinners and balls. She played dominoes with him after dinner, and carried out, in a desultory way, a scheme of reading him the daily papers. This observance was subject to fluctuations caused by the Count's invincible tendency to go to sleep – a failing his wife never attempted to disguise or palliate. She would sit and brush the flies from him while he lay statuesquely snoring, and, if I ventured near him, would place her finger on her lips and whisper that she thought her husband was as handsome asleep as awake. I confess I often felt tempted to reply that he was at least quite as entertaining, for the young man's happiness had not multiplied the topics on which he readily conversed. He had plenty of good sense, and his opinion on any practical matter was usually worth having. He would often come and sit near me while I worked at my easel, and offer a friendly criticism on what I was doing. His taste was a little crude, but his eye was excellent, and his measurement of the correspondence between some feature of my sketch and the object I was trying to reproduce, as trustworthy as that of a mathematical instrument. But he seemed to me to have either a strange reserve or a still stranger simplicity, to be fundamentally unfurnished with anything remotely resembling an idea. He had no beliefs nor hopes nor fears – nothing but senses, appetites, serenely luxurious tastes. As I watched him strolling about while he looked at his finger-nails, I often wondered whether he had anything that could properly be termed a soul, and whether good health and good nature were not the sum total of his advantages. 'It's lucky he's good natured,' I used to say to myself; 'for if he were not, there is nothing in his conscience to· keep him in order. If he had irritable nerves instead of quiet ones, he would strangle us as the infant Hercules strangled the poor little snakes. He's the natural man! Happily, his nature is gentle; I can mix my colours at my ease.' I wondered what he thought about and what passed through his mind in the sunny idleness that seemed to shut him in from the modern work-a-day world, of which, in spite of my passion for bedaubing old panels with ineffective portraiture of mouldy statues against screens of box, I still flattered myself I was a member. I went so far as to believe that he sometimes withdrew from the world altogether. He had moods in which his consciousness seemed so remote and his mind so irresponsive and inarticulate, that nothing but some fresh endearment or some sudden violence could have power to arouse him. Even his tenderness for his wife had a quality which made me uneasy. Whether or no he had a soul himself, he seemed not to suspect that she had one. I took a godfatherly interest in the development of her immortal part. I fondly believed her to be a creature susceptible of a moral life. But what was becoming of her moral life in this interminable heathenish honeymoon? Some fine day she would find herself tired of the Count's *beaux yeux* and make an appeal to his mind. She had, to my knowledge, plans of study, of charity, of worthily playing her part as a Contessa Valerio – a position as to which the family records furnished the most inspiring examples. But if the Count found the newspapers soporific, I doubted whether he would turn Dante's pages very fast for his wife, or smile with much zest at the anecdotes of Vasari. How could he advise her, instruct her, sustain her? And if she should become a mother, how could he share her responsibilities? He doubtless would transmit his little son and heir a stout pair of arms and legs and a magnificent crop of curls, and sometimes remove his cigarette to kiss a dimpled spot; but I found it hard to picture him lending his voice to teach the lusty urchin his alphabet or his prayers, or the rudiments of infant virtue. One accomplishment indeed the Count possessed which would make him an agreeable play-fellow: he carried in his pocket a collection of precious fragments of antique pavement – bits of porphyry and malachite and lapis and basalt – disinterred on his own soil and brilliantly polished by use. With these you might see him occupied by the half-hour, playing the simple game of catch-and-toss, ranging them in a circle, tossing them in rotation, catching them on the back of his hand. His skill was remarkable; he would send a stone five feet into the air, and pitch and catch and transpose the rest before he received it again. I watched with affectionate jealousy for the signs of a dawning sense, on Martha's part, that she was the least bit oddly mated. Once or twice, as the weeks went by, I fancied I read them, and that she looked at me with eyes which seemed to remember certain old talks of mine in which I had declared – with such verity as you please – that a Frenchman, an Italian, a Spaniard, might be a very good fellow, but that he never really respected the woman he pretended to love. For the most part, however, my alarms, suspicions, prejudices, spent them-selves easily in the charmed atmosphere of our romantic, our classical home. We were out of the modern world and had no business with modern scruples. The place was so bright, so still, so sacred to the silent, imperturbable past, that drowsy content-ment seemed a natural law; and sometimes when, as I sat at my work, I saw my companions passing arm in arm across the end of one of the long-drawn vistas, and, turning back to my palette, found my colours dimmer for the radiant vision, I could easily have believed that I was some old monkish chronicler or copyist, engaged in illuminating a medieval legend.

It was a help to ungrudging feelings that the Count, yielding to his wife's urgency, had undertaken a series of systematic excavations. To excavate is an expensive luxury, and neither Marco nor his later forefathers had possessed the means for a disinterested pursuit of archaeology. But his young wife had persuaded herself that the much-trodden soil of the Villa was as full of buried treasures as a bride-cake of plums, and that it would be a pretty compliment to the ancient house which had accepted her as mistress to devote a portion of her dowry to bring its mouldly honours to the light. I think she was not without a fancy that this liberal process would help to disinfect her Yankee dollars of the impertinent odour of trade. She took learned advice on the subject, and was soon ready to swear to you, proceeding from irrefutable premises, that a colossal gilt-bronze Minerva, mentioned by Strabo, was placidly awaiting resurrection at a point twenty rods from the north-west angle of the house. She had a couple of asthmatic old antiquaries to lunch, whom, having plied with unwonted potations, she walked off their legs in the grounds; and though they agreed on nothing else in the world, they individually assured her that researches properly conducted would probably yield an unequalled harvest of discoveries. The Count had been not only indifferent but even unfriendly to the scheme, and had more than once arrested his wife's complacent allusions to it by an unaccustomed acerbity of tone. 'Let them lie, the poor disinherited gods, the Minerva, the Apollo, the Ceres you are so sure of finding,' he said, 'and don't break their rest. What do you want of them? We can't worship them. Would you put them on pedestals to stare and mock at them? If you can't believe in them, don't disturb them. Peace be with them!' I remember being a good deal impressed by a confession drawn from him by his wife's playfully declaring, in answer to some remonstrances in this strain, that he was really and truly superstitious. 'Yes, by Bacchus, I *am* superstitious!' he cried. 'Too much so, perhaps! But I'm an old Italian, and you must take me as you find me. There have been things seen and done here which leave strange influences behind! They don't touch you, doubtless, who come of another race. But me they touch often, in the whisper of the leaves and the odour of the mouldly soil and the blank eyes of the old statues. I can't bear to look the statues in the face. I seem to see other strange eyes in the empty sockets, and I hardly know what they say to me. I call the poor old statues ghosts. In conscience, we have enough on the place already, lurking and peering in every shady nook. Don't dig up any more, or I won't answer for my wits!'

This account of Marco's sensibilities was too fantastic not to seem to his wife almost a joke; and though I imagined there was more in it, he made a joke so seldom that I should have been sorry to convert the poor girl's smile into a suspicion. With her smile she carried her point, and in a few days arrived a kind of archaeological expert, or commissioner, with a dozen workmen, who bristled with pickaxes and spades. For myself, I was secretly vexed at these energetic measures, for, though fond of disinterred statues, I disliked to see the soil disturbed, and deplored the profane sounds which were henceforth to jar upon the sleepy stillness of the gardens. I especially objected to the personage who conducted the operations – a little ugly, dwarfish man, who seemed altogether a subterranean genius, an earthy gnome of the underworld, and went prying about the grounds with a malicious smile which suggested more delight in the money the Signor Conte was going to bury than in the expected marbles and bronzes. When the first sod had been turned the Count's mood seemed to change very much, and his curiosity got the better of his scruples. He sniffed delightedly the odour of the humid earth, and stood watching the workmen, as they struck constantly deeper, with a kindling wonder in his eyes. Whenever a pickaxe rang against a stone he would utter a sharp cry, and be deterred from jumping into the trench only by some assurance on the part of the little expert that it was a false alarm. The near prospect of discoveries seemed to act upon his nerves, and I met him more than once strolling restlessly among his cedarn alleys, as if at last he too had learned how to reflect. He took me by the arm and made me walk with him, having much to say about the chance of a 'find'. I rather wondered at his sudden eagerness, and asked myself whether he had an eye to the past or to the future – to the intrinsic interest of possible Minervas and Apollos, or to their market value. Whenever the Count came down to the place and – as he very often did – began to berate his little army of spadesmen for dawdling, the diminutive person who superintended the operations would glance at me with a sarcastic twinkle which seemed to hint that excavations were sometimes a snare. We were kept a good while in suspense, for several false beginnings were made – the earth probed in the wrong places. The Count was discouraged – the resumption of his naps testified to it. But the master digger, who had his own ideas, shrewdly continued his labours; and as I sat at my easel I heard the spades making their gay sound as they touched the dislodged stones. Now and then I would pause, with an uncontrollable acceleration of my heart-beats. 'It *may* be,' I would say, 'that some marble masterpiece is stirring there beneath its lightening weight of earth! There are as good fish in the sea as ever were caught! What if I should be summoned to welcome another Antinous back to fame – a Venus, a Faun, an Augustus?'

One morning it seemed to me that I had been hearing for half an hour a livelier movement of voices than usual; but as I was preoccupied with a puzzling bit of work I made no inquiries. Suddenly a shadow fell across my canvas, and I turned round. The little excavator stood beside me, with a glittering eye, cap in hand, his forehead bathed in perspiration. Resting in the hollow of his arm was an earth-stained fragment of marble. In answer to my questioning glance he held it up to me, and I saw it was a woman's shapely hand. 'Come!' he simply said, and led the way to the excavation. The workmen were so closely gathered round the open trench that I saw nothing till he made them divide. Then, full in the sun, and flashing it back, almost, in spite of her dusky incrustations, I beheld, propped up with stones against a heap of earth, a majestic marble image. She seemed to me almost colossal, though I afterwards perceived that she was only of the proportions of a woman exceptionally tall. My pulses began to throb, for I felt that she was something great and it was a high privilege to be among the first to know her. Her finished beauty gave her an almost human look, and her absent eyes seemed to wonder back at us. She was amply draped, so that I saw that she was not a Venus. 'She's a Juno,' said the expert, decisively; and she seemed indeed an embodiment of celestial supremacy and repose. Her beautiful head, bound with a single band, could have bent only to give the nod of command; her eyes looked straight before her; her mouth was implacably grave; one hand, outstretched, appeared to have held a kind of imperial wand; the arm from which the other had been broken hung at her side with the most queenly majesty. The workmanship was of the greatest delicacy, and though perhaps there was more in her than usual of a certain personal expression, she was wrought, as a whole, in the large and simple manner of the great Greek period. She was a masterpiece of skill and a marvel of preservation. 'Does the Count know?' I soon asked, for I had a guilty sense that our eyes were taking something from her.

'The Signor Conte is at his siesta,' said the *padrone*, with his sceptical grin. 'We don't like to disturb him.'

'Here he comes!' cried one of the workmen, and we promptly made way for him. His siesta had evidently been suddenly broken, for his face was flushed and his hair disordered.

'Ah, my dream – my dream was right, then!' he cried, and stood staring at the image.

'What was your dream?' I asked, as his face seemed to betray more dismay than delight.

'That they had found a wonderful Juno, and that she rose and came and laid her marble hand on mine. Is that it?' said the Count, excitedly.

An awestruck '*Santissima Vergine!*' burst from one of the listening workmen.

'Yes, Signor Conte, this is the hand!' said the superintendent, holding up his perfect fragment. 'I have had it safe here this half-hour, so it can't have touched you!'

'But you are apparently right as to her being a Juno,' I said. 'Admire her at your leisure.' And I turned away; for if the Count was superstitious I didn't wish to embarrass him by my observation. I repaired to the house to carry the news to my goddaughter, whom I found slumbering – dreamlessly, it appeared – over a great archaeological octavo. 'They have touched bottom,' I said. 'They have found something Phidian or Praxitelian, at the very least!' She dropped her octavo, and rang for a parasol. I described the statue, but not graphically, I presume, for Martha gave a little sarcastic grimace.

'A long, fluted peplum?' she said. 'How very odd! I don't believe she's beautiful.'

'She's beautiful enough to make you jealous, *figlioccia mia*,' I replied.

We found the Count standing before the resurgent goddess in fixed contemplation, with folded arms. He seemed to have recovered from the impression of his dream, but I thought his face betrayed a still deeper emotion. He was pale, and gave no response as his wife affectionately clasped his arm. I am not sure, however, that his wife's attitude was not a livelier tribute to the perfection of the image. She had been laughing at my rhapsody as we walked from the house, and I had bethought myself of an assertion I had somewhere seen, that women lack the perception of the purest beauty. Martha, however, seemed slowly to measure our Juno's infinite stateliness. She gazed a long time, silently, leaning against her husband, and then stepped, half timidly, down upon the stones which formed a rough base for the figure. She laid her two rosy, ungloved hands upon the stony fingers of the goddess, and remained for some moments pressing them in her warm grasp and fixing her living eyes upon the sightless brow. When she turned round, her eyes were bright with the tear which deep admiration sometimes calls forth and which, in this case, her husband was too much absorbed to notice. He had apparently given orders that the workmen should be treated to a cask of wine, in honour of their discovery. It was now brought and opened on the spot, and the little expert, having drawn the first glass, stepped forward, hat in hand, and obsequiously presented it to the Countess. She only moistened her lips with it and passed it to her husband. He raised it mechanically to his own; then suddenly he stopped, held it a moment aloft, and poured it out slowly and solemnly at the feet of the Juno.

'Why, it's a libation!' I cried. He made no answer, and walked slowly away.

There was no more work done that day. The labourers lay on the grass, gazing with the native Roman relish of a fine piece of sculpture, but wasting no wine in pagan ceremonies. In the evening the Count paid the Juno another visit, and gave orders that on the morrow she should be transferred to the casino. The casino was a deserted garden-house, built in not ungraceful imitation of an Ionic temple, in which Marco's ancestors must often have assembled to drink cool syrups from Venetian glasses and listen to madrigals and other *concetti*. It contained several dusty fragments of antique sculpture, and it was spacious enough to enclose that richer collection of which I began fondly to regard the Juno as but the nucelus. Here, with short delay, this fine creature was placed, serenely upright, a reversed funereal *cippus* forming a sufficiently solid pedestal. The small superintendent, who seemed a thorough adept in all the offices of restoration, rubbed her and scraped her with mysterious art, removed her earthy stains, gave her back the lustre of her beauty. Her firm, fine surface seemed to glow with a kind of renascent purity and bloom, and but for her broken hand you might have fancied she had just received the last stroke of the chisel. Her presence remained no secret. Within two or three days half a dozen inquisitive *conoscenti* posted out to obtain sight of her. I happened to be present when the first of these gentlemen (a German in blue spectacles, with a portfolio under his arm) presented himself at the Villa. The Count, hearing his voice at the door, came forward and eyed him coldly from head to foot.

'Your new Juno, Signor Conte,' began the German, 'is, in my opinion, much more likely to be a certain Proserpine – '

'I have neither a Juno nor a Proserpine to discuss with you,' said the Count, curtly. 'You are misinformed.'

'You have dug up no statue?' cried the German. 'What a scandalous hoax!'

'None worthy of your learned attention. I am sorry you should have the trouble of carrying your little notebook so far.' The Count had suddenly become witty!

'But you have something, surely. The rumour is running through Rome.'

'The rumour be damned!' cried the Count, savagely. 'I have *nothing* – do you understand? Be so good as to say so to your friends!'

The answer was explicit, and the poor archaeologist departed, tossing his flaxen mane. But I pitied him, and vetured to remonstrate with the Count. 'She might as well be still in the earth, if no one is to see her,' I said.

'*I* am to see her: that's enough!' he answered with the same unnatural harshness. Then, in a moment, as he caught me eyeing him askance, in troubled surprise, 'I hated his great portfolio. He was going to make some hideous drawing of her.'

'Ah, that touches me,' I said. 'I too have been planning to make a little sketch.'

He was silent for some moments, after which he turned and grasped my arm, with less irritation, but with extraordinary gravity. 'Go in there towards twilight,' he said, 'and sit for an hour and look at her. I think you will give up your sketch. If you don't, my good old friend – you are welcome!'

I followed his advice, and, as a friend, I gave up my sketch. But an artist is an artist, and I secretly longed to attempt one. Orders strictly in accordance with the Count's reply to our German friend were given to the servants, who, with an easy Italian conscience and a gracious Italian persuasiveness, assured all subsequent inquirers that they had been lamentably misinformed. I have no doubt, indeed, that, in default of larger opportunity, they made condolence remunerative. Further operations were, for the present, suspended, as implying an affront to the incomparable Juno. The workmen departed, but the little adept still haunted the premises and sounded the soil for his own entertainment. One day he came to me with his usual ambiguous grimace. 'The beautiful hand of the Juno,' he murmured; 'what has become of it?'

'I have not seen it since you called me to look at her. I remember that when I went away it was lying on the grass, near the excavation.'

'Where I placed it myself! After that it disappeared. *Pare impossibile!*'

'Do you suspect one of your workmen? Such a fragment as that would bring more scudi than most of them ever looked at.'

'Some, perhaps, are greater thieves than the others. But if I were to call up the greatest rascal of the lot and accuse him, the Count would interfere.'

'He must value that beautiful hand, nevertheless.'

My friend the resurrectionist looked about him and winked.

'He values it so much that he himself purloined it. That's my belief, and I think that the less we say about it the better.'

'Purloined it, my dear sir? After all, it's his own property.'

'Not so much as that comes to! So beautiful a creature is more or less the property of everyone; we have all a right to look at her. But the Count treats her as if she were a sacrosanct image of the Madonna. He keeps her under lock and key, and pays her solitary visits. What does he do, after all? When a beautiful woman is in stone, all one can do is to look at her. And what does he do with that precious hand? He keeps it in a silver box; he has made a relic of it!' And this cynical personage began to chuckle grotesquely as he walked away.

He left me musing, uncomfortably, and wondering what the deuce he meant. The Count certainly chose to make a mystery of the Juno, but this seemed a natural incident of the first rapture of possession. I was willing to wait for permission to approach her, and in the meantime I was glad to find that there was a limit to his constitutional apathy. But as the days elapsed I began to be conscious that his enjoyment was not communicative, but strangely cold and shy and sombre. That he should admire a marble goddess was no reason for his despising mankind; yet he really seemed to be making invidious comparisons between us. From this ridiculous proscription his charming wife was not excepted. At moments when I tried to persuade myself that he was neither worse nor better company than usual, the expression of her face contradicted this superficial view. She said nothing, but she wore a look of really touching perplexity. She sat at times with her eyes fixed on him with a kind of imploring curiosity, as if for the present she were too much surprised to be angry. What passed between them in private, I had, of course, no warrant to inquire. Nothing, I suspected – and that was the misery! It was part of the misery, too, that he was impenetrable to these mute glances, and looked over her head with an air of superb abstraction. Occasionally he seemed to notice that I too didn't know what to make of his condition, and then for a moment his dull eye would sparkle, half, as it appeared, with a kind of sinister irony, and half with an impulse strangely stifled, as soon as he felt it, to justify himself. But from his wife he kept his face inexorably averted; and when she approached him with some melancholy attempt at fondness he received it with an ill-concealed shudder. The situation struck me as tremendously queer, and I grew to hate the Count and everything that belonged to him. 'I was a thousand times right,' I cried; 'an Italian count may be mighty fine, but he won't *wear*! Give us some wholesome young fellow of our own blood, who will play us none of these dusky old-world tricks. Artist as I have aspired to be, I will never again recommend a husband with traditions!' I lost my pleasure in the Villa, in the violet shadows and amber lights, the mossy marbles and the long-trailing profile of the Alban Hills. My painting stood still; everything looked ugly. I sat and fumbled with my palette, and seemed to be mixing mud with my colours. My head was stuffed with dismal thoughts; an intolerable weight settled itself on my heart. The poor Count became, to my imagination, a dark efflorescence of the evil germs which history had implanted in his line. No wonder he was foredoomed to be cruel. Was not cruelty a tradition in his race, and crime an example? The unholy passions of his forefathers revived, incurably, in his untaught nature and clamoured dumbly for an issue. What a heavy heritage it seemed to me, as I reckoned it up in my melancholy musings, the Count's interminable ancestry! Back to the profligate revival of arts and vices – back to the bloody medley of medieval wars – back through the long, fitfully glaring dusk of the early ages to its ponderous origin in the solid Roman state – back through all the darkness of history it stretched itself, losing every claim on my sympathies as it went. Such a record was in itself a curse, and my dear girl had expected it to sit as lightly and gratefully on her consciousness as her feather on her hat! I have little idea how long this painful situation lasted. It seemed the longer from my goddaughter's persistent reticence and my inability to offer her a word of consolation. A sensitive woman, disappointed in marriage, exhausts her own ingenuity before she takes counsel of others. The Count's preoccupations, whatever they were, made him increasingly restless; he came and went at random, with nervous abruptness; he took long rides alone, and, as I inferred, rarely went through the form of excusing himself to his wife; and still, as time went on, he came no nearer explaining his mystery. With the lapse of the months, however, I confess that my anxiety began to be tempered with compassion. If I had expected to see him propitiate his inexorable ancestry by the commission of a misdeed, now that his honest nature appeared to have refused them this satisfaction, I felt a sort of grudging gratitude. A man couldn't be so infernally blue without being, however little he might confess it, in want of sympathy. He had always treated me with that antique deference to a grizzled beard for which elderly men reserve the cream of their general tenderness for waning fashions, and I thought it possible he would suffer me at last to lay a healing hand upon his trouble. One evening, when I had taken leave of my goddaughter .and given her, in a silent kiss, my rather ineffectual blessing, I came out and found the Count sitting in the garden in the mild star-light, and staring at a mouldy Hermes, planted in a clump of oleander. I sat down by him and informed him in definite terms that his conduct required an explanation. He half turned his head, and his dark pupil gleamed an instant.

'I understand,' he said; 'you think me crazy!' And he tapped his forehead.

'No, not crazy, but unhappy. And if unhappiness runs its course too freely, of course, it's a great strain upon the mind.'

He was silent awhile, and then – 'I am not unhappy!' he cried, abruptly. 'I am tremendously happy. You wouldn't believe the satisfaction I take in sitting here and staring at that old weather-worn Hermes. Formerly I used to be afraid of him; his frown used to remind me of a bushy-browed old priest who taught me Latin and looked at me terribly over the book when I stumbled in my Virgil. But now it seems to me the friendliest, jolliest thing in the world, and suggests the most delightful images. He stood pouting his great lips in some old Roman's garden two thousand years ago. He saw the sandalled feet treading the alleys, and the rose-crowned heads bending over the wine; he knew the old feasts and the old worships, the old believers and the old gods. As I sit here he speaks to me, in his own dumb way, and des-cribes it all! No, no, my friend, I am the happiest of men!'

I had denied that I thought he was crazy, but I suddenly began to suspect it, for I found nothing reassuring in this singular rhapsody. The Hermes, for a wonder, had kept his nose; and when I reflected that my dear Countess was being neglected for this senseless pagan block, I secretly promised myself to come the next day with a hammer and deal him such a lusty blow as would make him too ridiculous for a sentimental *tête-à-tête*. Meanwhile, however, the Count's infatuation was no laughing matter, and I expressed my sincerest conviction when I said, after a pause, that I should recommend him to see either a priest or a physician.

He burst into uproarious laughter. 'A priest! What should I do with a priest, or he with me? I never loved them, and I feel less like beginning than ever. A priest, my dear friend,' he repeated, laying his hand on my arm, 'don't set a priest at me, if you value *his* sanity! My confession would frighten the poor man out of his wits. As for a doctor, I never was better in my life; and unless,' he added abruptly, rising and eyeing me askance, 'you want to poison me, in Christian charity I advise you to leave me alone.'

Decidedly, the Count *was* unsound, and I had no heart, for some days, to go back to the Villa. How should I treat him, what stand should I take, what course did Martha's happiness and dignity demand? I wandered about Rome, turning over these questions, and one afternoon found myself in the Pantheon. A light spring shower had begun to fall, and I hurried for refuge into the big rotunda which its Christian altars have but half converted into a church. No Roman monument retains a deeper impress of ancient life, or has more of the form of the antique faiths whose temples were nobler than their gods. The huge dusky dome seems to the spiritual ear to hold a vague reverberation of pagan worship, as a shell picked up on the beach holds the rumour of the sea. Three or four persons were scattered before the various altars; another stood near the centre, beneath the aperture in the dome. As I drew near I perceived this was the Count. He was planted with his hands behind him, looking up first at the heavy rain-clouds, as they crossed the great bull's-eye, and then down at the besprinkled circle on the pavement. In those days the pavement was rugged and cracked and magnificently old, and this ample space, in free communion with the weather, had become as mouldy and mossy and verdant as a strip of garden-soil. A tender herbage had sprung up in the crevices of the slabs, and the little microscopic shoots were twinkling in the rain. This great weather-current, through the uncapped vault, deadens effectively the customary odours of incense and tallow, and transports one to a faith that was on terms of reciprocity with nature. It seemed to have performed this office for the Count; his face wore an indefinable expression of ecstasy, and he was so rapt in contemplation that it was some time before he noticed me. The sun was struggling through the clouds without, and yet a thin rain continued to fall, and came drifting down into our gloomy enclosure in a sort of illuminated drizzle. The Count watched it with the fascinated stare of a child watching a fountain, and then turned away, pressing his hand to his brow, and walked over to one of the rather perfunctory altars. Here he again stood staring, but in a moment wheeled about and returned to his former place. Just then he recognized me, and perceived, I suppose, the curious gaze I must have fixed on him. He waved me a greeting with his hand, and at last came towards me. He was in a state of nervous exaltation – doing his best to appear natural.

'This is the best place in Rome,' he murmured. 'It is worth fifty St Peter's. But do you know I never came here till the other day? I left it to the *forestieri*. They go about with their red books and their opera-glasses, and read about this and that, and think they know it. Ah! you must *feel* it – feel the beauty and fitness of that great open skylight. Now, only the wind and the rain, the sun and the cold, come down; but of old – of old' – and he touched my arm and gave me a strange smile – 'the pagan gods and goddesses used to descend through it and take their places at their altars. What a procession, when the eyes of faith could see it! Those are the things they have given us instead!' And he gave a pitiful shrug. 'I should like to pull down their pictures, overturn their candlesticks, and poison their holy-water!'

'My dear Count,' I said gently, 'you should tolerate people's honest beliefs. Would you renew the Inquisition, and in the interest of Jupiter and Mercury?'

'People wouldn't tolerate *my* belief, if they guessed it!' he cried. 'There's been a great talk about the pagan persecutions;

but the Christians persecuted as well, and the old gods were worshipped in caves and woods as well as the new. And none the worse for that! It was in caves and woods and streams, in earth and air and water, they dwelt. And there – and here, too, in spite of all your Christian lustrations – a son of old Italy may find them still!'

He had said more than he meant, and his mask had fallen. I looked at him hard, and felt a sudden outgush of the compassion we always feel for a creature irresponsibly excited. I seemed to touch the source of his trouble, and my relief was great, for my discovery made me feel like bursting into laughter. But I contented myself with smiling benignantly. He looked back at me suspiciously, as if to judge how far he had betrayed himself; and in his glance I read, somehow, that he had a conscience we could take hold of. In my gratitude I was ready to thank any gods he pleased. 'Take care, take care,' I said, 'you are saying things which if the sacristan there were to hear and report – !' and I passed my hand through his arm and led him away.

I was startled and shocked, but I was also amused and comforted. The Count had suddenly become for me a delightfully curious phenomenon, and I passed the rest of the day in meditating on the strange ineffaceability of race-characteristics. A sturdy young Latin I had called poor Marco, and he was sturdier, indeed, than I had dreamed him! Discretion was now out of place, and on the morrow I spoke to my goddaughter. She had lately been hoping, I think, that I would help her to unburden her heart, for she immediately gave way to tears and confessed that she was miserable. 'At first,' she said, 'I thought it was all fancy, and not his affection that was growing less but my exactions that were growing greater. But suddenly it settled upon me like a mortal chill – the conviction that he had ceased to care for me, that something had come between us. And the puzzling thing has been the want of possible cause in my own conduct, or of any sign that there is another woman in the case. I have racked my brain to discover what I had said, or done, or thought, to displease him! And yet he goes about like a man too deeply injured to complain. He has never uttered a harsh word or given me a reproachful look. He has simply renounced me. I have dropped out of his life.'

She spoke with such a pathetic little quiver in her voice that I was on the point of telling her that I had guessed the riddle, and that this was half the battle. But I was afraid of her incredulity. My solution was so fantastic, so apparently far-fetched, so absurd, that I resolved to wait for convincing evidence. To obtain it I continued to watch the Count, covertly and cautiously but with a vigilance which disinterested curiosity now made intensely keen. I returned to my painting, and neglected no pretext for hovering about the gardens and the neighbourhood of the casino. The Count, I think, suspected my designs, or at least my suspicions, and would have been glad to remember just what he had suffered himself to say to me in the Pantheon. But it deepened my interest in his extraordinary situation that, in so far as I could read his deeply brooding face, he seemed – half contemptuously – to have forgiven me. He gave me a glance occasionally, as he passed me, in which a kind of dumb desire for help appeared to struggle with the conviction that such a one as I would never even understand him. I was willing enough to help him, but the case was exceedingly delicate, and I wished to master the symptoms. Meanwhile, I worked and waited and wondered. Ah! I wondered, you may be sure, with an interminable wonder, and, turn it over as I would, I couldn't get used to my idea. Sometimes it offered itself to me with a perverse fascination which deprived me of all wish to interfere. The Count took the form of a precious psychological study, and refined feeling seemed to dictate a tender respect for his delusion. I envied him the force of his imagination, and I used sometimes to close my eyes with a vague desire that when I opened them I might find Apollo under the opposite tree, lazily kissing his flute, or see Diana hurrying with long steps down the ilex-walk. But for the most part my host seemed to me simply an unhappy young man, with a morbid mental twist which ought to be smoothed away as speedily as possible. If the remedy was to match the disease, however, it would have to be an extraordinary dose!

One evening, having bidden my goddaughter good night, I started on my usual walk to my lodgings in the Corso. Five minutes after leaving the villa gate I discovered that I had left my eye-glass – an object in constant use – behind me. I immediately remembered that, while painting, I had broken the string which fastened it round my neck, and had hooked it provisionally upon the twig of a flowering-almond which happened to be near me. Shortly afterwards I had gathered up my things and retired, unmindful of the glass; and now, as I needed it to read the evening paper at the Caffé Greco, there was no alternative but to retrace my steps and detach it from its twig. I easily found it, and lingered awhile to note the curious night-aspect of the spot I had been studying by daylight. The night was magnificent, and full-charged with the breath of the early Roman spring. The moon was rising fast and flinging her silver chequers into the heavy masses of shadow. Watching her at play, I strolled farther and suddenly came in sight of the casino.

Just then the moon, which for a moment had been concealed, touched with a white ray a small marble figure which adorned the pediment of this rather factitious little structure. The way it leaped into prominence suggested that a rarer spectacle was at hand, and that the same influence must be vastly becoming to the imprisoned Juno. The door of the casino was, as usual, locked, but the moonlight flooded the high-placed windows so generously that my curiosity became obstinate and inventive. I dragged a garden-seat round from the portico, placed it on end, and succeeded in climbing to the top of it and bringing myself abreast of one of the windows. The casement yielded to my pressure, turned on its hinges, and showed me what I had been looking for – a transfiguration. The beautiful image stood bathed in the cold radiance, shining with a purity that made her convincingly divine. If by day her rich paleness suggested faded gold, she now had a complexion like silver slightly dimmed. The effect was almost terrible; beauty so expressive could hardly be inanimate. This was my foremost observation – I leave you to fancy whether my next was less interesting. At some distance from the foot of the statue, just out of the light, I perceived a figure lying flat on the pavement, prostrate apparently with devotion. I can hardly tell you how it completed the impressiveness of the scene. It marked the shining image as a goddess indeed, and seemed to throw a sort of conscious pride into her stony mask. Of course, in this recumbent worshipper I immediately recognized the Count, and while I lingered there, as if to help me to read the full meaning of his attitude, the moonlight travelled forward and covered his breast and face. Then I saw that his eyes were closed, and that he was either asleep or swooning. Watching him attentively, I perceived his even respirations, and judged there was no reason for alarm. The moonlight blanched his face, which seemed already pale with weariness. He had come into the presence of the Juno in obedience to that fabulous passion of which the symptoms had given us so much to wonder at, and, exhausted either by compliance or resistance, he had sunk down at her feet in a stupid sleep. The lunar influence soon roused him, however; he muttered something and raised himself, vaguely staring. Then, recognizing his situation, he rose and stood for some time gazing fixedly at the brilliant image, with an expression which I suspected was not that of wholly unprotesting devotion. He uttered a string of broken words, of which I was unable to catch the meaning, and then, after another pause and a long, melancholy moan, he turned slowly to the door. As rapidly and noiseless as possible I descended from my post of vigilance and passed behind the casino, and in a moment I heard the sound of the closing lock and of his departing footsteps.

The next day, meeting in the garden the functionary who had conducted the excavation, I shook my finger at him with an intention of portentous gravity. But he only grinned like the malicious earth-gnome to which I had always compared him, and twisted his moustache as if my menace were a capital joke. 'If you dig any more holes here,' I said, 'you shall be thrust into the deepest of them, and have the earth packed down on top of you. We have made enough discoveries, and we want no more statues. Your Juno has almost ruined us.'

He burst out laughing. 'I expected as much – I had my notion!'

'What was your notion?'

'That the Signor Conte would begin and say his prayers to her.'

'Good heavens! Is the case so common? Why did you expect it?'

'On the contrary, the case is rare. But I have fumbled so long in the monstrous heritage of antiquity that I have learned a multitude of secrets – learned that ancient relics may work modern miracles. There is a pagan element in all of us – I don't speak for you, *illustrissimi forestieri* – and the old gods have still their worshippers. The old spirit still throbs here and there, and the Signor Conte has his share of it. He's a good fellow, but, between ourselves, he's an impossible Christian!' And this singular personage resumed his impertinent hilarity.

'If your previsions were so distinct, you ought to have given me a hint of them,' I said. 'I should have sent your spadesmen walking.'

'Ah, but the Juno is so beautiful!'

'Her beauty be blasted! Can you tell me what has become of the Contessa's? To rival the Juno she is turning to marble herself.'

He shrugged his shoulders. 'Ah, but the Juno is worth fifty thousand scudi!'

'I would give a hundred thousand to have her annihilated! Perhaps, after all, I shall want you to dig another hole.'

'At your service!' he answered, with a flourish, while I turned my back upon him.

A couple of days later I dined, as I often did, with my host and hostess, and met the Count face to face for the first time since his prostration in the casino. He bore the traces of it, and was uncommonly taciturn and absent. It appeared to me that the path of the antique faith was not strewn with flowers, and that the Juno was becoming daily a harder mistress to serve. Dinner was scarcely over before he rose from table and took up his hat. As he did so, passing near his wife, he faltered a moment, stopped, and gave her – for the first time I imagine – that vaguely imploring look which I myself had often caught. She moved her lips in inarticulate sympathy and put out her hands. He drew her towards him, kissed her with an almost brutal violence, and strode away. The occasion was propitious, and further delay unnecessary.

'What I have to tell you is very strange,' I said to the Countess, 'very improbable, very incredible. But perhaps you will not find it so bad as you feared. There *is* a woman in the case! Your enemy is the Juno. The Count – how shall I say it? – the Count takes her *au sérieux*.' She was silent; but after a moment she touched my arm with her hand, and I knew she meant that I had spoken her own belief. 'You admired his antique simplicity: you see how far it goes! He has reverted to the faith of his fathers. Dormant for so many centuries, that imperious image has silently evoked it. He believes in the pedigrees you used to dog's-ear your school-mythology with trying to get by heart. In a word, dear child, Marco is an anthropomorphist. Do you know what that means?

'I suppose you will be terribly shocked,' she answered, 'if I say that he is welcome to any faith, if he will only share it with me. I will believe in Jupiter, if he'll bid me! My sorrow is not for that: let my husband be himself! My sorrow is for the gulf of silence and indifference that has opened itself between us. His Juno is the reality; I am the fiction!'

'I have lately become reconciled to this gulf of silence, and to your losing for a while your importance. After the fable the moral! The poor fellow has but half succumbed; the other half protests. The modern man is shut out in the darkness with his irreproachable wife. How can he have failed to feel – vaguely and grossly, if it must have been, but in every throb of his heart– that you are a more perfect experiment of nature, a riper fruit of time, than those primitive persons for whom Juno was a terror and Venus a model? He pays you the compliment of believing you an unconvertible modern. He has crossed the Acheron, but he has left you behind, as a pledge to the present. We will bring him back to redeem it. The old ancestral ghosts ought to be propitiated when a pretty creature like you has sacrified the best elements of her life. He has proved himself one of the Valerii; we shall see to it that he is the last, and yet that his passing away shall leave the Conte Marco in excellent health.'

I spoke with confidence, and partly felt it, for it seemed to me that if the Count was to be touched it must be by the sense that his strange spiritual excursion had not made his wife detest him. We talked long and to a hopeful end, for before I went away my goddaughter expressed the desire to go out and look at the Juno. 'I was afraid of her almost from the first,' she said, 'and have hardly seen her since she was set up in the casino. Perhaps I can learn a lesson from her – perhaps I can guess how she charms him!'

For a moment I hesitated, from the fear that we might intrude upon the Count's devotions. Then, as something in the poor girl's face suggested that she too had thought of this and felt a sudden impulse to pluck victory from the heart of danger, I bravely offered her my arm. The night was cloudy, and on this occasion, apparently, the triumphant goddess was to depend upon her own lustre. But as we approached the casino I saw that the door was ajar and that there was lamp-light within. The lamp was suspended in front of the image, and it showed us that the place was empty. But evidently the Count had lately been there. Before the statue stood a roughly extemporized altar, composed of a shapeless fragment of antique marble, engraved with an illegible Greek inscription. We seemed really to stand in a pagan temple, and as we gazed at the serene divinity I think we each of us felt for a moment the breath of superstition. It ought to have been quickened, I suppose, but it was rudely arrested, by our observing a curious glitter on the face of the low altar. A second glance showed us it was blood!

My companion looked at me in pale horror, and turned away with a cry. A swarm of hideous conjectures pressed into my mind, and for a moment I was sickened. But at last I remembered that there is blood and blood, and that in the best time the ancient Romans offered no human victims.

'Be sure it's very innocent,' I said; 'a lamb, a kid, or a sucking calf!' But it was enough for her nerves and her conscience that it was a crimson trickle, and she returned to the house in immense agitation. The rest of the night was not passed in a way to restore her to calmness. The Count had not come in, and she sat up for him from hour to hour. I remained with her – smoking my cigar as composedly as I might; but internally I wondered what in horror's name had become of him. Gradually, as the hours wore away, I arrived at a vague interpretation of these strange practices – an interpretation none the less valid and less welcome for being comparatively cheerful. The blood-drops on the altar, I mused, were the last instalment of his debt and the end of his delusion. They had been a happy necessity, for he was after all too generous a creature not to hate himself for having shed them, not to abhor so cruelly insistent an idol. He had wandered away to recover himself in solitude, and he would come back to us with a repentant heart and an inquiring mind! I should certainly have believed all this more easily, however, if I could have heard his footstep in the hall. Toward dawn scepticism threatened to creep in with the grey light, and I restlessly betook myself to the portico. Here in a few moments I saw him cross the grass, heavy-footed, splashed with mud, and evidently excessively tired. He must have been walking all night, and his face denoted that his spirit had been as restless as his body. He passed near me, and before he entered the house he stopped, looked at me a moment, and then held out his hand. I grasped it warmly, and it seemed to me to throb with all that he was unable to utter.

'Will you see your wife?' I asked.

He passed his hand over his eyes and shook his head. 'Not now – not yet – some time!' he answered.

I was disappointed, but I convinced her, I think, that he had cast out the devil. She felt, poor girl, a pardonable desire to celebrate the event. I returned to my lodging, spent the day in Rome, and came back to the Villa toward dusk. I was told that the Countess was in the grounds. I looked for her cautiously at first, for I thought it just possible I might intrude upon the natural consequences of a reconciliation; but, failing to meet her, I turned toward the casino, and found myself face to face with the mocking little commissioner.

'Does your excellency happen to have twenty yards of stout rope about him?' he asked, gravely.

'Do you want to hang yourself for the trouble you have stood sponsor to?' I answered.

'It's a hanging matter, I promise you. The Countess has given orders. You will find her in the casino. Sweet-voiced as she is, she knows how to make her orders understood.'

At the door of the casino stood half a dozen of the labourers on the place, looking vaguely solemn, like outstanding dependants at a superior funeral. The Countess was within, in a position which was an answer to the surveyor's riddle. She stood with her eyes fixed on the Juno, who had been removed from her pedestal and lay stretched in her magnificent length upon a rude litter.

'Do you understand?' she said. 'She's beautiful, she's noble, she's precious, but she must go back!' And, with a passionate gesture, she seemed to represent an open grave.

I was hugely delighted, but I thought it discreet to stroke my chin and look scrupulous. 'She is worth fifty thousand scudi.'

She shook her head sadly. 'If we were to sell her to the Pope and give the money to the poor, it wouldn't profit us. She must go back – she must go back! We must smother her beauty in the dreadful earth. It makes me feel almost as if she were alive; but it came to me last night with overwhelming force, when my husband came in and refused to see me, that he will not be himself so long as she is above ground. To cut the knot we must bury her! If I had only thought of it before!'

'Not before!' I said, shaking my head in turn. 'Heaven reward our sacrifice now!'

The little expert, when he reappeared, seemed hardly like an agent of the celestial influences, but he was deft and active, which was more to the point. Every now and then he uttered some half-articulate lament, by way of protest against the Countess's cruelty; but I saw him privately scanning the recumbent image with an eye which seemed to foresee a malicious glee in standing on a certain unmarked spot on the turf and grinning till people stared. He had brought back an abundance of rope, and, having summoned his assistants, who vigorously lifted the litter, he led the way to the original excavation, which had been left unclosed, owing to the project of further researches. By the time we reached the edge of the grave the evening had fallen and the beauty of our marble victim was shrouded in a dusky veil. No one spoke – if not exactly for shame, at least for regret. Whatever our plea, our performance looked, at least, monstrously profane. The ropes were adjusted and the Juno was slowly lowered into her earthy bed. The Countess took a handful of earth and dropped it solemnly on her breast. 'May it lie lightly, but for ever!' she said.

'Amen!' cried the little surveyor, with a strange, sneering inflection; and he gave us a bow, as he departed, which betrayed an agreeable consciousness of knowing where fifty thousand scudi were buried. His underlings had another cask of wine, the result of which, for them, was a suspension of all consciousness, and a subsequent irreparable confusion of memory as to where they had plied their spades.

The Countess had not yet seen her husband, who had again apparently betaken himself to communion with the great god Pan. I was of course unwilling to leave her to encounter alone the results of her momentous deed. She wandered into the drawing-room and pretended to occupy herself with a bit of embroidery, but in reality she was bravely composing herself for an 'explanation'. I took up a book, but it held my attention as feebly. As the evening wore away I heard a movement on the threshold, and saw the Count lifting the tapestried curtain which masked the door and looking silently at his wife. His eyes were brilliant, but not angry. He had missed the Juno – and drawn a long breath! The Countess kept her eyes fixed on her work, and drew her silken threads like an image of domestic tranquillity. The image seemed to fascinate him; he came in slowly, almost on tiptoe, walked to the chimney-piece, and stood there awhile, giving her, askance, an immense deal of attention. What had passed, what was passing, in his mind, I leave to your own apprehension. My goddaughter's hand trembled as it rose and fell, and the colour came into her cheek. At last she raised her eyes and sustained the gaze in which all his returning faith seemed concentrated. He hesitated a moment, as if her very forgiveness kept the gulf open between them, and then he strode forward, fell on his two knees, and buried his head in her lap. I departed as the Count had come in, on tiptoe.

He never became, if you will, a thoroughly modern man; but one day, years after, when a visitor to whom he was showing his cabinet became inquisitive as to a marble hand, suspended in one of its inner recesses, he looked grave and turned the lock on it. 'It is the hand of a beautiful creature,' he said, 'whom I once greatly admired.'

'Ah – a Roman?' asked the gentleman, with a smirk.

'A Greek,' said the Count, with a frown.

The Real Thing

1

WHEN the porter's wife (she used to answer the house-bell), announced 'A gentleman – with a lady, sir,' I had, as I often had in those days, for the wish was father to the thought, an immediate vision of sitters. Sitters my visitors in this case proved to be; but not in the sense I should have preferred. However, there was nothing at first to indicate that they might not have come for a portrait. The gentleman, a man of fifty, very high and very straight, with a moustache slightly grizzled and a dark grey walking-coat admirably fitted, both of which I noted professionally – I don't mean as a barber or yet as a tailor – would have struck me as a celebrity if celebrities often were striking. It was a truth of which I had for some time been conscious that a figure with a good deal of frontage was, as one might say, almost never a public institution. A glance at the lady helped to remind me of this paradoxical law: she also looked too distinguished to be a 'personality'. Moreover one would scarcely come across two variations together.

Neither of the pair spoke immediately – they only prolonged the preliminary gaze which suggested that each wished to give the other a chance. They were visibly shy; they stood there letting me take them in – which, as I afterwards perceived, was the most practical thing they could have done. In this way their embarrassment served their cause. I had seen people painfully reluctant to mention that they desired anything so gross as to be represented on canvas; but the scruples of my new friends appeared almost insurmountable. Yet the gentleman might have said 'I should like a portrait of my wife', and the lady might have said 'I should like a portrait of my husband'. Perhaps they were not husband and wife – this naturally would make the matter more delicate. Perhaps they wished to be done together – in which case they ought to have brought a third person to break the news.

'We come from Mr Rivet,' the lady said at last, with a dim

smile which had the effect of a moist sponge passed over a
'sunk' piece of painting, as well as of a vague allusion to vanished
beauty. She was as tall and straight, in her degree, as her companion, and with ten years less to carry. She looked as sad as a
woman could look whose face was not charged with expression;
that is her tinted oval mask showed friction as an exposed surface shows it. The hand of time had played over her freely, but
only to simplify. She was slim and stiff, and so well dressed,
in dark blue cloth, with lappets and pockets and buttons, that
it was clear she employed the same tailor as her husband. The
couple had an indefinable air of prosperous thrift – they evidently got a good deal of luxury for their money. If I was to
be one of their luxuries it would behove me to consider my
terms.

'Ah, Claude Rivet recommended me,' I inquired; and I added
that it was very kind of him, though I could reflect that, as he
only painted landscape, this was not a sacrifice.

The lady looked very hard at the gentleman, and the gentleman
looked round the room. Then staring at the floor a moment
and stroking his moustache, he rested his pleasant eyes on me
with the remark: 'He said you were the right one.'

'I try to be, when people want to sit.'

'Yes, we should like to,' said the lady anxiously.

'Do you mean together?'

My visitors exchanged a glance. 'If you could do anything
with *me*, I suppose it would be double,' the gentleman stammered.

'Oh yes, there's naturally a higher charge for two figures
than for one.'

'We would like to make it pay,' the husband confessed.

'That's very good of you,' I returned, appreciating so unwonted a sympathy – for I supposed he meant pay the artist.

A sense of strangeness seemed to dawn on the lady. 'We mean
for the illustrations – Mr Rivet said you might put one in.'

'Put one in – an illustration?' I was equally confused.

'Sketch her off, you know,' said the gentleman, colouring.

It was only then that I understood the service Claude Rivet
had rendered me; he had told them that I worked in black and

white, for magazines, for story-books, for sketches of contemporary life, and consequently had frequent employment for models. These things were true, but it was not less true (I may confess it now – whether because the aspiration was to lead to everything or to nothing I leave the reader to guess), that I couldn't get the honours, to say nothing of the emoluments, of a great painter of portraits out of my head. My 'illustrations' were my pot-boilers; I looked to a different branch of art (far and away the most interesting it had always seemed to me), to perpetuate my fame. There was no shame in looking to it also to make my fortune; but that fortune was by so much further from being made from the moment my visitors wished to be 'done' for nothing. I was disappointed, for in the pictorial sense I had immediately *seen* them. I had seized their type – I had already settled what I would do with it. Something that wouldn't absolutely have pleased them, I afterwards reflected.

'Ah, you're – you're – a – ?' I began, as soon as I had mastered my surprise. I couldn't bring out the dingy word 'models'; it seemed to fit the case so little.

'We haven't had much practice,' said the lady.

'We've got to *do* something, and we've thought that an artist in your line might perhaps make something of us,' her husband threw off. He further mentioned that they didn't know many artists and that they had gone first, on the off-chance (he painted views of course, but sometimes put in figures – perhaps I remembered), to Mr Rivet, whom they had met a few years before at a place in Norfolk where he was sketching.

'We used to sketch a little ourselves,' the lady hinted.

'It's very awkward, but we absolutely *must* do something,' her husband went on.

'Of course, we're not so *very* young,' she admitted, with a wan smile.

With the remark that I might as well know something more about them, the husband had handed me a card extracted from a neat new pocket-book (their appurtenances were all of the freshest) and inscribed with the words 'Major Monarch'. Impressive as these words were they didn't carry my knowledge much further; but my visitor presently added: 'I've left the army, and we've had the misfortune to lose our money. In fact our means are dreadfully small.'

'It's an awful bore,' said Mrs Monarch.

They evidently wished to be discreet – to take care not to swagger because they were gentlefolks. I perceived they would have been willing to recognize this as something of a drawback, at the same time that I guessed at an underlying sense – their consolation in adversity – that they *had* their points. They certainly had; but these advantages struck me as preponderantly social; such for instance as would help to make a drawing-room look well. However, a drawing-room was always, or ought to be, a picture.

In consequence of his wife's allusion to their age Major Monarch observed: 'Naturally, it's more for the figure that we thought of going in. We can still hold ourselves up.' On the instant I saw that the figure was indeed their strong point. His 'naturally' didn't sound vain, but it lighted up the question. '*She* has got the best,' he continued, nodding at his wife, with a pleasant after-dinner absence of circumlocution. I could only reply, as if we were in fact sitting over our wine, that this didn't prevent his own from being very good; which led him in turn to rejoin: 'We thought that if you ever have to do people like us, we might be something like it. *She*, particularly – for a lady in a book, you know.'

I was so amused by them that, to get more of it, I did my best to take their point of view; and though it was an embarrassment to find myself appraising physically, as if they were animals on hire or useful blacks, a pair of whom I should have expected to meet only in one of the relations in which criticism is tacit, I looked at Mrs Monarch judicially enough to be able to exclaim, after a moment, with conviction: 'Oh yes, a lady in a book!' She was singularly like a bad illustration.

'We'll stand up, if you like,' said the Major; and he raised himself before me with a really grand air.

I could take his measure at a glance – he was six feet two and a perfect gentleman. It would have paid any club in process of formation and in want of a stamp to engage him at a salary to stand in the principal window. What struck me immediately was that in coming to me they had rather missed their vocation; they could surely have been turned to better account for advertising purposes. I couldn't of course see the thing in detail, but I could see them make someone's fortune – I don't mean their own. There was something in them for a waistcoat-maker, an hotel-keeper, or a soap-vendor. I could imagine 'We always use it' pinned on their bosoms with the greatest effect; I had a vision of the promptitude with which they would launch a *table d'hôte*.

Mrs Monarch sat still, not from pride but from shyness, and presently her husband said to her: 'Get up my dear and show how smart you are.' She obeyed, but she had no need to get up to show it. She walked to the end of the studio, and then she came back blushing, with her fluttered eyes on her husband. I was reminded of an incident I had accidentally had a glimpse of in Paris – being with a friend there, a dramatist about to produce a play – when an actress came to him to ask to be intrusted with a part. She went through the paces before him, walked up and down as Mrs Monarch was doing. Mrs Monarch did it quite as well, but I abstained from applauding. It was very odd to see such people apply for such poor pay. She looked as if she had ten thousand a year. Her husband had used the word that described her: she was, in the London current jargon, essentially and typically 'smart'. Her figure was, in the same order of ideas, conspicuously and irreproachably 'good'. For a woman of her age her waist was surprisingly small; her elbow moreover had the orthodox crook. She held her head at the conventional angle; but why did she come to *me*? She ought to have tried on jackets at a big shop. I feared my visitors were not only destitute, but 'artistic' – which would be a great complication. When she sat down again I thanked her, observing that what a draughtsman most valued in his model was the faculty of keeping quiet.

'Oh, *she* can keep quiet,' said Major Monarch. Then he added, jocosely: 'I've always kept her quiet.'

'I'm not a nasty fidget, am I?' Mrs Monarch appealed to her husband.

He addressed his answer to me. 'Perhaps it isn't out of place to mention – because we ought to be quite businesslike, oughtn't we? – that when I married her she was known as the Beautiful Statue.'

'Oh dear!' said Mrs Monarch, ruefully.

'Of course I should want a certain amount of expression,' I rejoined.

'Of *course*!' they both exclaimed.

'And then I suppose you know that you'll get awfully tired.'

'Oh, we *never* get tired!' they eagerly cried.

'Have you had any kind of practice?'

They hesitated – they looked at each other. 'We've been photographed, *immensely*,' said Mrs Monarch.

'She means the fellows have asked us,' added the Major.

'I see – because you're so good-looking.'

'I don't know what they thought, but they were always after us.'

'We always got our photographs for nothing,' smiled Mrs Monarch.

'We might have brought some, my dear,' her husband remarked.

'I'm not sure we have any left. We've given quantities away,' she explained to me.

'With our autographs and that sort of thing,' said the Major.

'Are they to be got in the shops?' I inquired, as a harmless pleasantry.

'Oh, yes; *hers* – they used to be.'

'Not now,' said Mrs Monarch, with her eyes on the floor.

2

I could fancy the 'sort of thing' they put on the presentation-copies of their photographs, and I was sure they wrote a beautiful hand. It was odd how quickly I was sure of everything that concerned them. If they were now so poor as to have to earn shillings and pence, they never had had much of a margin. Their good looks had been their capital, and they had good-humouredly made the most of the career that this resource marked out for them. It was in their faces, the blankness, the deep intellectual repose of the twenty years of country-house visiting which had given them pleasant intonations. I could see the sunny drawing-rooms, sprinkled with periodicals she didn't read, in which Mrs Monarch had continuously sat; I could see the wet shrubberies in which she had walked, equipped to admiration for either exercise. I could see the rich covers the Major had helped to shoot and the wonderful garments in which, late at night, he repaired to the smoking-room to talk about them. I could imagine their leggings and waterproofs, their knowing tweeds and rugs, their rolls of sticks and cases of tackle and neat umbrellas; and I could evoke the exact appearance of their servants and the compact variety of their luggage on the platforms of country stations.

They gave small tips, but they were liked; they didn't do anything themselves, but they were welcome. They looked so well everywhere; they gratified the general relish for stature, complexion, and 'form'. They knew it without fatuity or vulgarity, and they respected themselves in consequence. They were not superficial; they were thorough and kept themselves up – it had been their line. People with such a taste for activity had to have some line. I could feel how, even in a dull house, they could have been counted upon for cheerfulness. At present something had happened – it didn't matter what, their little income had grown less, it had grown least – and they had to do something for pocket-money. Their friends liked them, but didn't like to support them. There was something about them that represented credit – their clothes, their manners, their type; but if credit is a large empty pocket in which an occasional chink reverberates, the chink at least must be audible. What they wanted of me was to help to make it so. Fortunately they had no children – I soon divined that. They would also perhaps wish our relations to be kept secret: this was why it was 'for the figure' – the reproduction of the face would betray them.

I liked them – they were so simple; and I had no objection to them if they would suit. But, somehow, with all their perfections I didn't easily believe in them. After all they were amateurs, and the ruling passion of my life was the detestation of the amateur.

Combined with this was another perversity – an innate preference for the represented subject over the real one: the defect of the real one was so apt to be a lack of representation. I liked things that appeared; then one was sure. Whether they *were* or not was a subordinate and almost always a profitless question. There were other considerations, the first of which was that I already had two or three people in use, notably a young person with big feet, in alpaca, from Kilburn, who for a couple of years had come to me regularly for my illustrations and with whom I was still – perhaps ignobly – satisfied. I frankly explained to my visitors how the case stood; but they had taken more precautions than I supposed. They had reasoned out their opportunity, for Claude Rivet had told them of the projected *édition de luxe* of one of the writers of our day – the rarest of the novelists – who, long neglected by the multitudinous vulgar and dearly prized by the attentive (need I mention Philip Vincent?) had had the happy fortune of seeing, late in life, the dawn and then the full light of a higher criticism – an estimate in which, on the part of the public, there was something really of expiation. The edition in question, planned by a publisher of taste, was practically an act of high reparation; the woodcuts with which it was to be enriched were the homage of English art to one of the most independent representatives of English letters. Major and Mrs Monarch confessed to me that they had hoped I might be able to work *them* into my share of the enterprise. They knew I was to do the first of the books, *Rutland Ramsay*, but I had to make clear to them that my participation in the rest of the affair – this first book was to be a test – was to depend on the satisfaction I should give. If this should be limited my employers would drop me without a scruple. It was therefore a crisis for me, and naturally I was making special preparation, looking about for new people, if they should be necessary, and securing the best types. I admitted however that I should like to settle down to two or three good models who would do for everything.

'Should we have often to – a – put on special clothes?' Mrs Monarch timidly demanded.

'Dear, yes – that's half the business.'

'And should we be expected to supply our own costumes?'

'Oh, no; I've got a lot of things. A painter's models put on – or put off – anything he likes.'

'And do you mean – a – the same?'

'The same?'

Mrs Monarch looked at her husband again.

'Oh, she was just wondering,' he explained, 'if the costumes are in *general* use.' I had to confess that they were, and I mentioned further that some of them (I had a lot of genuine, greasy last-century things) had served their time, a hundred years ago, on living, world-stained men and women. 'We'll put on anything that *fits*,' said the Major.

'Oh, I arrange that – they fit in the pictures.'

'I'm afraid I should do better for the modern books. I would come as you like,' said Mrs Monarch.

'She has got a lot of clothes at home: they might do for contemporary life,' her husband continued.

'Oh, I can fancy scenes in which you'd be quite natural.' And indeed I could see the slipshod rearrangements of stale properties – the stories I tried to produce pictures for without the exasperation of reading them – whose sandy tracts the good lady might help to people. But I had to return to the fact that for this sort of work – the daily mechanical grind – I was already equipped; the people I was working with were fully adequate.

'We only thought we might be more like *some* characters,' said Mrs Monarch mildly, getting up.

Her husband also rose; he stood looking at me with a dim wistfulness that was touching in so fine a man. 'Wouldn't it be rather a pull sometimes to have – a – to have – ?' He hung fire; he wanted me to help him by phrasing what he meant. But I couldn't – I didn't know. So he brought it out, awkwardly: 'The *real* thing; a gentleman, you know, or a lady.' I was quite ready to give a general assent – I admitted that there was a great deal in that. This encouraged Major Monarch to say, following up his appeal with an unacted gulp: 'It's awfully hard – we've tried everything.' The gulp was communicative; it proved too much for his wife. Before I knew it Mrs Monarch had dropped again upon a divan and burst into tears. Her husband sat down beside her, holding one of her hands; whereupon she quickly dried her eyes with the other, while I felt embarrassed as she looked up at me. 'There isn't a confounded job I haven't applied for – waited for – prayed for. You can fancy we'd be pretty bad at first. Secretaryships and that sort of thing? You might as well ask for a peerage. I'd be *anything* – I'm strong; a messenger or a coalheaver. I'd put on a gold-laced cap and open carriage doors in front of the haberdasher's; I'd hang about a station, to carry portmanteaux; I'd be a postman. But they won't *look* at you; there are thousands, as good as yourself, already on the ground. *Gentlemen*, poor beggars, who have drunk their wine, who have kept their hunters!'

I was as reassuring as I knew how to be, and my visitors were presently on their feet again while, for the experiment, we agreed on an hour. We were discussing it when the door opened and Miss Churm came in with a wet umbrella. Miss Churm had to take the omnibus to Maida Vale and then walk half a mile. She looked a trifle blowsy and slightly splashed. I scarcely ever saw her come in without thinking afresh how odd it was that, being so little in herself, she should yet be so much in others. She was a meagre little Miss Churm, but she was an ample heroine of romance. She was only a freckled cockney, but she could represent everything from a fine lady to a shepherdess; she had the faculty, as she might have had a fine voice or long hair. She couldn't spell, and she loved beer, but she had two or three 'points', and practice, and a knack, and mother-wit, and a kind of whimsical sensibility, and a love of the theatre, and seven sisters, and not an ounce of respect, especially for the 'h'. The first thing my visitors saw was that her umbrella was wet, and in their spotless perfection they visibly winced at it. The rain had come on since their arrival.

'I'm all in a soak; there *was* a mess of people in the bus. I wish you lived near a station,' said Miss Churm. I requested her to get ready as quickly as possible, and she passed into the room in which she always changed her dress. But before going out she asked me what she was to get into this time.

'It's the Russian princess, don't you know?' I answered; 'the one with the "golden eyes", in black velvet, for the long thing in the *Cheapside*.'

'Golden eyes? I *say*!' cried Miss Churm, while my companions watched her with intensity as she withdrew. She always arranged herself, when she was late, before I could turn round; and I kept my visitors a little, on purpose, so that they might get an idea, from seeing her, what would be expected of themselves. I mentioned that she was quite my notion of an excellent model – she was really very clever.

'Do you think she looks like a Russian princess?' Major Monarch asked, with lurking alarm.

'When I make her, yes.'

'Oh, if you have to *make* her – !' He reasoned, acutely.

'That's the most you can ask. There are so many that are not makeable.'

'Well now, *here's* a lady' – and with a persuasive smile he passed his arm into his wife's – 'who's already made!'

'Oh, I'm not a Russian princess,' Mrs Monarch protested, a little coldly. I could see that she had known some and didn't like them. There, immediately, was a complication of a kind that I never had to fear with Miss Churm.

This young lady came back in black velvet – the gown was rather rusty and very low on her lean shoulders – and with a Japanese fan in her red hands. I reminded her that in the scene I was doing she had to look over someone's head. 'I forget whose it is; but it doesn't matter. Just look over a head.'

'I'd rather look over a stove,' said Miss Churm; and she took her station near the fire. She fell into position, settled herself into a tall attitude, gave a certain backward inclination to her head and a certain forward drop to her fan, and looked, at least to my prejudiced sense, distinguished and charming, foreign and dangerous. We left her looking so, while I went downstairs with Major and Mrs Monarch.

'I think I could come about as near it as that,' said Mrs Monarch.

'Oh, you think she's shabby, but you must allow for the alchemy of art.'

However, they went off with an evident increase of comfort, founded on their demonstrable advantage in being the real thing. I could fancy them shuddering over Miss Churm. She was very droll about them when I went back, for I told her what they wanted.

'Well, if *she* can sit I'll tyke to book-keeping,' said my model.

'She's very lady-like,' I replied, as an innocent form of aggravation.

'So much the worse for *you*. That means she can't turn round.'

'She'll do for the fashionable novels.'

'Oh yes, she'll *do* for them!' my model humorously declared. 'Ain't they bad enough without her?' I had often sociably denounced them to Miss Churm.

3

It was for the elucidation of a mystery in one of these works that I first tried Mrs Monarch. Her husband came with her, to be useful if necessary – it was sufficiently clear that as a general thing he would prefer to come with her. At first I wondered if this were for 'propriety's' sake – if he were going to be jealous and meddling. The idea was too tiresome, and if it had been confirmed it would speedily have brought our acquaintance to a close. But I soon saw there was nothing in it and that if he accompanied Mrs Monarch it was (in addition to the chance of being wanted) simply because he had nothing else to do. When she was away from him his occupation was gone – she never *had* been away from him. I judged, rightly, that in their awkward situation their close union was their main comfort and that this union had no weak spot. It was a real marriage, an encouragement for the hesitating, a nut for pessimists to crack. Their address was humble (I remember afterwards thinking it had been the only thing about them that was really professional), and I could fancy the lamentable lodgings in which the Major would have been left alone. He could bear them with his wife – he couldn't bear them without her.

He had too much tact to try and make himself agreeable when he couldn't be useful; so he simply sat and waited, when I was too absorbed in my work to talk. But I liked to make him talk – it made my work, when it didn't interrupt it, less sordid, less special. To listen to him was to combine the excitement of going out with the economy of staying at home. There was only one hindrance: that I seemed not to know any of the people he and his wife had known. I think he wondered extremely, during the term of our intercourse, whom the deuce I *did* know. He hadn't a stray sixpence of an idea to fumble for; so we didn't spin it very fine – we confined ourselves to questions of leather and even of liquor (saddlers and breeches-makers and how to get good claret cheap), and matters like 'good trains' and the habits of small game. His lore on these last subjects was astonishing, he managed to interweave the stationmaster with the ornithologist. When he couldn't talk about greater things he could talk cheerfully about smaller, and since I couldn't accompany him into reminiscences of the fashionable world he could lower the conversation without a visible effort to my level.

So earnest a desire to please was touching in a man who could so easily have knocked one down. He looked after the fire and had an opinion on the draught of the stove, without my asking him, and I could see that he thought many of my arrangements not half clever enough. I remember telling him that if I were only rich I would offer him a salary to come and teach me how to live. Sometimes he gave a random sigh, of which the essence was: 'Give me even such a bare old barrack as *this*, and I'd do something with it!' When I wanted to use him he came alone; which was an illustration of the superior courage of women. His wife could bear her solitary second floor, and she was in general more discreet; showing by various small reserves that she was alive to the propriety of keeping our relations markedly professional – not letting them slide into sociability. She wished it to remain clear that she and the Major were employed, not cultivated, and if she approved of me as a superior, who could be kept in his place, she never thought me quite good enough for an equal.

She sat with great intensity, giving the whole of her mind to it, and was capable of remaining for an hour almost as motionless as if she were before a photographer's lens. I could see she had been photographed often, but somehow the very habit that made her good for that purpose unfitted her for mine. At first I was extremely pleased with her lady-like air, and it was a satisfaction, on coming to follow her lines, to see how good they were and how far they could lead the pencil. But after a few times I began to find her too insurmountably stiff; do what I would with it my drawing looked like a photograph or a copy of a photograph. Her figure had no variety of expression – she herself had no sense of variety. You may say that this was my business, was only a question of placing her. I placed her in every conceivable position, but she managed to obliterate their differences. She was always a lady certainly, and into the bargain was always the same lady. She was the real thing, but always the same thing. There were moments when I was oppressed by the serenity of her confidence that she *was* the real thing. All her dealings with me and all her husband's were an implication that this was lucky for *me*. Meanwhile I found myself trying to invent types that approached her own, instead of making her own transform itself – in the clever way that was not impossible, for instance, to poor Miss Churm. Arrange as I would and take the precautions I would, she always, in my pictures, came out too tall – landing me in the dilemma of having represented a fascinating woman as seven feet high, which, out of respect perhaps to my own very much scantier inches, was far from my idea of such a personage.

The case was worse with the Major – nothing I could do would keep *him* down, so that he became useful only for the representation of brawny giants. I adored variety and range, I cherished human accidents, the illustrative note; I wanted to characterize closely, and the thing in the world I most hated was the danger of being ridden by a type. I had quarrelled with some of my friends about it – I had parted company with them for maintaining that one *had* to be, and that if the type was beautiful (witness Raphael and Leonardo), the servitude was only a gain. I was neither Leonardo nor Raphael; I might only be a presumptuous young modern searcher, but I held that everything was to be sacrificed sooner than character. When they averred that the haunting type in question could easily *be* character, I retorted, perhaps superficially: 'Whose?' It couldn't be everybody's – it might end in being nobody's.

After I had drawn Mrs Monarch a dozen times I perceived more clearly than before that the value of such a model as Miss Churm resided precisely in the fact that she had no positive stamp, combined of course with the other fact that what she did have was a curious and inexplicable talent for imitation. Her usual appearance was like a curtain which she could draw up at a request for a capital performance. This performance was simply suggestive; but it was a word to the wise – it was vivid and pretty. Sometimes, even, I thought it, though she was plain herself, too insipidly pretty; I made it a reproach to her that the figures drawn from her were monotonously (*bêtement*, as we used to say) graceful. Nothing made her more angry: it was so much her pride to feel that she could sit for characters that had nothing in common with each other. She would accuse me at such moments of taking away her 'reputytion'.

It suffered a certain shrinkage, this queer quality, from the repeated visits of my new friends. Miss Churm was greatly in demand, never in want of employment, so I had no scruple in putting her off occasionally, to try them more at my ease. It was certainly amusing at first to do the real thing – it was amusing to do Major Monarch's trousers. They *were* the real thing, even if he did come out colossal. It was amusing to do his wife's back hair (it was so mathematically neat) and the particular 'smart' tension of her tight stays. She lent herself especially to positions in which the face was somewhat averted or blurred; she abounded in ladylike back views and *profils perdus*. When she stood erect she took naturally one of the attitudes in which court painters represent queens and princesses; so that I found myself wondering whether, to draw out this accomplishment, I couldn't get the editor of the *Cheapside* to publish a really royal romance, 'A Tale of Buckingham Palace'. Sometimes, however, the real thing and the make-believe came into contact; by which I mean that Miss Churm, keeping an appointment or coming to make one on days when I had much work in hand, encountered her invidious rivals. The encounter was not on their part, for they noticed her no more than if she had been the housemaid; not from intentional loftiness, but simply because, as yet, professionally, they didn't know how to fraternize as I could guess that they would have liked – or at least that the Major would. They couldn't talk about the omnibus – they always walked; and they didn't know what else to try – she wasn't interested in good trains or cheap claret. Besides, they must have felt – in the air – that she was amused at them, secretly derisive of their ever knowing how. She was not a person to conceal her scepticism if she had had a chance to show it. On the other hand Mrs Monarch didn't think her tidy; for why else did she take pains to say to me (it was going out of the way, for Mrs Monarch) that she didn't like dirty women?

One day when my young lady happened to be present with my other sitters (she even dropped in, when it was convenient, for a chat), I asked her to be as good as to lend a hand in getting tea – a service with which she was familiar and which was one of a class that, living as I did in a small way, with slender domestic resources, I often appeal to my models to render. They liked to lay hands on my property, to break the sitting, and some-times the china – I made them feel Bohemian. The next time I saw Miss Churm after this incident she surprised me greatly by making a scene about it – she accused me of having wished to humiliate her. She had not resented the outrage at the time, but had seemed obliging and amused, enjoying the comedy of asking Mrs Monarch, who sat vague and silent, whether she would have cream and sugar, and putting an exaggerated simper into the question. She had tried intonations – as if she too wished to pass for the real thing; till I was afraid my other visitors would take offence.

Oh, *they* were determined not to do this; and their touching patience was the measure of their great need. They would sit by the hour, uncomplaining, till I was ready to use them; they would come back on the chance of being wanted and would walk away cheerfully if they were not. I used to go to the door with them to see in what magnificent order they retreated. I tried to find other employment for them – I introduced them to several artists. But they didn't 'take', for reasons I could appreciate, and I became conscious, rather anxiously, that after such disappoint-ments they fell back upon me with a heavier weight. They did me the honour to think that it was I who was most *their* form.

They were not picturesque enough for the painters, and in those days there were not so many serious workers in black and white. Besides, they had an eye to the great job I had mentioned to them – they had secretly set their hearts on supplying the right essence for my pictorial vindication of our fine novelist. They knew that for this undertaking I should want no costume-effects, none of the frippery of past ages – that it was a case in which everything would be contemporary and satirical and, presumably, genteel. If I could work them into it their future would be assured, for the labour would of course be long and the occupation steady.

One day Mrs Monarch came without her husband – she explained his absence by his having had to go to the City. While she sat there in her usual anxious stiffness there came, at the door, a knock which I immediately recognized as the subdued appeal of a model out of work. It was followed by the entrance of a young man whom I easily perceived to be a foreigner and who proved in fact an Italian acquainted with no English word but my name, which he uttered in a way that made it seem to include all others. I had not then visited his country, nor was I proficient in his tongue; but as he was not so meanly constituted – what Italian is? – as to depend only on that member for expression he conveyed to me, in familiar but graceful mimicry, that he was in search of exactly the employment in which the lady before me was engaged. I was not struck with him at first, and while I continued to draw I emitted rough sounds of discouragement and dismissal. He stood his ground, however, not importunately, but with a dumb, dog-like fidelity in his eyes which amounted to innocent impudence – the manner of a devoted servant (he might have been in the house for years) unjustly suspected. Suddenly I saw that this very attitude and expression made a picture, whereupon I told him to sit down and wait till I should be free. There was another picture in the way he obeyed me, and I observed as I worked that there were others still in the way he looked wonderingly, with his head thrown back, about the high studio. He might have been crossing himself in St Peter's. Before I finished I said to myself: 'The fellow's a bankrupt orange-monger, but he's a treasure.'

When Mrs Monarch withdrew he passed across the room like a

flash to open the door for her, standing there with the rapt, pure gaze of the young Dante spellbound by the young Beatrice. As I never insisted, in such situations, on the blankness of the British domestic, I reflected that he had the making of a servant (and I needed one, but couldn't pay him to be only that), as well as of a model; in short I made up my mind to adopt my bright adventurer if he would agree to officiate in the double capacity. He jumped at my offer, and in the event my rashness (for I had known nothing about him) was not brought home to me. He proved a sympathetic though a desultory ministrant, and had in a wonderful degree the *sentiment de la pose*. It was uncultivated, instinctive; a part of the happy instinct which had guided him to my door and helped him to spell out my name on the card nailed to it. He had had no other introduction to me than a guess, from the shape of my high north window, seen outside, that my place was a studio and that as a studio it would contain an artist. He had wandered to England in search of fortune, like other itinerants, and had embarked, with a partner and a small green handcart, on the sale of penny ices. The ices had melted away and the partner had dissolved in their train. My young man wore tight yellow trousers with reddish stripes and his name was Oronte. He was sallow but fair, and when I put him into some old clothes of my own he looked like an Englishman. He was as good as Miss Churm, who could look, when required, like an Italian.

4

I thought Mrs Monarch's face slightly convulsed when, on her coming back with her husband, she found Oronte installed. It was strange to have to recognize in a scrap of a *lazzarone* a competitor to her magnificent Major. It was she who scented danger first, for the Major was anecdotically unconscious. But Oronte gave us tea, with a hundred eager confusions (he had never seen such a queer process), and I think she thought better of me for having at last an 'establishment'. They saw a couple of drawings that I had made of the establishment, and Mrs

Monarch hinted that it never would have struck her that he had sat for them. 'Now the drawings you make from *us*, they look exactly like us,' she reminded me, smiling in triumph; and I recognized that this was indeed just their defect. When I drew the Monarchs I couldn't, somehow, get away from them – get into the character I wanted to represent; and I had not the least desire my model should be discoverable in my picture. Miss Churm never was, and Mrs Monarch thought I hid her, very properly because she was vulgar; whereas if she was lost it was only as the dead who go to heaven are lost – in the gain of an angel the more.

By this time I had got a certain start with *Rutland Ramsay*, the first novel in the great projected series; that is I had produced a dozen drawings, several with the help of the Major and his wife, and I had sent them in for approval. My understanding with the publishers, as I have already hinted, had been that I was to be left to do my work, in this particular case, as I liked, with the whole book committed to me; but my connexion with the rest of the series was only contingent. There were moments when, frankly, it *was* a comfort to have the real thing under one's hand; for there were characters in *Rutland Ramsay* that were very much like it. There were people presumably as straight as the Major and women of as good a fashion as Mrs Monarch. There was a great deal of country-house life – treated, it is true, in a fine, fanciful, ironical, generalized way – and there was a considerable implication of knickerbockers and kilts. There were certain things I had to settle at the outset; such things for instance as the exact appearance of the hero, the particular bloom of the heroine. The author of course gave me a lead, but there was a margin for interpretation. I took the Monarchs into my confidence, I told them frankly what I was about, I mentioned my embarrassments and alternatives. 'Oh, take *him*!' Mrs Monarch murmured sweetly, looking at her husband; and 'What could you want better than my wife?' the Major inquired, with the comfortable candour that now prevailed between us.

I was not obliged to answer these remarks – I was only obliged to place my sitters. I was not easy in mind, and I postponed, a little timidly perhaps, the solution of the question. The book was a large canvas, the other figures were numerous, and I worked off at first some of the episodes in which the hero and the heroine were not concerned. When once I had set *them* up I should have to stick to them – I couldn't make my young man seven feet high in one place and five feet nine in another. I inclined on the whole to the latter measurements, though the major more than once reminded me that *he* looked about as young as anyone. It was indeed quite impossible to arrange him, for the figure, so that it would have been difficult to detect his age. After the spontaneous Oronte had been with me a month, and after I had given him to understand several different times that his native exuberance would presently constitute an insurmountable barrier to our further intercourse, I waked to a sense of his heroic capacity. He was only five feet seven, but the remaining inches were latent. I tried him almost secretly at first, for I was really rather afraid of the judgement my other models would pass on such a choice. If they regarded Miss Churm as little better than a snare, what would they think of the representation by a person so little the real thing as an Italian street-vendor of a protagonist formed by a public school?

If I went a little in fear of them it was not because they bullied me, because they had got an oppressive foothold, but because in their really pathetic decorum and mysteriously permanent newness they counted on me so intensely. I was therefore very glad when Jack Hawley came home: he was always of such good counsel. He painted badly himself, but there was no one like him for putting his finger on the place. He had been absent from England for a year; he had been somewhere – I don't remember where – to get a fresh eye. I was in a good deal of dread of any such organ, but we were old friends; he had been away for months and a sense of emptiness was creeping into my life. I hadn't dodged a missile for a year.

He came back with a fresh eye, but with the same old black velvet blouse, and the first evening he spent in my studio we smoked cigarettes till the small hours. He had done no work himself, he had only got the eye; so the field was clear for the production of my little things. He wanted to see what I had done for the *Cheapside*, but he was disappointed in the exhibition.

That at least seemed the meaning of two or three comprehensive groans which, as he lounged on my big divan, on a folded leg, looking at my latest drawings, issued from his lips with the smoke of the cigarette.

'What's the matter with you?' I asked.

'What's the matter with *you*?'

'Nothing save that I'm mystified.'

'You are indeed. You're quite off the hinge. What's the meaning of this new fad?' And he tossed me, with visible irreverence, a drawing in which I happened to have depicted both my majestic models. I asked if he didn't think it good, and he replied that it struck him as execrable, given the sort of thing I had always represented myself to him as wishing to arrive at; but I let that pass, I was so anxious to see exactly what he meant. The two figures in the picture looked colossal, but I supposed this was *not* what he meant, inasmuch as, for aught he knew to the contrary, I might have been trying for that. I maintained that I was working exactly in the same way as when he last had done me the honour to commend me. 'Well, there's a big hole somewhere,' he answered; 'wait a bit and I'll discover it.' I depended upon him to do so: where else was the fresh eye? But he produced at last nothing more luminous than 'I don't know – I don't like your types.' This was lame, for a critic who had never consented to discuss with me anything but the question of execution, the direction of strokes, and the mystery of values.

'In the drawings you've been looking at I think my types are very handsome.'

'Oh, they won't do!'

'I've had a couple of new models.'

'I see you have. *They* won't do.'

'Are you very sure of that?'

'Absolutely – they're stupid.'

'You mean *I* am – for I ought to get round that.'

'You *can't* – with such people. Who are they?'

I told him, as far as was necessary, and he declared, heartlessly: '*Ce sont des gens qu'il faut mettre à la porte.*'

'You've never seen them; they're awfully good,' I compassionately objected.

'Not seen them. Why, all this recent work of yours drops to pieces with them. It's all I want to see of them.'

'No one else has said anything against it – the *Cheapside* people are pleased.'

'Everyone else is an ass, and the *Cheapside* people the biggest asses of all. Come, don't pretend, at this time of day, to have pretty illusions about the public, especially about publishers and editors. It's not for *such* animals you work – it's for those who know, *coloro che sanno*; so keep straight for *me* if you can't keep straight for yourself. There's a certain sort of thing you tried for from the first – and a very good thing it is. But this twaddle isn't *in* it.' When I talked with Hawley later about *Rutland Ramsay* and its possible successors he declared that I must get back into my boat again or I would go to the bottom. His voice in short was the voice of warning.

I noted the warning, but I didn't turn my friends out of doors. They bored me a good deal; but the very fact that they bored me admonished me not to sacrifice them – if there was anything to be done with them – simply to irritation. As I look back at this phase they seem to me to have pervaded my life not a little. I have a vision of them as most of the time in my studio, seated, against the wall, on an old velvet bench to be out of the way, and looking like a pair of patient courtiers in a royal ante-chamber. I am convinced that during the coldest weeks of the winter they held their ground because it saved them fire. Their newness was losing its gloss, and it was impossible not to feel that they were objects of charity. Whenever Miss Churm arrived they went away, and after I was fairly launched in *Rutland Ramsay* Miss Churm arrived pretty often. They managed to express to me tacitly that they supposed I wanted her for the low life of the book, and I let them suppose it, since they had attempted to study the work – it was lying about the studio – without discovering that it dealt only with the highest circles. They had dipped into the most brilliant of our novelists without deciphering many passages. I still took an hour from them, now and again, in spite of Jack Hawley's warning: it would be time enough to dismiss them, if dismissal should be necessary, when the rigour of the season was over. Hawley had made their acquaintance – he had met them at my fireside – and thought them a ridiculous pair. Learning that he was a painter they tried to approach him, to show him too that they were the real thing; but he looked at them, across the big room, as if they were miles away: they were a compendium of everything that he most objected to in the social system of his country. Such people as that, all convention and patent-leather, with ejaculations that stopped conversation, had no business in a studio. A studio was a place to learn to see, and how could you see through a pair of feather beds?

The main inconvenience I suffered at their hands was that, at first, I was shy of letting them discover how my artful little servant had begun to sit for me for *Rutland Ramsay*. They knew that I had been odd enough (they were prepared by this time to allow oddity to artists) to pick a foreign vagabond out of the streets, when I might have had a person with whiskers and credentials; but it was some time before they learned how high I rated his accomplishments. They found him in an attitude more than once, but they never doubted I was doing him as an organ-grinder. There were several things they never guessed, and one of them was that for a striking scene in the novel, in which a footman briefly figured, it occurred to me to make use of Major Monarch as the menial. I kept putting this off, I didn't like to ask him to don the livery – besides the difficulty of finding a livery to fit him. At last, one day late in the winter, when I was at work on the despised Oronte (he caught one's idea in an instant), and was in the glow of feeling that I was going very straight, they came in, the Major and his wife, with their society laugh about nothing (there was less and less to laugh at), like country-callers – they always reminded me of that – who have walked across the park after church and are presently persuaded to stay to luncheon. Luncheon was over, but they could stay to tea – I knew they wanted it. The fit was on me, however, and I couldn't let my ardour cool and my work wait, with the fading daylight, while my model prepared it. So I asked Mrs Monarch if she would mind laying it out – a request which, for an instant, brought all the blood to her face. Her eyes were on her husband's for a second, and some mute telegraphy passed between them.

Their folly was over the next instant; his cheerful shrewdness put an end to it. So far from pitying their wounded pride, I must add, I was moved to give it as complete a lesson as I could. They bustled about together and got out the cups and saucers and made the kettle boil. I know they felt as if they were waiting on my servant, and when the tea was prepared I said: 'He'll have a cup, please – he's tired.' Mrs Monarch brought him one where he stood, and he took it from her as if he had been a gentleman at a party, squeezing a crush-hat with an elbow.

Then it came over me that she had made a great effort for me – made it with a kind of nobleness – and that I owed her a compensation. Each time I saw her after this I wondered what the compensation could be. I couldn't go on doing the wrong thing to oblige them. Oh, it *was* the wrong thing, the stamp of the work for which they sat – Hawley was not the only person to say it now. I sent in a large number of the drawings I had made for *Rutland Ramsay*, and I received a warning that was more to the point than Hawley's. The artistic adviser of the house for which I was working was of opinion that many of my illustrations were not what had been looked for. Most of these illustrations were the subjects in which the Monarchs had figured. Without going into the question of what *had* been looked for, I saw at this rate I shouldn't get the other books to do. I hurled myself in despair upon Miss Churm, I put her through all her paces. I not only adopted Oronte publicly as my hero, but one morning when the Major looked in to see if I didn't require him to finish a figure for the *Cheapside*, for which he had begun to sit the week before, I told him that I had changed my mind – I would do the drawing from my man. At this my visitor turned pale and stood looking at me. 'Is *he* your idea of an English gentleman?' he asked.

I was disappointed, I was nervous, I wanted to get on with my work; so I replied with irritation: 'Oh, my dear Major – I can't. be ruined for *you*!'

He stood another moment; then, without a word, he quitted the studio. I drew a long breath when he was gone, for I said to myself that I shouldn't see him again. I had not told him definitely that I was in danger of having my work rejected, but I was vexed at his not having felt the catastrophe in the air, read with me the moral of our fruitless collaboration, the lesson that, in the deceptive atmosphere of art, even the highest respectability may fail of being plastic.

I didn't owe my friends money, but I did see them again. They re-appeared together, three days later, and under the circumstances there was something tragic in the fact. It was a proof to me that they could find nothing else in life to do. They had threshed the matter out in a dismal conference – they had digested the bad news that they were not in for the series. If they were not useful to me even for the *Cheapside* their function seemed difficult to determine, and I could only judge at first that they had come, forgivingly, decorously, to take a last leave. This made me rejoice in secret that I had little leisure for a scene; for I had placed both my other models in position together and I was pegging away at a drawing from which I hoped to derive glory. It had been suggested by the passage in which Rutland Ramsay, drawing up a chair to Artemisia's piano-stool, says extraordinary things to her while she ostensibly fingers out a difficult piece of music. I had done Miss Churm at the piano before – it was an attitude in which she knew how to take on an absolutely poetic grace. I wished the two figures to 'compose' together, intensely, and my little Italian had entered perfectly into my conception. The pair were vividly before me, the piano had been pulled out; it was a charming picture of blended youth and murmured love, which I had only to catch and keep. My visitors stood and looked at it, and I was friendly to them over my shoulder.

They made no response, but I was used to silent company and went on with my work, only a little disconcerted (even though exhilarated by the sense that *this* was at last the ideal thing) at not having got rid of them after all. Presently I heard Mrs Monarch's sweet voice beside, or rather above me: 'I wish her hair was a little better done.' I looked up and she was staring with a strange fixedness at Miss Churm, whose back was turned to her. 'Do you mind my just touching it?' she went on – a question which made me spring up for an instant, as with the instinctive fear that she might do the young lady a harm. But she quieted me with a glance I shall never forget – I confess I should like to have been able to paint *that* – and went for a moment to my model. She spoke to her softly, laying a hand upon her shoulder and bending over her; and as the girl, understanding, gratefully assented, she disposed her rough curls, with a few quick passes, in such a way as to make Miss Churm's head twice as charming. It was one of the most heroic personal services I have ever seen rendered. Then Mrs Monarch turned away with a low sigh and, looking about her as if for something to do, stooped to the floor with a noble humility and picked up a dirty rag that had dropped out of my paint-box.

The Major meanwhile had also been looking for something to do and, wandering to the other end of the studio, saw before him my breakfast things, neglected, unremoved. 'I say, can't I be useful *here*?' he called out to me with an irrepressible quaver. I assented with a laugh that I fear was awkward and for the next ten minutes, while I worked, I heard the light clatter of china and the tinkle of spoons and glass. Mrs Monarch assisted her husband – they washed up my crockery, they put it away. They wandered off into my little scullery, and I afterwards found that they had cleaned my knives and that my slender stock of plate had an unprecedented surface. When it came over me, the latent eloquence of what they were doing, I confess that my drawing was blurred for a moment – the picture swam. They had accepted their failure, but they couldn't accept their fate. They had bowed their heads in bewilderment to the perverse and cruel law in virtue of which the real thing could be so much less precious than the unreal; but they didn't want to starve. If my servants were my models, my models might be my servants. They would reverse the parts – the others would sit for the ladies and gentlemen, and *they* would do the work. They would still be in the studio – it was an intense dumb appeal to me not to turn them out. 'Take us on,' they wanted to say – 'we'll do *anything*.'

When all this hung before me the *afflatus* vanished – my pencil dropped from my hand. My sitting was spoiled and I got rid of my sitters, who were also evidently rather mystified and awestruck. Then, alone with the Major and his wife, I had a most uncomfortable moment. He put their prayer into a single sentence: 'I say, you know – just let *us* do for you, can't you?'

I couldn't – it was dreadful to see them emptying my slops; but I pretended I could to oblige them for about a week. Then I gave them a sum of money to go away; and I never saw them again. I obtained the remaining books, but my friend Hawley repeats that Major and Mrs Monarch did me a permanent harm, got me into a second-rate trick. If it be true I am content to have paid the price – for the memory.

The Lesson of the Master

1

HE had been told the ladies were at church, but this was corrected by what he saw from the top of the steps – they descended from a great height in two arms, with a circular sweep of the most charming effect – at the threshold of the door which, from the long bright gallery, overlooked the immense lawn. Three gentlemen, on the grass, at a distance, sat under the great trees, while the fourth figure showed a crimson dress that told as a 'bit of colour' amid the fresh rich green. The servant had so far accompanied Paul Overt as to introduce him to this view, after asking him if he wished first to go to his room. The young man declined that privilege conscious of no disrepair from so short and easy a journey and always liking to take at once a general perceptive possession of a new scene. He stood there a little with his eyes on the group and on the admirable picture, the wide grounds of an old country house near London – that only made it better – on a splendid Sunday in June. 'But that lady, who's *she*?' he said to the servant before the man left him.

'I think she's Mrs St George, sir.'

'Mrs St George, the wife of the distinguished –' Then Paul Overt checked himself, doubting if a footman would know.

'Yes, sir – probably, sir,' said his guide, who appeared to wish to intimate that a person staying at Summersoft would naturally be, if only by alliance, distinguished. His tone, however, made poor Overt himself feel for the moment scantly so.

'And the gentlemen?' Overt went on.

'Well, sir, one of them's General Fancourt.'

'Ah yes, I know; thank you.' General Fancourt was distinguished, there was no doubt of that, for something he had done, or perhaps even hadn't done – the young man couldn't remember which – some years before in India. The servant went away, leaving the glass doors open into the gallery, and Paul Overt remained at the head of the wide double staircase, saying to himself that the place was sweet and promised a pleasant visit, while he leaned on the balustrade of fine old ironwork which, like all the other details, was of the same period as the house. It all went together and spoke in one voice – a rich English voice of the early part of the eighteenth century. It might have been church-time on a summer's day in the reign of Queen Anne; the stillness was too perfect to be modern, the nearness counted so as distance, and there was something so fresh and sound in the originality of the large smooth house, the expanse of beautiful brickwork that showed for pink rather than red and that had been kept clear of messy creepers by the law under which a woman with a rare complexion disdains a veil. When Paul Overt became aware that the people under the trees had noticed him he turned back through the open doors into the great gallery which was the pride of the place. It marched across from end to end and seemed – with its bright colours, its high panelled windows, its faded flowered chintzes, its quickly-recognized portraits and pictures, the blue-and-white china of its cabinets and the attenuated festoons and rosettes of its ceiling – a cheerful upholstered avenue into the other century.

Our friend was slightly nervous; that went with his character as a student of fine prose, went with the artist's general disposition to vibrate; and there was a particular thrill in the idea that Henry St George might be a member of the party. For the young aspirant he had remained a high literary figure, in spite of the lower range of production to which he had fallen after his first three great successes, the comparative absence of quality in his later work. There had been moments when Paul Overt almost shed tears for this; but now that he was near him – he had never met him – he was conscious only of the fine original source and of his own immense debt. After he had taken a turn or two up and down the gallery he came out again and descended the steps. He was but slenderly supplied with a certain social boldness – it was really a weakness in him – so that, conscious of a want of acquaintance with the four persons in the distance, he gave way to motions recommended by their not committing him to a positive approach. There was a fine English awkwardness in this – he felt that too as he sauntered vaguely and obliquely across the lawn, taking an independent line. Fortunately there was an equally fine English directness in the way one of the gentlemen presently rose and made as if to 'stalk' him, though with an air of conciliation and reassurance. To this demonstration Paul Overt instantly responded, even if the gentleman were not his host. He was tall, straight, and elderly and had, like the great house itself, a pink smiling face, and into the bargain a white moustache. Our young man met him half-way while he laughed and said: 'Er – Lady Watermouth told us you were coming; she asked me just to look after you.' Paul Overt thanked him, liking him on the spot, and turned round with him to walk toward the others. 'They've all gone to church – all except us,' the stranger continued as they went; 'we're just sitting here – it's so jolly.' Overt pronounced it jolly indeed: it was such a lovely place. He mentioned that he was having the charming impression for the first time.

'Ah, you've not been here before?' said his companion. 'It's a nice little place – not much to *do*, you know.' Overt wondered what he wanted to 'do' – he felt that he himself was doing so much. By the time they came to where the others sat he had recognized his initiator for a military man and – such was the turn of Overt's imagination – had found him thus still more sympathetic. He would naturally have a need for action, for deeds at variance with the pacific pastoral scene. He was evidently so good-natured, however, that he accepted the inglorious hour for what it was worth. Paul Overt shared it with him and with his companions for the next twenty minutes; the latter looked at him and he looked at them without knowing much who they were, while the talk went on without much telling him even what it meant. It seemed indeed to mean nothing in particular; it wandered, with casual pointless pauses and short terrestrial flights, amid names of persons and places – names which, for our friend, had no great power of evocation. It was all sociable and slow, as was right and natural of a warm Sunday morning.

His first attention was given to the question, privately considered, of whether one of the two younger men would be Henry St George. He knew many of his distinguished contemporaries by their photographs, but had never, as happened, seen a portrait of the great misguided novelist. One of the gentlemen was unimaginable – he was too young; and the other scarcely looked clever enough, with such mild undiscriminating eyes. If those eyes were St George's the problem presented by the ill-matched parts of his genius would be still more difficult of solution. Besides, the deportment of their proprietor was not, as regards the lady in the red dress, such as could be natural, toward the wife of his bosom, even to a writer accused by several critics of sacrificing too much to manner. Lastly Paul Overt had a vague sense that if the gentleman with the expressionless eyes bore the name that had set his heart beating faster (he also had contradictory conventional whiskers – the young admirer of the celebrity had never in a mental vision seen *his* face in so vulgar a frame) he would have given him a sign of recognition or of friendliness, would have heard of him a little, would know something about *Ginistrella*, would have an impression of how that fresh fiction had caught the eye of real criticism. Paul Overt had a dread of being grossly proud, but even morbid modesty might view the authorship of *Ginistrella* as constituting a degree of identity. His soldierly friend became clear enough: he was 'Fancourt', but was also 'the General'; and he mentioned to the new visitor in the course of a few moments that he had but lately returned from twenty years' service abroad.

'And now you remain in England?' the young man asked.

'Oh yes; I've bought a small house in London.'

'And I hope you like it,' said Overt, looking at Mrs St George.

'Well, a little house in Manchester Square – there's a limit to the enthusiasm *that* inspires.'

'Oh I meant being at home again – being back in Piccadilly.'

'My daughter likes Piccadilly – that's the main thing. She's very fond of art and music and literature and all that kind of thing. She missed it in India and she finds it in London, or she hopes she'll find it. Mr St George has promised to help her – he has been awfully kind to her. She has gone to church – she's fond of that too – but they'll all be back in a quarter of an hour. You must let me introduce you to her – she'll be so glad to know you. I dare say she has read every blest word you've written.'

'I shall be delighted – I haven't written so very many,' Overt pleaded, feeling, and without resentment, that the General at least was vagueness itself about that. But he wondered a little why, expressing this friendly disposition, it didn't occur to the doubtless eminent soldier to pronounce the word that would put him in relation with Mrs St George. If it was a question of introductions Miss Fancourt – apparently as yet unmarried – was far away, while the wife of his illustrious confrère was almost between them. This lady struck Paul Overt as altogether pretty, with a surprising juvenility and a high smartness of aspect, something that – he could scarcely have said why – served for mystification. St George certainly had every right to a charming wife, but he himself would never have imagined the important little woman in the aggressively Parisian dress the partner for life, the *alter ego*, of a man of letters. That partner in general, he knew, that second self, was far from presenting herself in a single type: observation had taught him that she was not inveterately, not necessarily plain. But he had never before seen her look so much as if her prosperity had deeper foundations than an ink-spotted study-table littered with proof-sheets. Mrs St George might have been the wife of a gentleman who 'kept' books rather than wrote them, who carried on great affairs in the City and made better bargains than those that poets mostly make with publishers. With this she hinted at a success more personal – a success peculiarly stamping the age in which society, the world of conversation, is a great drawing-room with the City for its ante-chamber. Overt numbered her years at first as some thirty, and then ended by believing that she might approach her fiftieth. But she somehow in this case juggled away the excess and the difference – you only saw them in a rare glimpse, like the rabbit in the conjurer's sleeve. She was extraordinarily white, and her every element and item was pretty; her eyes, her ears, her hair, her voice, her hands, her feet – to which her relaxed attitude in her wicker chair gave a great publicity – and the numerous ribbons and trinkets with which she was bedecked. She looked as if she had put on her best clothes to go to church and then had decided they were too good for that and had stayed at home. She told a story of some length about the shabby way Lady Jane had treated the Duchess, as well as an anecdote in relation to a purchase she had made in Paris – on her way back from Cannes; made for Lady Egbert, who had never refunded the money. Paul Overt suspected her of a tendency to figure great people as larger than life, until he noticed the manner in which she handled Lady Egbert, which was so sharply mutinous that it reassured him. He felt he should have understood her better if he might have met her eye; but she scarcely so much as glanced at him. 'Ah here they come – all the good ones!' she said at last; and Paul Overt admired at his distance the return of the church-goers – several persons, in couples and threes, advancing in a flicker of sun and shade at the end of a large green vista formed by the level grass and the overarching boughs.

'If you mean to imply that *we're* bad, I protest,' said one of the gentlemen – 'after making one's self agreeable all the morning!'

'Ah, if they've found you agreeable –!' Mrs St George gaily cried. 'But if we're good the others are better.'

'They must be angels then,' said the amused General.

'Your husband was an angel, the way he went off at your bidding,' the gentleman who had first spoken declared to Mrs St George.

'At my bidding?'

'Didn't you make him go to church?'

'I never made him do anything in my life but once – when I made him burn up a bad book. That's all!' At her 'That's all!' our young friend broke into an irrepressible laugh; it lasted only a second, but it drew her eyes to him. His own met them, though not long enough to help him to understand her; unless it were a step towards this that he saw on the instant how the burnt book – the way she alluded to it! – would have been one of her husband's finest things.

'A bad book?' her interlocutor repeated.

'I didn't like it. He went to church because your daughter went,' she continued to General Fancourt. 'I think it my duty to call your attention to his extraordinary demonstrations to your daughter.'

'Well, if you don't mind them I don't,' the General laughed. '*Il s'attache à ses pas*. But I don't wonder – she's so charming.'

'I hope she won't make him burn any books!' Paul Overt ventured to exclaim.

'If she'd make him write a few it would be more to the purpose,' said Mrs St George. 'He has been of a laziness of late – !'

Our young man stared – he was so struck with the lady's phraseology. Her 'write a few' seemed to him almost as good as her 'That's all'. Didn't she, as the wife of a rare artist, know what it was to produce *one* perfect work of art? How in the world did she think they were turned off? His private conviction was that, admirably as Henry St George wrote, he had written for the last ten years, and especially for the last five, only too much, and there was an instant during which he felt inwardly solicited to make this public. But before he had spoken a diversion was effected by the return of the absentees. They strolled up dispersedly – there were eight or ten of them – and the circle under the trees rearranged itself as they took their place in it. They made it much larger, so that Paul Overt could feel – he was always feeling that sort of thing, as he said to himself – that if the company had already been interesting to watch the interest would now become intense. He shook hands with his hostess, who welcomed him without many words, in the manner of a woman able to trust him to understand and conscious that so pleasant an occasion would in every way speak for itself. She offered him no particular facility for sitting by her, and when they had all subsided again he found himself still next General Fancourt, with an unknown lady on his other flank.

'That's my daughter – that one opposite,' the General said to him without loss of time. Overt saw a tall girl, with magnificent red hair, in a dress of a pretty grey-green tint and of a limp silken texture, a garment that clearly shirked every modern effect. It had therefore somehow the stamp of the latest thing, so that our beholder quickly took her for nothing if not contemporaneous.

'She's very handsome – very handsome,' he repeated while he considered her. There was something noble in her head, and she appeared fresh and strong.

Her good father surveyed her with complacency, remarking

soon: 'She looks too hot – that's her walk. But she'll be all right presently. Then I'll make her come over and speak to you.'

'I should be sorry to give you that trouble. If you were to take me over *there* – !' the young man murmured.

'My dear sir, do you suppose I put myself out that way? I don't mean for you, but for Marian,' the General added.

'*I* would put myself out for her soon enough,' Overt replied; after which he went on: 'Will you be so good as to tell me which of those gentlemen is Henry St George?'

'The fellow talking to my girl. By Jove, he *is* making up to her – they're going off for another walk.'

'Ah, is that he – really?' Our friend felt a certain surprise, for the personage before him seemed to trouble a vision which had been vague only while not confronted with the reality. As soon as the reality dawned the mental image, retiring with a sigh, became substantial enough to suffer a slight wrong. Overt, who had spent a considerable part of his short life in foreign lands, made now, but not for the first time, the reflection that whereas in those countries he had almost always recognized the artist and the man of letters by his personal 'type', the mould of his face, the character of his head, the expression of his figure, and even the indications of his dress, so in England this identification was as little as possible a matter of course, thanks to the greater conformity, the habit of sinking the profession instead of advertising it, the general diffusion of the air of the gentleman – the gentleman committed to no particular set of ideas. More than once, on returning to his own country, he had said to himself about the people met in society: 'One sees them in this place and that, and one even talks with them; but to find out what they *do* one would really have to be a detective.' In respect to several individuals whose work he was the opposite of 'drawn to' – perhaps he was wrong – he found himself adding 'No wonder they conceal it – when it's so bad!' He noted that oftener than in France and in Germany his artist looked like a gentleman – that is like an English one – while, certainly outside a few exceptions, his gentleman didn't look like an artist. St George was not one of the exceptions; that circumstance he definitely apprehended before the great man had turned his back to walk off with Miss Fancourt. He certainly looked better behind than any foreign man of letters – showed for beautifully correct in his tall black hat and his superior frock coat. Somehow, all the same, these very garments – he wouldn't have minded them so much on a week-day – were disconcerting to Paul Overt, who forgot for the moment that the head of the profession was not a bit better dressed than himself. He had caught a glimpse of a regular face, a fresh colour, a brown moustache, and a pair of eyes surely never visited by a fine frenzy, and he promised himself to study these denotements on the first occasion. His superficial sense was that their owner might have passed for a lucky stock-broker – a gentleman driving eastward every morning from a sanitary suburb in a smart dog-cart. That carried out the impression already derived from his wife. Paul's glance, after a moment, travelled back to this lady, and he saw how her own had followed her husband as he moved off with Miss Fancourt. Overt permitted himself to wonder a little if she were jealous when another woman took him away. Then he made out that Mrs St George wasn't glaring at the indifferent maiden. Her eyes rested but on her husband, and with unmistakable serenity. That was the way she wanted him to be – she liked his conventional uniform. Overt longed to hear more about the book she had induced him to destroy.

2

As they all came out from luncheon General Fancourt took hold of him with an 'I say, I want you to know my girl!' as if the idea had just occurred to him and he hadn't spoken of it before. With the other hand he possessed himself all paternally of the young lady. 'You know all about him. I've seen you with his books. She reads everything – everything!' he went on to Paul. The girl smiled at him and then laughed at her father. The General turned away and his daughter spoke – 'Isn't papa delightful?'

'He is indeed, Miss Fancourt.'

'As if I read you because I read "everything"!'

'Oh I don't mean for saying that,' said Paul Overt. 'I liked him from the moment he began to be kind to me. Then he promised me this privilege.'

'It isn't for you he means it – it's for me. If you flatter yourself that he thinks of anything in life but me you'll find you're mistaken. He introduces everyone. He thinks me insatiable.'

'You speak just like him,' laughed our youth.

'Ah but sometimes I want to' – and the girl coloured. 'I don't read everything – I read very little. But I *have* read you.'

'Suppose we go into the gallery,' said Paul Overt. She pleased him greatly, not so much because of this last remark – though that of course was not too disconcerting – as because, seated opposite to him at luncheon, she had given him for half an hour the impression of her beautiful face. Something else had come with it – a sense of generosity, of an enthusiasm which, unlike many enthusiasms, was not all manner. That was not spoiled for him by his seeing that the repast had placed her again in familiar contact with Henry St George. Sitting next her this celebrity was also opposite our young man, who had been able to note that he multiplied the attentions lately brought by his wife to the General's notice. Paul Overt had gathered as well that this lady was not in the least discomposed by these fond excesses and that she gave every sign of an unclouded spirit. She had Lord Masham on one side of her and on the other the accomplished Mr Mulliner, editor of the new high-class lively evening paper which was expected to meet a want felt in circles increasingly conscious that Conservatism must be made amusing, and unconvinced when assured by those of another political colour that it was already amusing enough. At the end of an hour spent in her company Paul Overt thought her still prettier than at the first radiation, and if her profane allusions to her husband's work had not still rung in his ears he should have liked her – so far as it could be a question of that in connexion with a woman to whom he had not yet spoken and to whom probably he should never speak if it were left to her. Pretty women were a clear need to this genius, and for the hour it was Miss Fancourt who supplied the want. If Overt had promised himself a closer

view the occasion was now of the best, and it brought consequences felt by the young man as important. He saw more in
St George's face, which he liked the better for its not having
told its whole story in the first three minutes. That story came
out as one read, in short instalments – it was excusable that one's
analogies should be somewhat professional – and the text was a
style considerably involved, a language not easy to translate at
sight. There were shades of meaning in it and a vague perspective of history which receded as you advanced. Two facts
Paul had particularly heeded. The first of these was that he liked
the measured mask much better at inscrutable rest than in social
agitation; its almost convulsive smile above all displeased him
(as much as any impression from that source could), whereas
the quiet face had a charm that grew in proportion as stillness
settled again. The change to the expression of gaiety excited,
he made out, very much the private protest of a person sitting
gratefully in the twilight when the lamp is brought in too soon.
His second reflection was that, though generally averse to the
flagrant use of ingratiating arts by a man of age 'making up' to
a pretty girl, he was not in this case too painfully affected: which
seemed to prove either that St George had a light hand or the
air of being younger than he was, or else that Miss Fancourt's
own manner somehow made everything right.

Overt walked with her into the gallery, and they strolled to
the end of it, looking at the pictures, the cabinets, the charming
vista, which harmonized with the prospect of the summer afternoon, resembling it by a long brightness, with great divans and
old chairs that figured hours of rest. Such a place as that had the
added merit of giving those who came into it plenty to talk about.
Miss Fancourt sat down with her new acquaintance on a flowered
sofa, the cushions of which, very numerous, were tight ancient
cubes of many sizes, and presently said: 'I'm so glad to have a
chance to thank you.'

'To thank me – ?' He had to wonder.

'I liked your book so much. I think it splendid.'

She sat there smiling at him, and he never asked himself which
book she meant; for after all he had written three or four. That
seemed a vulgar detail, and he wasn't even gratified by the idea

of the pleasure she told him – her handsome bright face told him – he had given her. The feeling she appealed to, or at any rate the feeling she excited, was something larger, something that had little to do with any quickened pulsation of his own vanity. It was responsive admiration of the life she embodied, the young purity and richness of which appeared to imply that real success was to resemble *that*, to live, to bloom, to present the perfection of a fine type, not to have hammered out headachy fancies with a bent back at an ink-stained table. While her grey eyes rested on him – there was a widish space between these, and the division of her rich-coloured hair, so thick that it ventured to be smooth, made a free arch above them – he was almost ashamed of that exercise of the pen which it was her present inclination to commend. He was conscious he should have liked better to please her in some other way. The lines of her face were those of a woman grown, but the child lingered on in her complexion and in the sweetness of her mouth. Above all she was natural – that was indubitable now; more natural than he had supposed at first, perhaps on account of her aesthetic toggery, which was conventionally unconventional, suggesting what he might have called a tortuous spontaneity. He had feared that sort of thing in other cases, and his fears had been justified; for, though he was an artist to the essence, the modern reactionary nymph, with the brambles of the woodland caught in her folds and a look as if the satyrs had toyed with her hair, made him shrink not as a man of starch and patent leather, but as a man potentially himself a poet or even a faun. The girl was really more candid than her costume, and the best proof of it was her supposing her liberal character suited by any uniform. This was a fallacy, since if she was draped as a pessimist he was sure she liked the taste of life. He thanked her for her appreciation – aware at the same time that he didn't appear to thank her enough and that she might think him ungracious. He was afraid she would ask him to explain something he had written, and he always winced at that – perhaps too timidly – for to his own ear the explanation of a work of art sounded fatuous. But he liked her so much as to feel a confidence that in the long run he should be able to show her he wasn't rudely evasive. Moreover she surely wasn't quick to take offence, wasn't irritable; she could be trusted to wait. So when he said to her, 'Ah, don't talk of anything I've done, don't talk of it *here*; there's another man in the house who's the actuality!' – when he uttered this short sincere protest it was with the sense that she would see in the words neither mock humility nor the impatience of a successful man bored with praise.

'You mean Mr St George – isn't he delightful?'

Paul Overt met her eyes, which had a cool morning light that would have half broken his heart if he hadn't been so young. 'Alas I don't know him. I only admire him at a distance.'

'Oh you *must* know him – he wants so to talk to you,' returned Miss Fancourt, who evidently had the habit of saying the things that, by her quick calculation, would give people pleasure. Paul saw how she would always calculate on everything's being simple between others.

'I shouldn't have supposed he knew anything about me,' he professed.

'He does then – everything. And if he didn't I should be able to tell him.'

'To tell him everything?' our friend smiled.

'You talk just like the people in your book!' she answered.

'Then they must all talk alike.'

She thought a moment, not a bit disconcerted. 'Well, it must be so difficult. Mr St George tells me it *is* – terribly. I've tried too – and I find it so. I've tried to write a novel.'

'Mr St George oughtn't to discourage you,' Paul went so far as to say.

'You do much more – when you wear that expression.'

'Well, after all, why try to be an artist?' the young man pursued. 'It's so poor – so poor!'

'I don't know what you mean,' said Miss Fancourt, who looked grave.

'I mean as compared with being a person of action – as living your works.'

'But what's art but an intense life – if it be real?' she asked. 'I think it's the only one – everything else is so clumsy!' Her companion laughed and she brought out with her charming serenity what next struck her. 'It's so interesting to meet so many celebrated people.'

'So I should think – but surely it isn't new to you.'

'Why I've never seen anyone – anyone: living always in Asia.'

The way she talked of Asia somehow enchanted him. 'But doesn't that continent swarm with great figures? Haven't you administered provinces in India and had captive rajahs and tributary princes chained to your car?'

It was as if she didn't care even *should* he amuse himself at her cost. 'I was with my father after I left school to go out there. It was delightful being with him – we're alone together in the world he and I – but there was none of the society I like best. One never heard of a picture – never of a book except bad ones.'

'Never of a picture? Why, wasn't all life a picture?'

She looked over the delightful place where they sat. 'Nothing to compare to this. I adore England!' she cried.

It fairly stirred in him the sacred chord. 'Ah of course I don't deny that we must do something with her, poor old dear, yet.'

'She hasn't been touched, really,' said the girl.

'Did Mr St George say that?'

There was a small, as he felt, harmless spark of irony in his question; which, however, she answered very simply, not noticing the insinuation. 'Yes, he says England hasn't been touched – not considering all there is,' she went on eagerly. 'He's so interesting about our country. To listen to him makes one want so to do something.'

'It would make *me* want to,' said Paul Overt, feeling strongly, on the instant, the suggestion of what she said and that of the emotion with which she said it, and well aware of what an incentive, on St George's lips, such a speech might be.

'Oh you – as if you hadn't! I should like so to hear you talk together,' she added ardently.

'That's very genial of you; but he'd have it all his own way. I'm prostrate before him.'

She had an air of earnestness. 'Do you think then he's so perfect?'

'Far from it. Some of his later books seem to me of a queer-ness – !'

'Yes, yes – he knows that.'

Paul Overt stared. 'That they seem to me of a queerness –!'

'Well yes, or at any rate that they're not what they should be. He told me he didn't esteem them. He has told me such wonderful things – he's so interesting.'

There was a certain shock for Paul Overt in the knowledge that the fine genius they were talking of had been reduced to so explicit a confession and had made it, in his misery, to the first comer; for though Miss Fancourt was charming what was she after all but an immature girl encountered at a country house? Yet precisely this was part of the sentiment he himself had just expressed; he would make way completely for the poor peccable great man not because he didn't read him clear, but altogether because he did. His consideration was half composed of tenderness for superficialities which he was sure their perpetrator judged privately, judged more ferociously than anyone, and which represented some tragic intellectual secret. He would have his reasons for his psychology *à fleur de peau*, and these reasons could only be cruel ones, such as would make him dearer to those who already were fond of him. 'You excite my envy. I have my reserves, I discriminate – but I love him,' Paul said in a moment. 'And seeing him for the first time this way is a great event for me.'

'How momentous – how magnificent!' cried the girl. 'How delicious to bring you together!'

' *Your* doing it – that makes it perfect,' our friend returned.

'He's as eager as you,' she went on. 'But it's so odd you shouldn't have met.'

'It's not really so odd as it strikes you. I've been out of England so much – made repeated absences all these last years.'

She took this in with interest. 'And yet you write of it as well as if you were always here.'

'It's just the being away perhaps. At any rate the best bits, I suspect, are those that were done in dreary places abroad.'

'And why were they dreary?'

'Because they were health resorts – where my poor mother was dying.'

'Your poor mother?' – she was all sweet wonder.

'We went from place to place to help her to get better. But

she never did. To the deadly Riviera (I hate it!), to the high Alps, to Algiers, and far away – a hideous journey – to Colorado.'

'And she isn't better?' Miss Fancourt went on.

'She died a year ago.'

'Really? like mine! Only that's years since. Some day you must tell me about your mother,' she added.

He could at first, on this, only gaze at her. 'What right things you say! If you say them to St George I don't wonder he's in bondage.'

It pulled her up for a moment. 'I don't know what you mean. He doesn't make speeches and professions at all – he isn't ridiculous.'

'I'm afraid you consider then that I am.'

'No, I don't' – she spoke it rather shortly. And then she added: 'He understands – understands everything.'

The young man was on the point of saying jocosely: 'And I don't – is that it?' But these words, in time, changed themselves to others slightly less trivial: 'Do you suppose he understands his wife?'

Miss Fancourt made no direct answer, but after a moment's hesitation put it: 'Isn't she charming?'

'Not in the least!'

'Here he comes. Now you must know him,' she went on. A small group of visitors had gathered at the other end of the gallery and had been there overtaken by Henry St George, who strolled in from a neighbouring room. He stood near them a moment, not falling into the talk but taking up an old miniature from a table and vaguely regarding it. At the end of a minute he became aware of Miss Fancourt and her companion in the distance; whereupon, laying down his miniature, he approached them with the same proscrastinating air, his hands in his pockets and his eyes turned, right and left, to the pictures. The gallery was so long that this transit took some little time, especially as there was a moment when he stopped to admire the fine Gainsborough. 'He says Mrs St George has been the making of him,' the girl continued in a voice slightly lowered.

'Ah, he's often obscure!' Paul laughed.

'Obscure?' she repeated as if she heard it for the first time. Her eyes rested on her other friend, and it wasn't lost upon Paul that they appeared to send out great shafts of softness. 'He's going to speak to us!' she fondly breathed. There was a sort of rapture in her voice, and our friend was startled. 'Bless my soul, does she care for him like *that*? – is she in love with him?' he mentally inquired. 'Didn't I tell you he was eager?' she had meanwhile asked of him.

'It's eagerness dissimulated,' the young man returned as the subject of their observation lingered before his Gainsborough. 'He edges towards us shyly. Does he mean that she saved him by burning that book?'

'That book? what book did she burn?' The girl quickly turned her face to him.

'Hasn't he told you then?'

'Not a word.'

'Then he doesn't tell you everything!' Paul had guessed that she pretty much supposed he did. The great man had now resumed his course and come nearer; in spite of which his more qualified admirer risked a profane observation: 'St George and the Dragon is what the anecdote suggests!'

His companion, however, didn't hear it: she smiled at the dragon's adversary. 'He *is* eager – he is!' she insisted.

'Eager for you – yes.'

But meanwhile she had called out: 'I'm sure you want to know Mr Overt. You'll be great friends and it will always be delightful to me to remember I was here when you first met and that I had something to do with it.'

There was a freshness of intention in the words that carried them off; nevertheless our young man was sorry for Henry St George, as he was sorry at any time for any person publicly invited to be responsive and delightful. He would have been so touched to believe that a man he deeply admired should care a straw for him that he wouldn't play with such a presumption if it were possibly vain. In a single glance of the eye of the pardonable Master he read – having the sort of divination that belonged to his talent – that this personage had ever a store of friendly patience, which was part of his rich outfit, but was versed in no printed page of a rising scribbler. There was even a relief, a simplification, in that: liking him so much already for what he had done, how could one have liked him any more for a perception which must at the best have been vague? Paul Overt got up, trying to show his compassion, but at the same instant he found himself encompassed by St George's happy personal art – a manner of which it was the essence to conjure away false positions. It all took place in a moment. Paul was conscious that he knew him now, conscious of his handshake and of the very quality of his hand; of his face, seen nearer and consequently seen better, of a general fraternizing assurance, and in particular of the circumstance that St George didn't dislike him (as yet at least) for being imposed by a charming but too gushing girl, attractive enough without such danglers. No irritation at any rate was reflected in the voice with which he questioned Miss Fancourt as to some project of a walk – a general walk of the company round the park. He had soon said something to Paul about a talk – 'We must have a tremendous lot of talk; there are so many things, aren't there?' – but our friend could see this idea wouldn't in the present case take very immediate effect. All the same he was extremely happy, even after the matter of the walk had been settled – the three presently passed back to the other part of the gallery, where it was discussed with several members of the party; even when, after they had all gone out together, he found himself for half an hour conjoined with Mrs St George. Her husband had taken the advance with Miss Fancourt, and this pair were quite out of sight. It was the prettiest of rambles for a summer afternoon – a grassy circuit, of immense extent, skirting the limit of the park within. The park was completely surrounded by its old mottled but perfect red wall, which, all the way on their left, constituted in itself an object of interest. Mrs St George mentioned to him the surprising number of acres thus enclosed, together with numerous other facts relating to the property and the family, and the family's other properties: she couldn't too strongly urge on him the importance of seeing their other houses. She ran over the names of these and rang the changes on them with the facility of practice, making them appear an almost endless list. She had received Paul Overt very amiably on his breaking ground with her by the mention of his joy in having just made her husband's acquaint-

ance, and struck him as so alert and so accommodating a little
woman that he was rather ashamed of his *mot* about her to Miss
Fancourt; though he reflected that a hundred other people, on
a hundred occasions, would have been sure to make it. He got
on with Mrs St George, in short, better than he expected;
but this didn't prevent her suddenly becoming aware that she
was faint with fatigue and must take her way back to the house
by the shortest cut. She professed that she hadn't the strength of
a kitten and was a miserable wreck; a character he had been too
preoccupied to discern in her while he wondered in what sense
she could be held to have been the making of her husband. He
had arrived at a glimmering of the answer when she announced
that she must leave him, though this perception was of course
provisional. While he was in the very act of placing himself at her
disposal for the return the situation underwent a change; Lord
Masham had suddenly turned up, coming back to them, over-
taking them, emerging from the shrubbery – Overt could scarcely
have said how he appeared – and Mrs St George had protested
that she wanted to be left alone and not to break up the party.
A moment later she was walking off with Lord Masham. Our
friend fell back and joined Lady Watermouth, to whom he
presently mentioned that Mrs St George had been obliged to
renounce the attempt to go further.

'She oughtn't to have come out at all,' her ladyship rather
grumpily remarked.

'Is she so very much of an invalid?'

'Very bad indeed.' And his hostess added with still greater
austerity: 'She oughtn't really to come to one!' He wondered
what was implied by this, and presently gathered that it was not
a reflection on the lady's conduct or her moral nature: it only
represented that her strength was not equal to her aspirations.

3

The smoking-room at Summersoft was on the scale of the rest
of the place; high, light, commodious, and decorated with such

refined old carvings and mouldings that it seemed rather a bower
for ladies who should sit at work at fading crewels than a par-
liament of gentlemen smoking strong cigars. The gentlemen
mustered there in considerable force on the Sunday evening,
collecting mainly at one end, in front of one of the cool fair
fireplaces of white marble, the entablature of which was adorned
with a delicate little Italian 'subject'. There was another in
the wall that faced it, and, thanks to the mild summer night, a
fire in neither; but a nucleus for aggregation was furnished on
one side by a table in the chimney-corner laden with bottles,
decanters, and tall tumblers. Paul Overt was a faithless smoker;
he would puff a cigarette for reasons with which tobacco had
nothing to do. This was particularly the case on the occasion of
which I speak; his motive was the vision of a little direct talk
with Henry St George. The 'tremendous' communion of which
the great man had held out hopes to him earlier in the day had
not yet come off, and this saddened him considerably, for the
party was to go its several ways immediately after breakfast on
the morrow. He had, however, the disappointment of finding
that apparently the author of *Shadowmere* was not disposed
to prolong his vigil. He wasn't among the gentlemen assembled
when Paul entered, nor was he one of those who turned up, in
bright habiliments, during the next ten minutes. The young man
waited a little, wondering if he had only gone to put on something
extraordinary; this would account for his delay as well as
contribute further to Overt's impression of his tendency to do the
approved superficial thing. But he didn't arrive – he must have
been putting on something more extraordinary than was probable.
Our hero gave him up, feeling a little injured, a little wounded, at
this loss of twenty coveted words. He wasn't angry, but he puffed
his cigarette sighingly, with the sense of something rare possibly
missed. He wandered away with his regret and moved slowly
round the room, looking at the old prints on the walls. In this
attitude he presently felt a hand on his shoulder and a friendly
voice in his ear. 'This is good. I hoped I should find you. I
came down on purpose.' St George was there without a change
of dress and with a fine face – his graver one – to which our
young man all in a flutter responded. He explained that it was

only for the Master – the idea of a little talk – that he had sat up, and that, not finding him, he had been on the point of going to bed.

'Well, you know, I don't smoke – my wife doesn't let me,' said St George, looking for a place to sit down. 'It's very good for me – very good for me. Let us take that sofa.'

'Do you mean smoking's good for you?'

'No, no – her not letting me. It's a great thing to have a wife who's so sure of all the things one can do without. One might never find them out one's self. She doesn't allow me to touch a cigarette.' They took possession of a sofa at a distance from the group of smokers, and St George went on: 'Have you got one yourself?'

'Do you mean a cigarette?'

'Dear no – a wife.'

'No; and yet I'd give up my cigarette for one.'

'You'd give up a good deal more than that,' St George returned. 'However, you'd get a great deal in return. There's a something to be said for wives,' he added, folding his arms and crossing his outstretched legs. He declined tobacco altogether and sat there without returning fire. His companion stopped smoking, touched by his courtesy; and after all they were out of the fumes, their sofa was in a far-away corner. It would have been a mistake, St George went on, a great mistake for them to have separated without a little chat; 'for I know all about you,' he said. 'I know you're very remarkable. You've written a very distinguished book.'

'And how do you know it?' Paul asked.

'Why, my dear fellow, it's in the air, it's in the papers, it's everywhere.' St George spoke with the immediate familiarity of a confrère – a tone that seemed to his neighbour the very rustle of the laurel. 'You're on all men's lips and, what's better, on all women's. And I've just been reading your book.'

'Just? You hadn't read it this afternoon,' said Overt.

'How do you know that?'

'I think you should know how I know it,' the young man laughed.

'I suppose Miss Fancourt told you.'

'No indeed – she led me rather to suppose you had.'

'Yes – that's much more what she'd do. Doesn't she shed a rosy glow over life? But you didn't believe her?' asked St George.

'No, not when you came to us there.'

'Did I pretend? Did I pretend badly?' But without waiting for an answer to this St George went on: 'You ought always to believe such a girl as that – always, always. Some women are meant to be taken with allowances and reserves; but you must take *her* just as she is.'

'I like her very much,' said Paul Overt.

Something in his tone appeared to excite on his companion's part a momentary sense of the absurd; perhaps it was the air of deliberation attending this judgement. St George broke into a laugh to reply. 'It's the best thing you can do with her. She's a rare young lady! In point of fact, however, I confess I hadn't read you this afternoon.'

'Then you see how right I was in this particular case not to believe Miss Fancourt.'

'How right? how can I agree to that when I lost credit by it?'

'Do you wish to pass exactly for what she represents you? Certainly you needn't be afraid,' Paul said.

'Ah, my dear young man, don't talk about passing – for the likes of me! I'm passing away – nothing else than that. She has a better use for her young imagination (isn't it fine?) than in "representing" in any way such a weary wasted used-up animal!' The Master spoke with a sudden sadness that produced a protest on Paul's part; but before the protest could be uttered he went on, reverting to the latter's striking novel: 'I had no idea you were so good – one hears of so many things. But you're surprisingly good.'

'I'm going to be surprisingly better,' Overt made bold to reply.

'I see that, and it's what fetches me. I don't see so much else – as one looks about – that's going to be surprisingly better. They're going to be consistently worse – most of the things. It's so much easier to be worse – heaven knows I've found it so. I'm not in a great glow, you know, about what's breaking out all over the place. But you *must* be better – you really must keep it up. I haven't of course. It's very difficult – that's the devil of the whole thing, keeping it up. But I see you'll be able to. It will be a great disgrace if you don't.'

'It's very interesting to hear you speak of yourself; but I don't know what you mean by your allusions to your having fallen off,' Paul Overt observed with pardonable hypocrisy. He liked his companion so much that the fact of any decline of talent or of care had ceased for the moment to be vivid to him.

'Don't say that – don't say that,' St George returned gravely, his head resting on the top of the sofa-back and his eyes on the ceiling. 'You know perfectly what I mean. I haven't read twenty pages of your book without seeing that you can't help it.'

'You make me very miserable,' Paul ecstatically breathed.

'I'm glad of that, for it may serve as a kind of warning. Shocking enough it must be, especially to a young fresh mind, full of faith – the spectacle of a man meant for better things sunk at my age in such dishonour.' St George, in the same contemplative attitude, spoke softly but deliberately, and without perceptible emotion. His tone indeed suggested an impersonal lucidity that was practically cruel – cruel to himself – and made his young friend lay an argumentative hand on his arm. But he went on while his eyes seemed to follow the graces of the eighteenth-century ceiling: 'Look at me well, take my lesson to heart – for it *is* a lesson. Let that good come of it at least that you shudder with your pitiful impression, and that this may help to keep you straight in the future. Don't become in your old age what I have in mine – the depressing, the deplorable illustration of the worship of false gods!'

'What do you mean by your old age?' the young man asked.

'It has made me old. But I like your youth.'

Paul answered nothing – they sat for a minute in silence. They heard the others going on about the governmental majority. Then 'What do you mean by false gods?' he inquired.

His companion had no difficulty whatever in saying, 'The idols of the market; money and luxury and "the world"; placing one's children and dressing one's wife; everything that drives one to the short and easy way. Ah the vile things they make one do!'

'But surely one's right to want to place one's children.'

'One has no business to have any children,' St George placidly declared. 'I mean of course if one wants to do anything good.'

'But aren't they an inspiration – an incentive?'

'An incentive to damnation, artistically speaking.'

'You touch on very deep things – things I should like to discuss with you,' Paul said. 'I should like you to tell me volumes about yourself. This is a great feast for *me*!'

'Of course it is, cruel youth. But to show you I'm still not incapable, degraded as I am, of an act of faith, I'll tie my vanity to the stake for you and burn it to ashes. You must come and see me – you must come and see us,' the Master quickly substituted. 'Mrs St George is charming; I don't know whether you've had any opportunity to talk with her. She'll be delighted to see you; she likes great celebrities, whether incipient or predominant. You must come and dine – my wife will write to you. Where are you to be found?'

'This is my little address' – and Overt drew out his pocketbook and extracted a visiting-card. On second thoughts, however, he kept it back, remarking that he wouldn't trouble his friend to take charge of it but would come and see him straightway in London and leave it at his door if he should fail to obtain entrance.

'Ah you'll probably fail; my wife's always out – or when she isn't out is knocked up from having *been* out. You must come and dine – though that won't do much good either, for my wife insists on big dinners.' St George turned it over further, but then went on: 'You must come down and see us in the country, that's the best way; we've plenty of room, and it isn't bad.'

'You've a house in the country?' Paul asked enviously.

'Ah not like this! But we have a sort of place we go to – an hour from Euston. That's one of the reasons.'

'One of the reasons?'

'Why my books are so bad.'

'You must tell me all the others!' Paul longingly laughed.

His friend made no direct rejoinder to this, but spoke again abruptly. 'Why have I never seen you before?'

The tone of the question was singularly flattering to our hero, who felt it to imply the great man's now perceiving he had for years missed something. 'Partly, I suppose, because there has been no particular reason why you should see me. I haven't lived in the world – in your world. I've spent many years out of England, in different places abroad.'

'Well, please don't do it any more. You must do England – there's such a lot of it.'

'Do you mean I must write about it?' and Paul struck the note of the listening candour of a child.

'Of course you must. And tremendously well, do you mind? That takes off a little of my esteem for this thing of yours – that it goes on abroad. Hang "abroad"! Stay at home and do things here – do subjects we can measure.'

'I'll do whatever you tell me,' Overt said, deeply attentive. 'But pardon me if I say I don't understand how you've been reading my book,' he added. 'I've had you before me all the afternoon, first in that long walk, then at tea on the lawn, till we went to dress for dinner, and all the evening at dinner and in this place.'

St George turned his face about with a smile. 'I gave it but a quarter of an hour.'

'A quarter of an hour's immense, but I don't understand where you put it in. In the drawing-room after dinner you weren't reading – you were talking to Miss Fancourt.'

'It comes to the same thing, because we talked about *Ginistrella*. She described it to me – she lent me her copy.'

'Lent it to you?'

'She travels with it.'

'It's incredible,' Paul blushed.

'It's glorious for you, but it also turned out very well for me. When the ladies went off to bed she kindly offered to send the book down to me. Her maid brought it to me in the hall and I went to my room with it. I hadn't thought of coming here, I do that so little. But I don't sleep early, I always have to read an hour or two. I sat down to your novel on the spot, without undressing, without taking off anything but my coat. I think that's a sign my curiosity had been strongly roused about it. I read a quarter of an hour, as I tell you, and even in a quarter of an hour I was greatly struck.'

'Ah the beginning isn't very good – it's the whole thing!' said Overt, who had listened to this recital with extreme interest. 'And you laid down the book and came after me?' he asked.

'That's the way it moved me. I said to myself, "I see it's off his own bat, and he's there, by the way, and the day's over and I haven't said twenty words to him." It occurred to me that you'd probably be in the smoking-room and that it wouldn't be too late to repair my omission. I wanted to do something civil to you, so I put on my coat and came down. I shall read your book again when I go up.'

Our friend faced round in his place – he was touched as he had scarce ever been by the picture of such a demonstration in his favour. 'You're really the kindest of men. *Cela s'est passé comme ça?* – and I've been sitting here with you all this time and never apprehended it and never thanked you!'

'Thank Miss Fancourt – it was she who wound me up. She has made me feel as if I had read your novel.'

'She's an angel from heaven!' Paul declared.

'She is indeed. I've never seen anyone like her. Her interest in literature's touching – something quite peculiar to herself; she takes it all so seriously. She feels the arts and she wants to feel them more. To those who practise them it's almost humiliating – her curiosity, her sympathy, her good faith. How can anything be as fine as she supposes it?'

'She's a rare organization,' the younger man sighed.

'The richest I've ever seen – an artistic intelligence really of the first order. And lodged in such a form!' St George exclaimed.

'One would like to represent such a girl as that,' Paul continued.

'Ah, there it is – there's nothing like life!' said his companion. 'When you're finished, squeezed dry and used up and you think the sack's empty, you're still appealed to, you still get touches and thrills, the idea springs up – out of the lap of the actual – and shows you there's always something to be done. But I shan't do it – she's not for me!'

'How do you mean, not for you?'

'Oh, it's all over – she's for you, if you like.'

'Ah, much less!' said Paul. 'She's not for a dingy little man of letters; she's for the world, the bright rich world of bribes and rewards. And the world will take hold of her – it will carry her away.'

'It will try – but it's just a case in which there may be a fight. It would be worth fighting, for a man who had it in him, with youth and talent on his side.'

These words rang not a little in Paul Overt's consciousness – they held him briefly silent. 'It's a wonder she has remained as she is; giving herself away so – with so much to give away.'

'Remaining, you mean, so ingenuous – so natural? Oh, she doesn't care a straw – she gives away because she overflows. She has her own feelings, her own standards; she doesn't keep remembering that she must be proud. And then she hasn't been here long enough to be spoiled; she has picked up a fashion or two, but only the amusing ones. She's a provincial – a provincial of genius,' St George went on; 'her very blunders are charming, her mistakes are interesting. She has come back from Asia with all sorts of excited curiosities and unappeased appetites. She's first-rate herself and she expends herself on the second-rate. She's life herself and she takes a rare interest in imitations. She mixes all things up, but there are none in regard to which she hasn't perceptions. She sees things in a perspective – as if from the top of the Himalayas – and she enlarges everything she touches. Above all she exaggerates – to herself, I mean. She exaggerates you and me!'

There was nothing in that description to allay the agitation caused in our younger friend by such a sketch of a fine subject. It seemed to him to show the art of St George's admired hand, and he lost himself in gazing at the vision – this hovered there before him – of a woman's figure which should be part of the glory of a novel. But at the end of a moment the thing had turned into smoke, and out of the smoke – the last puff of a big cigar – proceeded the voice of General Fancourt, who had left the others, and come and planted himself before the gentlemen on the sofa. 'I suppose that when you fellows get talking you sit up half the night.'

'Half the night? – *jamais de la vie!* I follow a hygiene' –
and St George rose to his feet.

'I see – you're hothouse plants,' laughed the General. 'That's
the way you produce your flowers.'

'I produce mine between ten and one every morning – I
bloom with a regularity!' St George went on.

'And with a splendour!' added the polite General, while Paul
noted how little the author of *Shadowmere* minded, as he phrased
it to himself, when addressed as a celebrated story-teller. The
young man had an idea *he* should never get used to that; it
would always make him uncomfortable – from the suspicion that
people would think they had to – and he would want to prevent
it. Evidently his great colleague had toughened and hardened –
had made himself a surface. The group of men had finished their
cigars and taken up their bedroom candlesticks; but before they
all passed out Lord Watermouth invited the pair of guests who
had been so absorbed together to 'have' something. It happened
that they both declined; upon which General Fancourt said:
'Is that the hygiene? You don't water the flowers?'

'Oh, I should drown them!' St George replied; but, leaving
the room still at his young friend's side, he added whimsically,
for the latter's benefit, in a lower tone: 'My wife doesn't let me.'

'Well, I'm glad I'm not one of you fellows!' the General
richly concluded.

The nearness of Summersoft to London had this consequence,
chilling to a person who had had a vision of sociability in a rail-
way carriage, that most of the company, after breakfast, drove
back to town, entering their own vehicles, which had come out
to fetch them, while their servants returned by train with their
luggage. Three or four young men, among whom was Paul Overt,
also availed themselves of the common convenience; but they
stood in the portico of the house and saw the others roll away.
Miss Fancourt got into a victoria with her father after she had
shaken hands with our hero and said, smiling in the frankest way
in the world, 'I *must* see you more. Mrs St George is so nice:
she has promised to ask us both to dinner together.' This lady and
her husband took their places in a perfectly appointed brougham
– she required a closed carriage – and as our young man waved

his hat to them in response to their nods and flourishes he reflected that, taken together, they were an honourable image of success, of the material rewards and the social credit of literature. Such things were not the full measure, but he nevertheless felt a little proud for literature.

4

Before a week had elapsed he met Miss Fancourt in Bond Street, at a private view of the works of a young artist in 'black-and-white' who had been so good as to invite him to the stuffy scene. The drawings were admirable, but the crowd in the one little room was so dense that he felt himself up to his neck in a sack of wool. A fringe of people at the outer edge endeavoured by curving forward their backs and presenting, below them, a still more convex surface of resistance to the pressure of the mass, to preserve an interval between their noses and the glazed mounts of the pictures; while the central body, in the comparative gloom projected by a wide horizontal screen hung under the skylight and allowing only a margin for the day, remained upright, dense and vague, lost in the contemplation of its own ingredients. This contemplation sat especially in the sad eyes of certain female heads, surmounted with hats of strange convolution and plumage, which rose on long necks above the others. One of the heads, Paul perceived, was much the most beautiful of the collection, and his next discovery was that it belonged to Miss Fancourt. Its beauty was enhanced by the glad smile she sent him across surrounding obstructions, a smile that drew him to her as fast as he could make his way. He had seen for himself at Summersoft that the last thing her nature contained was an affectation of indifference; yet even with this circumspection he took a fresh satisfaction in her not having pretended to await his arrival with composure. She smiled as radiantly as if she wished to make him hurry, and as soon as he came within earshot she broke out in her voice of joy: 'He's here – he's here – he's coming back in a moment!'

'Ah, your father?' Paul returned as she offered him her hand.

'Oh dear no, this isn't my poor father's line. I mean Mr St George. He has just left me to speak to someone – he's coming back. It's he who brought me – wasn't it charming?'

'Ah, that gives him a pull over me – I couldn't have "brought" you, could I?'

'If you had been so kind as to propose it – why not you as well as he?' the girl returned with a face that, expressing no cheap coquetry, simply affirmed a happy fact.

'Why he's a *père de famille*. They've privileges,' Paul explained. And then quickly: 'Will you go to see places with *me*?' he asked.

'Anything you like!' she smiled. 'I know what you mean, that girls have to have a lot of people –' Then she broke off: 'I don't know; I'm free. I've always been like that – I can go about with anyone. I'm so glad to meet you,' she added with a sweet distinctness that made those near her turn round.

'Let me at least repay that speech by taking you out of this squash,' her friend said. 'Surely people aren't happy here!'

'No, they're awfully *mornes*, aren't they? But I'm very happy indeed and I promised Mr St George to remain in this spot till he comes back. He's going to take me away. They send him invitations for things of this sort – more than he wants. It was so kind of him to think of me.'

'They also send me invitations of this kind – more than *I* want. And if thinking of *you* will do it – !' Paul went on.

'Oh, I delight in them – everything that's life – everything that's London!'

'They don't have private views in Asia, I suppose,' he laughed. 'But what a pity that for this year, even in this gorged city, they're pretty well over.'

'Well, next year will do, for I hope you believe we're going to be friends always. Here he comes!' Miss Fancourt continued before Paul had time to respond.

He made out St George in the gaps of the crowd, and this perhaps led to his hurrying a little to say: 'I hope that doesn't mean I'm to wait till next year to see you.'

'No, no – aren't we to meet at dinner on the twenty-fifth?' she panted with an eagerness as happy as his own.

'That's almost next year. Is there no means of seeing you before?'

She stared with all her brightness. 'Do you mean you'd *come*?'

'Like a shot, if you'll be so good as to ask me!'

'On Sunday then – this next Sunday?'

'What have I done that you should doubt it?' the young man asked with delight.

Miss Fancourt turned instantly to St George, who had now joined them, and announced triumphantly: 'He's coming on Sunday – this next Sunday!'

'Ah, my day – my day too!' said the famous novelist, laughing, to their companion.

'Yes, but not yours only. You shall meet in Manchester Square; you shall talk – you shall be wonderful!'

'We don't meet often enough,' St George allowed, shaking hands with his disciple. 'Too many things – ah too many things! But we must make it up in the country in September. You won't forget you've promised me that?'

'Why he's coming on the twenty-fifth – you'll see him then,' said the girl.

'On the twenty-fifth?' St George asked vaguely.

'We dine with you; I hope you haven't forgotten. He's dining out that day,' she added gaily to Paul.

'Oh bless me, yes – that's charming! And you're coming? My wife didn't tell me,' St George said to him. 'Too many things – too many things!' he repeated.

'Too many people – too many people!' Paul exclaimed, giving ground before the penetration of an elbow.

'You oughtn't to say that. They all read you.'

'Me? I should like to see them! Only two or three at most,' the young man returned.

'Did you ever hear anything like that? He knows, haughtily, how good he is!' St George declared, laughing to Miss Fancourt. 'They read *me*, but that doesn't make me like them any better. Come away from them, come away!' And he led the way out of the exhibition.

'He's going to take me to the Park,' Miss Fancourt observed

to Overt with elation as they passed along the corridor that led to the street.

'Ah, does he go there?' Paul asked, taking the fact for a somewhat unexpected illustration of St George's *mœurs*.

'It's a beautiful day – there'll be a great crowd. We're going to look at the people, to look at types,' the girl went on. 'We shall sit under the trees; we shall walk by the Row.'

'I go once a year – on business,' said St George, who had overheard Paul's question.

'Or with a country cousin, didn't you tell me? I'm the country cousin!' she continued over her shoulder to Paul as their friend drew her toward a hansom to which he had signalled. The young man watched them get in; he returned, as he stood there, the friendly wave of the hand with which, ensconced in the vehicle beside her, St George took leave of him. He even lingered to see the vehicle start away and lose itself in the confusion of Bond Street. He followed it with his eyes; it put to him embarrassing things. 'She's not for *me*!' the great novelist had said emphatically at Summersoft; but his manner of conducting himself toward her appeared not quite in harmony with such a conviction. How could he have behaved differently if she *had* been for him? An indefinite envy rose in Paul Overt's heart as he took his way on foot alone; a feeling addressed alike, strangely enough, to each of the occupants of the hansom. How much he should like to rattle about London with such a girl! How much he should like to go and look at 'types' with St George!

The next Sunday at four o'clock he called in Manchester Square, where his secret wish was gratified by his finding Miss Fancourt alone. She was in a large bright friendly occupied room, which was painted red all over, draped with the quaint cheap florid stuffs that are represented as coming from southern and eastern countries, where they are fabled to serve as the counterpanes of the peasantry, and bedecked with pottery of vivid hues, ranged on casual shelves, and with many water-colour drawings from the hand (as the visitor learned) of the young lady herself, commemorating with a brave breadth the sunsets, the mountains, the temples and palaces of India. He sat an hour – more than an hour, two hours – and all the while no one came in. His hostess was so good as to remark, with her liberal humanity, that it was delightful they weren't interrupted; it was so rare in London, especially at that season, that people got a good talk. But luckily now, of a fine Sunday, half the world went out of town, and that made it better for those who didn't go, when these others were in sympathy. It was the defect of London – one of two or three, the very short list of those she recognized in the teeming world-city she adored – that there were too few good chances for talk; you never had time to carry anything far.

'Too many things – too many things!' Paul said, quoting St George's exclamation of a few days before.

'Ah yes, for him there are too many – his life's too complicated.'

'Have you seen it *near*? That's what I should like to do; it might explain some mysteries,' her visitor went on. She asked him what mysteries he meant, and he said: 'Oh peculiarities of his work, inequalities, superficialities. For one who looks at it from the artistic point of view it contains a bottomless ambiguity.'

She became at this, on the spot, all intensity. 'Ah do describe that more – it's so interesting. There are no such suggestive questions. I'm so fond of them. He thinks he's a failure – fancy!' she beautifully wailed.

'That depends on what his ideal may have been. With his gifts it ought to have been high. But till one knows what he really proposed to himself – ? Do *you* know by chance?' the young man broke off.

'Oh he doesn't talk to me about himself. I can't make him. It's too provoking.'

Paul was on the point of asking what then he did talk about, but discretion checked it and he said instead: 'Do you think he's unhappy at home?'

She seemed to wonder. 'At home?'

'I mean in his relations with his wife. He has a mystifying little way of alluding to her.'

'Not to me,' said Marian Fancourt with her clear eyes. 'That wouldn't be right, would it?' she asked gravely.

'Not particularly; so I'm glad he doesn't mention her to you. To praise her might bore you, and he has no business to do anything else. Yet he knows you better than me.'

'Ah but he respects *you*!' the girl cried as with envy.

Her visitor stared a moment, then broke into a laugh. 'Doesn't he respect you?'

'Of course, but not in the same way. He respects what you've done – he told me so, the other day.'

Paul drank it in, but retained his faculties. 'When you went to look at types?'

'Yes – we found so many: he has such an observation of them! He talked a great deal about your book. He says it's really important.'

'Important! Ah the grand creature!' – and the author of the work in question groaned for joy.

'He was wonderfully amusing, he was inexpressibly droll, while we walked about. He sees everything; he has so many comparisons and images, and they're always exactly right. *C'est d'un trouvé*, as they say.'

'Yes, with his gifts, such things as he ought to have done!' Paul sighed.

'And don't you think he *has* done them?'

Ah it was just the point. 'A part of them, and of course even that part's immense. But he might have been one of the greatest. However, let us not make this an hour of qualifications. Even as they stand,' our friend earnestly concluded, 'his writings are a mine of gold.'

To this proposition she ardently responded, and for half an hour the pair talked over the Master's principal productions. She knew them well – she knew them even better than her visitor, who was struck with her critical intelligence and with something large and bold in the movement in her mind. She said things that startled him and that evidently had come to her directly; they weren't picked-up phrases – she placed them too well. St George had been right about her being first-rate, about her not being afraid to gush, not remembering that she must be proud. Suddenly something came back to her, and she said: 'I recollect that he did speak of Mrs St George to me once.

He said, apropos of something or other, that she didn't care for perfection.'

'That's a great crime in an artist's wife,' Paul returned.

'Yes, poor thing!' and the girl sighed with a suggestion of many reflections, some of them mitigating. But she presently added: 'Ah perfection, perfection – how one ought to go in for it! I wish *I* could.'

'Everyone can in his way,' her companion opined.

'In *his* way, yes – but not in hers. Women are so hampered – so condemned! Yet it's a kind of dishonour if you don't, when you want to *do* something, isn't it?' Miss Fancourt pursued, dropping one train in her quickness to take up another, an accident that was common with her. So these two young persons sat discussing high themes in their eclectic drawing-room, in their London 'season' – discussing, with extreme seriousness, the high theme of perfection. It must be said in extenuation of this eccentricity that they were interested in the business. Their tone had truth and their emotion beauty; they weren't posturing for each other or for someone else.

The subject was so wide that they found themselves reducing it; the perfection to which, for the moment, they agreed to confine their speculations was that of the valid, the exemplary work of art. Our young woman's imagination, it appeared, had wandered far in that direction, and her guest had the rare delight of feeling in their conversation a full interchange. This episode will have lived for years in his memory and even in his wonder; it had the quality that fortune distils in a single drop at a time – the quality that lubricates many ensuing frictions. He still, whenever he likes, has a vision of the room, the bright red sociable talkative room with the curtains that, by a stroke of successful audacity, had the note of vivid blue. He remembers where certain things stood, the particular book open on the table and the almost intense odour of the flowers placed, at the left, somewhere behind him. These facts were the fringe, as it were, of a fine special agitation which had its birth in those two hours and of which perhaps the main sign was in its leading him inwardly and repeatedly to breathe, 'I had no idea there was anyone like this – I had no idea there was anyone like this!' Her freedom amazed him and charmed him – it seemed so to simplify the practical question. She was on the footing of an independent personage – a motherless girl who had passed out of her teens and had a position and responsibilities, who wasn't held down to the limitations of a little miss. She came and went with no dragged duenna, she received people alone, and, though she was totally without hardness, the question of protection or patronage had no relevancy in regard to her. She gave such an impression of the clear and the noble combined with the easy and the natural that in spite of her eminent modern situation she suggested no sort of sisterhood with the 'fast' girl. Modern she was indeed, and made Paul Overt, who loved old colour, the golden glaze of time, think with some alarm of the muddled palette of the future. He couldn't get used to her interest in the arts he cared for; it seemed too good to be real – it was so unlikely an adventure to tumble into such a well of sympathy. One might stray into the desert easily – that was on the cards and that was the law of life; but it was too rare an accident to stumble on a crystal well. Yet if her aspirations seemed at one moment too extravagant to be real they struck him at the next as too intelligent to be false. They were both high and lame, and, whims for whims, he preferred them to any he had met in a like relation. It was probable enough she would leave them behind – exchange them for politics or 'smartness' or mere prolific maternity, as was the custom of scribbling daubing educated flattered girls in an age of luxury and a society of leisure. He noted that the water-colours on the walls of the room she sat in had mainly the quality of being naïve, and reflected that naïveté in art is like a zero in a number: its importance depends on the figure it is united with. Meanwhile, however, he had fallen in love with her. Before he went away, at any rate, he said to her: 'I thought St George was coming to see you today, but he doesn't turn up.'

For a moment he supposed she was going to cry '*Comment donc?* Did you come here only to meet him?' But the next he became aware of how little such a speech would have fallen in with any note of flirtation he had as yet perceived in her. She only replied: 'Ah yes, but I don't think he'll come. He recommended me not to expect him.' Then she gaily but all gently added: 'He said it wasn't fair to you. But I think I could manage two.'

'So could I,' Paul Overt returned, stretching the point a little to meet her. In reality his appreciation of the occasion was so completely an appreciation of the woman before him that another figure in the scene, even so esteemed a one as St George, might for the hour have appealed to him vainly. He left the house wondering what the great man had meant by its not being fair to him; and, still more than that, whether he had actually stayed away from the force of that idea. As he took his course through the Sunday solitude of Manchester Square, swinging his stick and with a good deal of emotion fermenting in his soul, it appeared to him he was living in a world strangely magnanimous. Miss Fancourt had told him it was possible she should be away, and that her father should be, on the following Sunday, but that she had the hope of a visit from him in the other event. She promised to let him know should their absence fail, and then he might act accordingly. After he had passed into one of the streets that open from the Square, he stopped, without definite intentions, looking sceptically for a cab. In a moment he saw a hansom roll through the place from the other side and come a part of the way toward him. He was on the point of hailing the driver when he noticed a 'fare' within; then he waited, seeing the man prepare to deposit his passenger by pulling up at one of the houses. The house was apparently the one he himself had just quitted; at least he drew that inference as he recognized Henry St George in the person who stepped out of the hansom. Paul turned off as quickly as if he had been caught in the act of spying. He gave up his cab – he preferred to walk; he would go nowhere else. He was glad St George hadn't renounced his visit altogether – that would have been too absurd. Yes, the world was magnanimous, and even he himself felt so as, on looking at his watch, he noted but six o'clock, so that he could mentally congratulate his successor on having an hour still to sit in Miss Fancourt's drawing-room. He himself might use that hour for another visit, but by the time he reached the Marble Arch the idea of such a course had become incongruous to him. He passed beneath that architectural effort and walked into the Park till he got upon the spreading grass. Here he continued to walk; he took his way across the elastic turf and came out by the Serpentine. He watched with a friendly eye the diversions of the London people, he bent a glance almost encouraging on the young ladies paddling their sweethearts about the lake and the guardsmen tickling tenderly with their bearskins the artificial flowers in the Sunday hats of their partners. He prolonged his meditative walk; he went into Kensington Gardens, he sat upon the penny chairs, he looked at the little sail-boats launched upon the round pond and was glad he had no engagement to dine. He repaired for this purpose, very late, to his club, where he found himself unable to order a repast and told the waiter to bring whatever there was. He didn't even observe what he was served with, and he spent the evening in the library of the establishment, pretending to read an article in an American magazine. He failed to discover what it was about; it appeared in a dim way to be about Marian Fancourt.

Quite late in the week she wrote to him that she was not to go into the country – it had only just been settled. Her father, she added, would never settle anything, but put it all on her. She felt her responsibility – she had to – and since she was forced this was the way she had decided. She mentioned no reasons, which gave our friend all the clearer field for bold conjecture about them. In Manchester Square on this second Sunday he esteemed his fortune less good, for she had three or four other visitors. But there were three or four compensations; perhaps the greatest of which was that, learning how her father had after all, at the last hour, gone out of town alone, the bold conjecture I just now spoke of found itself becoming a shade more bold. And then her presence was her presence, and the personal red room was there and was full of it, whatever phantoms passed and vanished, emitting incomprehensible sounds. Lastly, he had the resource of staying till everyone had come and gone and of believing this grateful to her, though she gave no particular sign. When they were alone together he came to his point. 'But St George did come – last Sunday. I saw him as I looked back.'

'Yes; but it was the last time.'

'The last time?'

'He said he would never come again.'

Paul Overt stared. 'Does he mean he wishes to cease to see you?'

'I don't know what he means,' the girl bravely smiled. 'He won't at any rate see me here.'

'And pray why not?'

'I haven't the least idea,' said Marian Fancourt, whose visitor found her more perversely sublime than ever yet as she professed this clear helplessness.

5

'Oh I say, I want you to stop a little,' Henry St George said to him at eleven o'clock the night he dined with the head of the profession. The company – none of it indeed *of* the profession – had been numerous and was taking its leave; our young man, after bidding good night to his hostess, had put out his hand in farewell to the master of the house. Besides drawing from the latter the protest I have cited this movement provoked a further priceless word about their chance now to have a talk, their going into his room, his having still everything to say. Paul Overt was all delight at this kindness; nevertheless he mentioned in weak jocose qualification the bare fact that he had promised to go to another place which was at a considerable distance.

'Well then you'll break your promise, that's all. You quite awful humbug!' St George added in a tone that confirmed our young man's ease.

'Certainly I'll break it – but it was a real promise.'

'Do you mean to Miss Fancourt? You're following her?' his friend asked.

He answered by a question. 'Oh is *she* going?'

'Base imposter!' his ironic host went on. 'I've treated you handsomely on the article of that young lady: I won't make another concession. Wait three minutes – I'll be with you.' He gave himself to his departing guests, accompanied the long-trained ladies to the door. It was a hot night, the windows were open, the sound of the quick carriages and of the linkmen's call came into the house. The affair had rather glittered; a sense of festal things was in the heavy air: not only the influence of that particular entertainment, but the suggestion of the wide hurry of pleasure which in London on summer nights fills so many of the happier quarters of the complicated town. Gradually Mrs St George's drawing-room emptied itself; Paul was left alone with his hostess, to whom he explained the motive of his waiting. 'Ah yes, some intellectual, some *professional*, talk,' she leered; 'at this season doesn't one miss it? Poor dear Henry, I'm so glad!' The young man looked out of the window a moment, at the called hansoms that lurched up, at the smooth broughams that rolled away. When he turned round Mrs St George had disappeared; her husband's voice rose to him from below – he was laughing and talking, in the portico, with some lady who awaited her carriage. Paul had solitary possession, for some minutes, of the warm deserted rooms where the covered tinted lamplight was soft, the seats had been pushed about and the odour of flowers lingered. They were large, they were pretty, they contained objects of value; everything in the picture told of a 'good house'. At the end of five minutes a servant came in with a request from the Master that he would join him downstairs; upon which, descending, he followed his conductor through a long passage to an apartment thrown out, in the rear of the habitation, for the special requirements, as he guessed, of a busy man of letters.

St George was in his shirt-sleeves in the middle of a large high room – a room without windows, but with a wide skylight at the top, that of a place of exhibition. It was furnished as a library, and the serried bookshelves rose to the ceiling, a surface of incomparable tone produced by dimly-gilt 'backs' interrupted here and there by the suspension of old prints and drawings. At the end farthest from the door of admission was a tall desk, of great extent, at which the person using it could write only in the erect posture of a clerk in a counting-house; and stretched from the entrance to this structure was a wide plain band of crimson cloth, as straight as a garden-path and almost as long, where, in his mind's eye, Paul at once beheld the Master pace to and fro during vexed hours – hours, that is, of admirable composition. The servant gave him a coat, an old jacket with a hang of experience, from a cupboard in the wall, retiring afterwards with the garment he had taken off. Paul Overt welcomed the coat; it was a coat for talk, it promised confidences – having visibly received so many – and had tragic literary elbows. 'Ah we're practical – we're practical!' St George said as he saw his visitor look the place over. 'Isn't it a good big cage for going round and round? My wife invented it and she locks me up here every morning.'

Our young man breathed – by way of tribute – with a certain oppression. 'You don't miss a window – a place to look out?'

'I did at first awfully; but her calculation was just. It saves time, it has saved me many months in these ten years. Here I stand, under the eye of day – in London of course, very often, it's rather a bleared old eye – walled in to my trade. I can't get away – so the room's a fine lesson in concentration. I've learnt the lesson, I think; look at that big bundle of proofs and acknowledge it.' He pointed to a fat roll of papers, on one of the tables, which had not been undone.

'Are you bringing out another – ?' Paul asked in a tone the fond deficiencies of which he didn't recognize till his companion burst out laughing, and indeed scarce even then.

'You humbug, you humbug!' – St George appeared to enjoy caressing him, as it were, with that opprobrium. 'Don't I know what you think of them?' he asked, standing there with his hands in his pockets and with a new kind of smile. It was as if he were going to let his young votary see him all now.

'Upon my word in that case you know more than I do!' the latter ventured to respond, revealing a part of the torment of being able neither clearly to esteem nor distinctly to renounce him.

'My dear fellow,' said the more and more interesting Master, 'don't imagine I talk about my books specifically; they're not a decent subject – *il ne manquerait plus que ça!* I'm not so bad as you may apprehend! About myself, yes, a little, if you like; though it wasn't for that I brought you down here. I want to ask you something – very much indeed; I value this chance.

Therefore sit down. We're practical, but there *is* a sofa, you see – for she does humour my poor bones so far. Like all really great administrators and disciplinarians she knows when wisely to relax.' Paul sank into the corner of a deep leathern couch, but his friend remained standing and explanatory. 'If you don't mind, in this room, this is my habit. From the door to the desk and from the desk to the door. That shakes up my imagination gently; and don't you see what a good thing it is that there's no window for her to fly out of? The eternal standing as I write (I stop at that bureau and put it down, when anything comes, and so we go on) was rather wearisome at first, but we adopted it with an eye to the long run; you're in better order – if your legs don't break down! – and you can keep it up for more years. Oh we're practical – we're practical!' St George repeated, going to the table and taking up all mechanically the bundle of proofs. But, pulling off the wrapper, he had a change of attention that appealed afresh to our hero. He lost himself a moment, examining the sheets of his new book, while the younger man's eyes wandered over the room again.

'Lord, what good things I should do if I had such a charming place as this to do them in!' Paul reflected. The outer world, the world of accident and ugliness, was so successfully excluded, and within the rich protecting square, beneath the patronizing sky, the dream-figures, the summoned company, could hold their particular revel. It was a fond prevision of Overt's rather than an observation on actual data, for which occasions had been too few, that the Master thus more closely viewed would have the quality, the charming gift, of flashing out, all surprisingly, in personal intercourse and at moments of suspended or perhaps even of diminished expectation. A happy relation with him would be a thing proceeding by jumps, not by traceable stages.

'Do you read them – really?' he asked, laying down the proofs on Paul's inquiring of him how soon the work would be published. And when the young man answered 'Oh yes, always,' he was moved to mirth again by something he caught in his manner of saying that. 'You go to see your grandmother on her birthday – and very proper it is, especially as she won't last for ever. She has lost every faculty and every sense; she neither sees, nor hears, nor speaks; but all customary pieties and kindly habits are respectable. Only you're strong if you *do* read 'em! *I* couldn't, my dear fellow. You *are* strong, I know; and that's just a part of what I wanted to say to you. You're very strong indeed. I've been going into your other things – they've interested me immensely. Someone ought to have told me about them before – someone I could believe. But whom can one believe? You're wonderfully on the right road – it's awfully decent work. Now do you mean to keep it up? – that's what I want to ask you.'

'Do I mean to do others?' Paul asked, looking up from his sofa at his erect inquisitor and feeling partly like a happy little boy when the schoolmaster is gay, and partly like some pilgrim of old who might have consulted a world-famous oracle. St George's own performance had been infirm, but as an adviser he would be infallible.

'Others – others? Ah the number won't matter; one other would do, if it were really a further step – a throb of the same effort. What I mean is have you it in your heart to go in for some sort of decent perfection?'

'Ah decency, ah perfection – !' the young man sincerely sighed. 'I talked of them the other Sunday with Miss Fancourt.'

It produced on the Master's part a laugh of odd acrimony. 'Yes, they'll "talk" of them as much as you like! But they'll do little to help one to them. There's no obligation of course; only you strike me as capable,' he went on. 'You must have thought it all over. I can't believe you're without a plan. That's the sensation you give me, and it's so rare that it really stirs one up – it makes you remarkable. If you haven't a plan, if you *don't* mean to keep it up, surely you're within your rights; it's nobody's business, no one can force you, and not more than two or three people will notice you don't go straight. The others – *all* the rest, every blest soul in England, will think you do – will think you *are* keeping it up: upon my honour they will! I shall be one of the two or three who know better. Now the question is whether you can do it for two or three. Is that the stuff you're made of?'

It locked his guest a minute as in closed throbbing arms. 'I could do it for one, if you were the one.'

'Don't say that; I don't deserve it; it scorches me,' he protested with eyes suddenly grave and glowing. 'The "one" is of course one's self, one's conscience, one's idea, the singleness of one's aim. I think of that pure spirit as a man thinks of a woman he has in some detested hour of his youth loved and forsaken. She haunts him with reproachful eyes, she lives for ever before him. As an artist, you know, I've married for money.' Paul stared and even blushed a little, confounded by this avowal; whereupon his host, observing the expression of his face, dropped a quick laugh and pursued: 'You don't follow my figure. I'm not speaking of my dear wife, who had a small fortune – which, however, was not my bribe. I fell in love with her, as many other people have done. I refer to the mercenary muse whom I led to the altar of literature. Don't, my boy, put your nose into *that* yoke. The awful jade will lead you a life!'

Our hero watched him, wondering and deeply touched. 'Haven't you been happy?'

'Happy? It's a kind of hell.'

'There are things I should like to ask you,' Paul said after a pause.

'Ask me anything in all the world. I'd turn myself inside out to save you.'

'To "save" me?' he quavered.

'To make you stick to it – to make you see it through. As I said to you the other night at Summersoft, let my example be vivid to you.'

'Why your books are not so bad as that,' said Paul, fairly laughing and feeling that if ever a fellow had breathed the air of art –!

'So bad as what?'

'Your talent's so great that it's in everything you do, in what's less good as well as in what's best. You've some forty volumes to show for it – forty volumes of wonderful life, of rare observation, of magnificent ability.'

'I'm very clever, of course I know that' – but it was a thing, in fine, this author made nothing of. 'Lord, what rot they'd all

be if I hadn't been! I'm a successful charlatan,' he went on –
'I've been able to pass off my system. But do you know what it
is? It's *carton-pierre*.'

'*Carton-pierre?*' Paul was struck, and gaped.

'Lincrusta-Walton!'

'Ah don't say such things – you make me bleed!' the younger
man protested. 'I see you in a beautiful fortunate home, living
in comfort and honour.'

'Do you call it honour?' – his host took him up with an
intonation that often comes back to him. 'That's what I want *you*
to go in for. I mean the real thing. This is brummagem.'

'Brummagem?' Paul ejaculated while his eyes wandered, by
a movement natural at the moment, over the luxurious room.

'Ah they make it so well today – it's wonderfully deceptive!'

Our friend thrilled with the interest and perhaps even more
with the pity of it. Yet he wasn't afraid to seem to patronize
when he could still so far envy. 'Is it deceptive that I find you
living with every appearance of domestic felicity – blest with a
devoted, accomplished wife, with children whose acquaintance
I haven't yet had the pleasure of making, but who *must* be
delightful young people, from what I know of their parents?'

St George smiled as for the candour of his question. 'It's
all excellent, my dear fellow – heaven forbid I should deny it.
I've made a great deal of money; my wife has known how to
take care of it, to use it without wasting it, to put a good bit of
it by, to make it fructify. I've got a loaf on the shelf; I've got
everything in fact but the great thing.'

'The great thing?' Paul kept echoing.

'The sense of having done the best – the sense which is the
real life of the artist and the absence of which is his death, of
having drawn from his intellectual instrument the finest music
that nature had hidden in it, of having played it as it should be
played. He either does that or he doesn't – and if he doesn't he
isn't worth speaking of. Therefore, precisely, those who really
know *don't* speak of him. He may still hear a great chatter, but
what he hears most is the incorruptible silence of Fame. I've
squared her, you may say, for my little hour – but what's my
little hour? Don't imagine for a moment,' the Master pursued,

'that I'm such a cad as to have brought you down here to abuse or to complain of my wife to you. She's a woman of distinguished qualities, to whom my obligations are immense; so that, if you please, we'll say nothing about her. My boys – my children are all boys – are straight and strong, thank God, and have no poverty of growth about them, no penury of needs. I receive periodically the most satisfactory attestation from Harrow, from Oxford, from Sandhurst – oh we've done the best for them! – of their eminence as living thriving consuming organisms.'

'It must be delightful to feel that the son of one's loins is at Sandhurst,' Paul remarked enthusiastically.

'It is – it's charming. Oh I'm a patriot!'

The young man then could but have the greater tribute of questions to pay. 'Then what did you mean – the other night at Summersoft – by saying that children are a curse?'

'My dear youth, on what basis are we talking?' and St George dropped upon the sofa at a short distance from him. Sitting a little sideways he leaned back against the opposite arm with his hands raised and interlocked behind his head. 'On the supposition that a certain perfection's possible and even desirable – isn't it so? Well, all I say is that one's children interfere with perfection. One's wife interferes. Marriage interferes.'

'You think then the artist shouldn't marry?'

'He does so at his peril – he does so at his cost.'

'Not even when his wife's in sympathy with his work?'

'She never is – she can't be! Women haven't a conception of such things.'

'Surely they on occasion work themselves,' Paul objected.

'Yes, very badly indeed. Oh, of course, often they think they understand, they think they sympathize. Then it is they're most dangerous. Their idea is that you shall do a great lot and get a great lot of money. Their great nobleness and virtue, their exemplary conscientiousness as British females, is in keeping you up to that. My wife makes all my bargains with my publishers for me, and has done so for twenty years. She does it consummately well – that's why I'm really pretty well off. Aren't you the father of their innocent babes, and will you withhold from them their natural sustenance? You asked me the other night if they're not an immense incentive. Of course they are – there's no doubt of that!'

Paul turned it over: it took, from eyes he had never felt open so wide, so much looking at. 'For myself I've an idea I need incentives.'

'Ah well then, *n'en parlons plus!*' his companion handsomely smiled.

'*You* are an incentive, I maintain,' the young man went on. 'You don't affect me in the way you'd apparently like to. Your great success is what I see – the pomp of Ennismore Gardens!'

'Success?' – St George's eyes had a cold fine light. 'Do you call it success to be spoken of as you'd speak of me if you were sitting here with another artist – a young man intelligent and sincere like yourself? Do you call it success to make you blush – as you *would* blush! – if some foreign critic (some fellow, of course I mean, who should know what he was talking about and should have shown you he did, as foreign critics like to show it) were to say to you: "He's the one, in this country, whom they consider the most perfect, isn't he?" Is it success to be the occasion of a young Englishman's having to stammer as you would have to stammer at such a moment for old England? No, no; success is to have made people wriggle to another tune. Do try it!'

Paul continued all gravely to glow. 'Try what?'

'Try to do some really good work.'

'Oh I want to, heaven knows!'

'Well, you can't do it without sacrifices – don't believe that for a moment,' the Master said. 'I've made none. I've had everything. In other words I've missed everything.'

'You've had the full rich masculine human general life, with all the responsibilities and duties and burdens and sorrows and joys – all the domestic and social initiations and complications. They must be immensely suggestive, immensely amusing,' Paul anxiously submitted.

'Amusing?'

'For a strong man – yes.'

'They've **given me** subjects without number, if that's what you mean; but they've taken away at the same time the power to use them. I've touched a thousand things, but which one of them have I turned into gold? The artist has to do only with that – he knows nothing of any baser metal. I've led the life of the world, with my wife and my progeny; the clumsy conventional expensive materialized vulgarized brutalized life of London. We've got everything handsome, even a carriage – we're perfect Philistines and prosperous hospitable eminent people. But, my dear fellow, don't try to stultify yourself and pretend you don't know what we *haven't* got. It's bigger than all the rest. Between artists – come!' the Master wound up. 'You know as well as you sit there that you'd put a pistol-ball into your brain if you had written my books!'

It struck his listener that the tremendous talk promised by him at Summersoft had indeed come off, and with a promptitude, a fulness, with which the latter's young imagination had scarcely reckoned. His impression fairly shook him and he throbbed with the excitement of such deep soundings and such strange confidences. He throbbed indeed with the conflict of his feelings – bewilderment and recognition and alarm, enjoyment and protest and assent, all commingled with tenderness (and a kind of shame in the participation) for the sores and bruises exhibited by so fine a creature, and with a sense of the tragic secret nursed under his trappings. The idea of *his*, Paul Overt's becoming the occasion of such an act of humility made him flush and pant, at the same time that his consciousness was in certain directions too much alive not to swallow – and not intensely to taste – every offered spoonful of the revelation. It had been his odd fortune to blow upon the deep waters, to make them surge and break in waves of strange eloquence. But how couldn't he give out a passionate contradiction of his host's last extravagance, how couldn't he enumerate to him the parts of his work he loved, the splendid things he had found in it, beyond the compass of any other writer of the day? St George listened a while, courteously; then he said, laying his hand on his visitor's: 'That's all very well; and if your idea's to do nothing better there's no reason you shouldn't have as many good things as I – as many human and material appendages, as many sons or daughters, a wife with as many gowns, a house with as many servants, a stable with as many horses, a heart with as many aches.' The Master got up when he had spoken thus – he stood a moment – near the sofa looking down on his agitated pupil. 'Are you possessed of any property?' it occurred to him to ask.

'None to speak of.'

'Oh well then there's no reason why you shouldn't make a goodish income – if you set about it the right way. Study *me* for that – study me well. You may really have horses.'

Paul sat there some minutes without speaking. He looked straight before him – he turned over many things. His friend had wandered away, taking up a parcel of letters from the table where the roll of proofs had lain. 'What was the book Mrs St George made you burn – the one she didn't like?' our young man brought out.

'The book she made me burn – how did you know that?' The Master looked up from his letters quite without the facial convulsion the pupil had feared.

'I heard her speak of it at Summersoft.'

'Ah yes – she's proud of it. I don't know – it was rather good.'

'What was it about?'

'Let me see.' And he seemed to make an effort to remember. 'Oh yes – it was about myself.' Paul gave an irrepressible groan for the disappearance of such a production, and the elder man went on: 'Oh but *you* should write it – *you* should do me.' And he pulled up – from the restless motion that had come upon him; his fine smile a generous glare. 'There's a subject, my boy: no end of stuff in it!'

Again Paul was silent, but it was all tormenting. 'Are there no women who really understand – who can take part in a sacrifice?'

'How can they take part? They themselves are the sacrifice. They're the idol and the altar and the flame.'

'Isn't there even *one* who sees farther?' Paul continued.

For a moment St George made no answer; after which, having torn up his letters, he came back to the point all ironic. 'Of course I know the one you mean. But not even Miss Fancourt.'

'I thought you admired her so much.'

'It's impossible to admire her more. Are you in love with her?' St George asked.

'Yes,' Paul Overt presently said.

'Well then give it up.'

Paul stared. 'Give up my "love"?'

'Bless me, no. Your idea.' And then as our hero but still gazed: 'The one you talked with her about. The idea of a decent perfection.'

'She'd help it – she'd help it!' the young man cried.

'For about a year – the first year, yes. After that she'd be as a millstone round its neck.'

Paul frankly wondered. 'Why she has a passion for the real thing, for good work – for everything you and I care for most.'

'"You and I" is charming, my dear fellow!' his friend laughed. 'She has it indeed, but she'd have a still greater passion for her children – and very proper too. She'd insist on everything's being made comfortable, advantageous, propitious for them. That isn't the artist's business.'

'The artist – the artist! Isn't he a man all the same?'

St George had a grand grimace. 'I mostly think not. You know as well as I what he has to do: the concentration, the finish, the independence he must strive for from the moment he begins to wish his work really decent. Ah my young friend, his relation to women, and especially to the one he's most intimately concerned with, is at the mercy of the damning fact that whereas he can in the nature of things have but one standard, they have about fifty. That's what makes them so superior,' St George amusingly added. 'Fancy an artist with a change of standards as you'd have a change of shirts or of dinner-plates. To *do* it – to do it and make it divine – is the only thing he has to think about. "Is it done or not?" is his only question. Not "Is it done as well as a proper solicitude for my dear little family will allow?" He has nothing to do with the relative – he has only to do with the absolute; and a dear little family may represent a dozen relatives.'

'Then you don't allow him the common passions and affections of men?' Paul asked.

'Hasn't he a passion, an affection, which includes all the rest? Besides, let him have all the passions he likes – if he only keeps his independence. He must be able to be poor.'

Paul slowly got up. 'Why then did you advise me to make up to her?'

St George laid his hand on his shoulder. 'Because she'd make a splendid wife! And I hadn't read you then.'

The young man had a strained smile. 'I wish you had left me alone!'

'I didn't know that that wasn't good enough for you,' his host returned.

'What a false position, what a condemnation of the artist, that he's a mere disfranchised monk and can produce his effect only by giving up personal happiness. What an arraignment of art!' Paul went on with a trembling voice.

'Ah you don't imagine by chance that I'm defending art? "Arraignment" – I should think so! Happy the societies in which it hasn't made its appearance, for from the moment it comes they have a consuming ache, they have an incurable corruption, in their breast. Most assuredly is the artist in a false position! But I thought we were taking him for granted. Pardon me,' St George continued: '*Ginistrella* made me!'

Paul stood looking at the floor – one o'clock struck, in the stillness, from a neighbouring church tower. 'Do you think she'd ever look at me?' he put to his friend at last.

'Miss Fancourt – as a suitor? Why shouldn't I think it? That's why I've tried to favour you – I've had a little chance or two of bettering your opportunity.'

'Forgive me asking you, but do you mean by keeping away yourself?' Paul said with a blush.

'I'm an old idiot – my place isn't there,' St George stated gravely.

'I'm nothing yet, I've no fortune; and there must be so many others,' his companion pursued.

The Master took this considerably in, but made little of it. 'You're a gentleman and a man of genius. I think you might do something.'

'But if I must give that up – the genius?'

'Lots of people, you know, think I've kept mine,' St George wonderfully grinned.

'You've a genius for mystification!' Paul declared; but grasping his hand gratefully in attenuation of this judgement.

'Poor dear boy, I do worry you! But try, try, all the same. I think your chances are good and you'll win a great prize.'

Paul held fast the other's hand a minute; he looked into the strange deep face. 'No, I *am* an artist – I can't help it!'

'Ah show it then!' St George pleadingly broke out. 'Let me see before I die the thing I most want, the thing I yearn for: a life in which the passion – ours – is really intense. If you can be rare don't fail of it! Think what it is – how it counts – how it lives!'

They had moved to the door and he had closed both his hands over his companion's. Here they paused again and our hero breathed deep. 'I want to live!'

'In what sense?'

'In the greatest.'

'Well then stick to it – see it through.'

'With your sympathy – your help?'

'Count on that – you'll be a great figure to me. Count on my highest appreciation, my devotion. You'll give me satisfaction – if that has any weight with you.' After which, as Paul appeared still to waver, his host added: 'Do you remember what you said to me at Summersoft?'

'Something infatuated, no doubt!'

'"I'll do anything in the world you tell me." You said that.'

'And you hold me to it?'

'Ah what am I?' the Master expressively sighed.

'Lord what things I shall have to do!' Paul almost moaned as he departed.

6

'It goes on too much abroad – hang abroad!' These or something like them had been the Master's remarkable words in relation to the action of *Ginistrella*; and yet, though they had made a sharp impression on the author of that work, like almost all spoken words from the same source, he a week after the conversation I have noted left England for a long absence and full of brave intentions. It is not a perversion of the truth to pronounce that encounter the direct cause of his departure. If the oral utterance of the eminent writer had the privilege of moving him deeply it was especially on his turning it over at leisure, hours and days later, that it appeared to yield him its full meaning and exhibit its extreme importance. He spent the summer in Switzerland and, having in September begun a new task, determined not to cross the Alps till he should have made a good start. To this end he returned to a quiet corner he knew well, on the edge of the Lake of Geneva and within sight of the towers of Chillon: a region and a view for which he had an affection that sprang from old associations and was capable of mysterious revivals and refreshments. Here he lingered late, till the snow was on the nearer hills, almost down to the limit to which he could climb when his stint, on the shortening after- noons, was performed. The autumn was fine, the lake was blue, and his book took form and direction. These felicities, for the time embroidered his life, which he suffered to cover him with its mantle. At the end of six weeks he felt he had learnt St George's lesson by heart, had tested and proved its doctrine. Nevertheless he did a very inconsistent thing: before crossing the Alps he wrote to Marian Fancourt. He was aware of the perversity of this act, and it was only as a luxury, an amusement, the reward of a strenuous autumn, that he justified it. She had asked of him no such favour when, shortly before he left London, three days after their dinner in Ennismoré Gardens, he went to take leave of her. It was true she had had no ground – he hadn't named his intention of absence. He had kept his counsel for want of due assurance: it was that particular visit that was, the next thing, to settle the matter. He had paid the visit to see how much he really cared for her, and quick departure, without so much as an explicit farewell, was the sequel to this inquiry, the answer to which had created within him a deep yearning. When he wrote her from Clarens he noted that he owed her an explanation (more than three months after!) for not having told her what he was doing.

She replied now briefly but promptly, and gave him a striking piece of news: that of the death, a week before, of Mrs St George. This exemplary woman had succumbed, in the country, to a violent attack of inflammation of the lungs – he would remember that for a long time she had been delicate. Miss Fancourt added that she believed her husband overwhelmed by the blow; he would miss her too terribly – she had been everything in life to him. Paul Overt, on this, immediately wrote to St George. He would from the day of their parting have been glad to remain in communication with him, but had hitherto lacked the right excuse for troubling so busy a man. Their long nocturnal talk came back to him in every detail, but this was no bar to an expression of proper sympathy with the head of the profession, for hadn't that very talk made it clear that the late accomplished lady was the influence that ruled his life? What catastrophe could be more cruel than the extinction of such an influence? This was to be exactly the tone taken by St George in answering his young friend upwards of a month later. He made no allusion of course to their important discussion. He spoke of his wife as frankly and generously as if he had quite forgotten that occasion, and the feeling of deep bereavement was visible in his words. 'She took everything off my hands – off my mind. She carried on our life with the greatest art, the rarest devotion, and I was free, as few men can have been, to drive my pen, to shut myself up with my trade. This was a rare service – the highest she could have rendered me. Would I could have acknowledged it more fitly!'

A certain bewilderment, for our hero, disengaged itself from these remarks: they struck him as a contradiction, a retraction, strange on the part of a man who hadn't the excuse of witlessness. He had certainly not expected his correspondent to rejoice in the death of his wife, and it was perfectly in order that the rupture of a tie of more than twenty years should have left him sore. But if she had been so clear a blessing what in the name of consistency had the dear man meant by turning *him* upside down that night – by dosing him to that degree, at the most sensitive hour of his life, with the doctrine of renunciation? If Mrs St George was an irreparable loss, then her husband's inspired advice had been a bad joke and renunciation was a mistake. Overt was on the point of rushing back to London to show that, for his part, he was perfectly willing to consider it so, and he went so far as to take the manuscript of the first chapters of his new book out of his table drawer, to insert it into a pocket of his portmanteau. This led to his catching a glimpse of certain pages he hadn't looked at for months, and that accident, in turn, to his being struck with the high promise they revealed – a rare result of such retrospections, which it was his habit to avoid as much as possible: they usually brought home to him that the glow of composition might be a purely subjective and misleading emotion. On this occasion a certain belief in himself disengaged itself whimsically from the serried erasures of his first draft, making him think it best after all to pursue his present trial to the end. If he could write as well under the rigour of privation it might be a mistake to change the conditions before that spell had spent itself. He would go back to London, of course, but he would go back only when he should have finished his book. This was the vow he privately made, restoring his manuscript to the table drawer. It may be added that it took him a long time to finish his book, for the subject was as difficult as it was fine, and he was literally embarrassed by the fulness of his notes. Something within him warned him that he must make it supremely good – otherwise he should lack, as regards his private behaviour, a handsome excuse. He had a horror of this deficiency and found himself as firm as need be on the question of the lamp and the file. He crossed the Alps at last and spent the winter, the spring, the ensuing summer, in Italy, where still, at the end of a twelvemonth, his task was unachieved. 'Stick to it – see it through': this general injunction of St George's was good also for the particular case. He applied it to the utmost, with the result that when in its slow order the summer had come round again he felt he had given all that was in him. This time he put his papers into his portmanteau, with the address of his publisher attached, and took his way northward.

He had been absent from London for two years – two years which, seeming to count as more, had made such a difference in his own life – through the production of a novel far stronger, he believed, than *Ginistrella* – that he turned out into Piccadilly, the morning after his arrival, with a vague expectation of changes, of finding great things had happened. But there were few transformations in Piccadilly – only three or four big red houses where there had been low black ones – and the brightness of the end of June peeped through the rusty railings of the Green Park and glittered in the varnish of the rolling carriages as he had seen it in other, more cursory Junes. It was a greeting he appreciated; it seemed friendly and pointed, added to the exhilaration of his finished book, of his having his own country and the huge oppressive amusing city that suggested everything, that contained everything, under his hand again. 'Stay at home and do things here – do subjects we can measure,' St George had said; and now it struck him he should ask nothing better than to stay at home for ever. Late in the afternoon he took his way to Manchester Square, looking out for a number he hadn't forgotten. Miss Fancourt, however, was not at home, so that he turned rather dejectedly from the door. His movement brought him face to face with a gentleman just approaching it and recognized on another glance as Miss Fancourt's father. Paul saluted this personage, and the General returned the greeting with his customary good manner – a manner so good, however, that you could never tell whether it meant he placed you. The disappointed caller felt the impulse to address him; then, hesitating, became both aware of having no particular remark to make, and convinced that though the old soldier remembered him he remembered him wrong. He therefore went his way without computing the irresistible effect his own evident recognition would have on the General, who never neglected a chance to gossip. Our young man's face was expressive, and observation seldom let it pass. He hadn't taken ten steps before he heard himself called after with a friendly semi-articulate 'Er – I beg your pardon!' He turned round and the General, smiling at him from the porch, said: 'Won't you come in? I won't leave you the advantage of me!' Paul declined to come in, and then

felt regret, for Miss Fancourt, so late in the afternoon, might
return at any moment. But her father gave him no second chance;
he appeared mainly to wish not to have struck him as ungracious.
A further look at the visitor had recalled something, enough at
least to enable him to say: 'You've come back, you've come
back?' Paul was on the point of replying that he had come back
the night before, but he suppressed, the next instant, this strong
light on the immediacy of his visit and, giving merely a general
assent, alluded to the young lady he deplored not having found.
He had come late in the hope she would be in. 'I'll tell her –
I'll tell her,' said the old man; and then he added quickly,
gallantly: 'You'll be giving us something new? It's a long time,
isn't it?' Now he remembered him right.

'Rather long. I'm very slow,' Paul explained. 'I met you at
Summersoft a long time ago.'

'Oh yes – with Henry St George. I remember very well.
Before his poor wife – ' General Fancourt paused a moment,
smiling a little less. 'I dare say you know.'

'About Mrs St George's death? Certainly – I heard at the
time.'

'Oh no, I mean – I mean he's to be married.'

'Ah I've not heard that!' But just as Paul was about to add
'To whom?' the General crossed his intention.

'When did you come back? I know you've been away – by
my daughter. She was very sorry. You ought to give her something new.'

'I came back last night,' said our young man, to whom
something had occurred which made his speech for the moment
a little thick.

'Ah most kind of you to come so soon. Couldn't you turn up
at dinner?'

'At dinner!' Paul just mechanically repeated, not liking to
ask whom St George was going to marry, but thinking only of
that.

'There are several people, I believe. Certainly St George.
Or afterwards if you like better. I believe my daughter expects –'
He appeared to notice something in the visitor's raised face
(on his steps he stood higher) which led him to interrupt himself

and the interruption gave him a momentary sense of awkwardness, from which he sought a quick issue. 'Perhaps then you
haven't heard she's to be married.'

Paul gaped again. 'To be married?'

'To Mr St George – it has just been settled. Odd marriage
isn't it?' Our listener uttered no opinion on this point: he only
continued to stare. 'But I dare say it will do – she's so awfully
literary!' said the General.

Paul had turned very red. 'Oh it's a surprise – very interesting,
very charming! I'm afraid I can't dine – so many thanks!'

'Well, you must come to the wedding!' cried the General.
'Oh I remember that day at Summersoft. He's a great man,
you know.'

'Charming – charming!' Paul stammered for retreat. He
shook hands with the General and got off. His face was red and
he had the sense of its growing more and more crimson. All the
evening at home – he went straight to his rooms and remained
there dinnerless – his cheek burned at intervals as if it had been
smitten. He didn't understand what had happened to him, what
trick had been played him, what treachery practised. 'None,
none,' he said to himself. 'I've nothing to do with it. I'm out of
it – it's none of my business.' But that bewildered murmur was
followed again and again by the incongruous ejaculations: 'Was
it a plan – was it a plan?' Sometimes he cried to himself, breath-
less, 'Have I been duped, sold, swindled?' If at all, he was an
absurd, an abject victim. It was as if he hadn't lost her till now.
He had renounced her, yes; but that was another affair – that
was a closed but not a locked door. Now he seemed to see the
door quite slammed in his face. Did he expect her to wait – was
she to give him his time like that: two years at a stretch? He
didn't know what he had expected – he only knew what he
hadn't. It wasn't this – it wasn't this. Mystification, bitterness,
and wrath rose and boiled in him when he thought of the deference, the devotion, the credulity with which he had listened to
St George. The evening wore on and the light was long; but even
when it had darkened he remained without a lamp. He had
flung himself on the sofa, where he lay through the hours with
his eyes either closed or gazing at the gloom, in the attitude of

a man teaching himself to bear something, to bear having been made a fool of. He had made it too easy – that idea passed over him like a hot wave. Suddenly, as he heard eleven o'clock strike, he jumped up, remembering what General Fancourt had said about his coming after dinner. He'd go – he'd see her at least; perhaps he should see what it meant. He felt as if some of the elements of a hard sum had been given him and the others were wanting: he couldn't do his sum till he had got all his figures.

He dressed and drove quickly, so that by half past eleven he was at Manchester Square. There were a good many carriages at the door – a party was going on; a circumstance which at the last gave him a slight relief, for now he would rather see her in a crowd. People passed him on the staircase; they were going away, going 'on' with the hunted herdlike movement of London society at night. But sundry groups remained in the drawing-room, and it was some minutes, as she didn't hear him announced, before he discovered and spoke to her. In this short interval he had seen St George talking to a lady before the fireplace; but he at once looked away, feeling unready for an encounter, and therefore couldn't be sure the author of *Shadowmere* noticed him. At all events he didn't come over; though Miss Fancourt did as soon as she saw him – she almost rushed at him, smiling rustling radiant beautiful. He had forgotten what her head, what her face offered to the sight; she was in white, there were gold figures on her dress, and her hair was a casque of gold. He saw in a single moment that she was happy, happy with an aggressive splendour. But she wouldn't speak to him of that, she would speak only of himself.

'I'm so delighted; my father told me. How kind of you to come!' She struck him as so fresh and brave, while his eyes moved over her, that he said to himself irresistibly: 'Why to *him*, why not to youth, to strength, to ambition, to a future? Why, in her rich young force, to failure, to abdication, to super-annuation?' In his thought at that sharp moment he blasphemed even against all that had been left of his faith in the peccable Master. 'I'm so sorry I missed you,' she went on. 'My father told me. How charming of you to have come so soon!'

'Does that surprise you?' Paul Overt asked.

'The first day? No, from you – nothing that's nice.' She was interrupted by a lady who bade her good night, and he seemed to read that it cost her nothing to speak to him in that tone; it was her old liberal lavish way, with a certain added amplitude that time had brought; and if this manner began to operate on the spot, at such a juncture in her history, perhaps in the other days too it had meant just as little or as much – a mere mechanical charity, with the difference now that she was satisfied, ready to give but in want of nothing. Oh she was satisfied – and why shouldn't she be? Why shouldn't she have been surprised at his coming the first day – for all the good she had ever got from him? As the lady continued to hold her attention Paul turned from her with a strange irritation in his complicated artistic soul and a sort of disinterested disappointment. She was so happy that it was almost stupid – a disproof of the extraordinary intelligence he had formerly found in her. Didn't she know how bad St George could be, hadn't she recognized the awful thinness – ? If she didn't she was nothing, and if she did why such an insolence of serenity? This question expired as our young man's eyes settled at last on the genius who had advised him in a great crisis. St George was still before the chimney-piece, but now he was alone – fixed, waiting, as if he meant to stop after everyone – and he met the clouded gaze of the young friend so troubled as to the degree of his right (the right his resentment would have enjoyed) to regard himself as a victim. Somehow the ravage of the question was checked by the Master's radiance. It was as fine in its way as Marian Fancourt's, it denoted the happy human being; but also it represented to Paul Overt that the author of *Shadowmere* had now definitely ceased to count – ceased to count as a writer. As he smiled a welcome across the place he was almost banal, was almost smug. Paul fancied that for a moment he hesitated to make a movement, as if for all the world he *had* his bad conscience; then they had already met in the middle of the room and had shaken hands – expressively, cordially on St George's part. With which they had passed back together to where the elder man had been standing, while St George said: 'I hope you're never going away again. I've been dining here; the

General told me.' He was handsome, he was young, he looked as if he had still a great fund of life. He bent the friendliest, most unconfessing eyes on his disciple of a couple of years before; asked him about everything, his health, his plans, his late occupations, the new book. 'When will it be out – soon, soon, I hope? Splendid, eh? That's right; you're a comfort, you're a luxury! I've read you all over again these last six months.' Paul waited to see if he would tell him what the General had told him in the afternoon and what Miss Fancourt, verbally at least, of course hadn't. But as it didn't come out he at last put the question.

'Is it true, the great news I hear – that you're to be married?'

'Ah you *have* heard it then?'

'Didn't the General tell you?' Paul asked.

The Master's face was wonderful. 'Tell me what?'

'That he mentioned it to me this afternoon?'

'My dear fellow, I don't remember. We've been in the midst of people. I'm sorry, in that case, that I lose the pleasure, myself, of announcing to you a fact that touches me so nearly. It *is* a fact, strange as it may appear. It has only just become one. Isn't it ridiculous?' St George made this speech without confusion, but on the other hand, so far as our friend could judge, without latent impudence. It struck his interlocutor that, to talk so comfortably and coolly, he must simply have forgotten what had passed between them. His next words, however, showed he hadn't, and they produced, as an appeal to Paul's own memory, an effect which would have been ludicrous if it hadn't been cruel. 'Do you recall the talk we had at my house that night, into which Miss Fancourt's name entered? I've often thought of it since.'

'Yes; no wonder you said what you did' – Paul was careful to meet his eyes.

'In the light of the present occasion? Ah but there was no light then. How could I have foreseen this hour?'

'Didn't you think it probable?'

'Upon my honour, no,' said Henry St George. 'Certainly I owe you that assurance. Think how my situation has changed.'

'I see – I see,' our young man murmured.

His companion went on as if, now that the subject had been broached, he was, as a person of imagination and tact, quite ready to give every satisfaction – being both by his genius and his method so able to enter into everything another might feel. 'But it's not only that; for honestly, at my age, I never dreamed – a widower with big boys and with so little else! It has turned out differently from anything one could have dreamed, and I'm fortunate beyond all measure. She has been so freė, and yet she consents. Better than anyone else perhaps – for I remember how you liked her before you went away, and how she liked you – you can intelligently congratulate me.'

'She has been so free!' Those words made a great impression on Paul Overt, and he almost writhed under that irony in them as to which it so little mattered whether it was designed or casual. Of course she had been free, and appreciably perhaps by his own act; for wasn't the Master's allusion to her having liked him a part of the irony too? 'I thought that by your theory you disapproved of a writer's marrying.'

'Surely – surely. But you don't call me a writer?'

'You ought to be ashamed,' said Paul.

'Ashamed of marrying again?'

'I won't say that – but ashamed of your reasons.'

The elder man beautifully smiled. 'You must let me judge of them, my good friend.'

'Yes; why not? For you judged wonderfully of mine.'

The tone of these words appeared suddenly, for St George, to suggest the unsuspected. He stared as if divining a bitterness. 'Don't you think I've been straight?'

'You might have told me at the time perhaps.'

'My dear fellow, when I say I couldn't pierce futurity – !'

'I mean afterwards.'

The Master wondered. 'After my wife's death?'

'When this idea came to you.'

'Ah never, never! I wanted to save you, rare and precious as you are.'

Poor Overt looked hard at him. 'Are you marrying Miss Fancourt to save me?'

'Not absolutely, but it adds to the pleasure. I shall be the making of you,' St George smiled. 'I was greatly struck, after our talk, with the brave devoted way you quitted the country, and still more perhaps with your force of character in remaining abroad. You're very strong – you're wonderfully strong.'

Paul tried to sound his shining eyes; the strange thing was that he seemed sincere – not a mocking fiend. He turned away, and as he did so heard the Master say something about his giving them all the proof, being the joy of his old age. He faced him again, taking another look. 'Do you mean to say you've stopped writing?'

'My dear fellow, of course I have. It's too late. Didn't I tell you?'

'I can't believe it!'

'Of course you can't – with your own talent! No, no; for the rest of my life I shall only read *you*.'

'Does she know that – Miss Fancourt?'

'She will – she will.' Did he mean this, our young man wondered, as a covert intimation that the assistance he should derive from that young lady's fortune, moderate as it was, would make the difference of putting it in his power to cease to work ungratefully an exhausted vein? Somehow, standing there in the ripeness of his successful manhood, he didn't suggest that any of his veins were exhausted. 'Don't you remember the moral I offered myself to you that night as pointing?' St George continued. 'Consider at any rate the warning I am at present.'

This was too much – he *was* the mocking fiend. Paul turned from him with a mere nod for good night and the sense in a sore heart that he might come back to him and his easy grace, his fine way of arranging things, some time in the far future, but couldn't fraternize with him now. It was necessary to his soreness to believe for the hour in the intensity of his grievance – all the more cruel for its not being a legal one. It was doubtless in the attitude of hugging this wrong that he descended the stairs without taking leave of Miss Fancourt, who hadn't been in view at the moment he quitted the room. He was glad to get out into the honest dusky unsophisticating night, to move fast, to take his way home on foot. He walked a long time, going astray, paying no attention. He was thinking of too many other things. His steps recovered their direction, however, and at the end of an hour he found himself before his door in the small inexpensive empty street. He lingered, questioning himself still before going in, with nothing around and above him but moonless blackness, a bad lamp or two and a few far-away dim stars. To these last faint creatures he raised his eyes; he had been saying to himself that he should have been 'sold' indeed, diabolically sold, if now, on his new foundation, at the end of a year, St George were to put forth something of his prime quality – something of the type of *Shadowmere* and finer than his finest. Greatly as he admired his talent Paul literally hoped such an incident wouldn't occur; it seemed to him just then that he shouldn't be able to bear it. His late adviser's words were still in his ears – ' You're very strong, wonderfully strong.' Was he really? Certainly he would have to be, and it might a little serve for revenge. *Is* he? the reader may ask in turn, if his interest has followed the perplexed young man so far. The best answer to that perhaps is that he's doing his best, but that it's too soon to say. When the new book came out in the autumn Mr and Mrs St George found it really magnificent. The former still has published nothing but Paul doesn't even yet feel safe. I may say for him, however, that if this event were to occur he would really be the very first to appreciate it: which is perhaps a proof that the Master was essentially right and that Nature had dedicated him to intellectual, not to personal passion.

Daisy Miller

1

AT the little town of Vevey, in Switzerland, there is a particularly comfortable hotel. There are, indeed, many hotels; for the entertainment of tourists is the business of the place, which, as many travellers will remember, is seated upon the edge of a remarkably blue lake – a lake that it behoves every tourist to visit. The shore of the lake presents an unbroken array of establishments of this order, of every category, from the 'grand hotel' of the newest fashion, with a chalk-white front, a hundred balconies, and a dozen flags flying from its roof, to the little Swiss *pension* of an elder day, with its name inscribed in German-looking lettering upon a pink or yellow wall, and an awkward summer-house in the angle of the garden. One of the hotels at Vevey, however, is famous, even classical, being distinguished from many of its upstart neighbours by an air both of luxury and of maturity. In this region, in the month of June, American travellers are extremely numerous; it may be said, indeed, that Vevey assumes at this period some of the characteristics of an American watering-place. There are sights and sounds which evoke a vision, an echo, of Newport and Saratoga. There is a flitting hither and thither of 'stylish' young girls, a rustling of muslin flounces, a rattle of dance-music in the morning hours, a sound of high-pitched voices at all times. You receive an impression of these things at the excellent inn of the Trois Couronnes, and are transported in fancy to the Ocean House or to Congress Hall. But at the Trois Couronnes, it must be added, there are other features that are much at variance with these suggestions: neat German waiters, who look like secretaries of legation; Russian princesses sitting in the garden; little Polish boys walking about, held by the hand, with their governors; a view of the snowy crest of the Dent du Midi and the picturesque towers of the Castle of Chillon.

I hardly know whether it was the analogies or the differences that were uppermost in the mind of a young American, who, two or three years ago, sat in the garden of the Trois Couronnes, looking about him, rather idly, at some of the graceful objects I have mentioned. It was a beautiful summer morning, and in whatever fashion the young American looked at things, they must have seemed to him charming. He had come from Geneva the day before, by the little steamer, to see his aunt, who was staying at the hotel – Geneva having been for a long time his place of residence. But his aunt had a headache – his aunt had almost always a headache – and now she was shut up in her room, smelling camphor, so that he was at liberty to wander about. He was some seven-and-twenty years of age; when his friends spoke of him, they usually said that he was at Geneva, 'studying'. When his enemies spoke of him they said – but, after all, he had no enemies; he was an extremely amiable fellow, and universally liked. What I should say is, simply, that when certain persons spoke of him they affirmed that the reason of his spending so much time at Geneva was that he was extremely devoted to a lady who lived there – a foreign lady – a person older than himself. Very few Americans – indeed I think none – had ever seen this lady, about whom there were some singular stories. But Winterbourne had an old attachment for the little metropolis of Calvinism; he had been put to school there as a boy, and he had afterwards gone to college there – circumstances which had led to his forming a great many youthful friendships. Many of these he had kept, and they were a source of great satisfaction to him.

After knocking at his aunt's door and learning that she was indisposed, he had taken a walk about the town, and then he had come in to his breakfast. He had now finished his breakfast, but he was drinking a small cup of coffee, which had been served to him on a little table in the garden by one of the waiters who looked like an attaché. At last he finished his coffee and lit a cigarette. Presently a small boy came walking along the path – an urchin of nine or ten. The child, who was diminutive for his years, had an aged expression of countenance, a pale complexion, and sharp little features. He was dressed in knickerbockers, with red stockings, which displayed his poor little spindleshanks; he also wore a brilliant red cravat. He carried in his hand a long alpenstock, the sharp point of which he thrust into everything that he approached – the flowerbeds, the garden-benches, the trains of the ladies' dresses. In front of Winterbourne he paused, looking at him with a pair of bright, penetrating little eyes.

'Will you give me a lump of sugar?' he asked, in a sharp, hard little voice – a voice immature, and yet, somehow, not young.

Winterbourne glanced at the small table near him, on which his coffee-service rested, and saw that several morsels of sugar remained. 'Yes, you may take one,' he answered; 'but I don't think sugar is good for little boys.'

This little boy stepped forward and carefully selected three of the coveted fragments, two of which he buried in the pocket of his knickerbockers, depositing the other as promptly in another place. He poked his alpenstock, lance-fashion, into Winterbourne's bench, and tried to crack the lump of sugar with his teeth.

'Oh, blazes; it's har-r-d!' he exclaimed, pronouncing the adjective in a peculiar manner.

Winterbourne had immediately perceived that he might have the honour of claiming him as a fellow-countryman. 'Take care you don't hurt your teeth,' he said, paternally.

'I haven't got any teeth to hurt. They have all come out. I have only got seven teeth. My mother counted them last night, and one came out right afterwards. She said she'd slap me if any more came out. I can't help it. It's this old Europe. It's the climate that makes them come out. In America they didn't come out. It's these hotels.'

Winterbourne was much amused. 'If you eat three lumps of sugar, your mother will certainly slap you,' he said.

'She's got to give me some candy, then,' rejoined his young interlocutor. 'I can't get any candy here – any American candy. American candy's the best candy.'

'And are American little boys the best little boys?' asked Winterbourne.

'I don't know. I'm an American boy,' said the child.

'I see you are one of the best!' laughed Winterbourne.

'Are you an American man?' pursued this vivacious infant.

And then, on Winterbourne's affirmative reply – 'American men are the best,' he declared.

His companion thanked him for the compliment; and the child, who had now got astride of his alpenstock, stood looking about him, while he attacked a second lump of sugar. Winterbourne wondered if he himself had been like this in his infancy, for he had been brought to Europe at about this age.

'Here comes my sister!' cried the child, in a moment. 'She's an American girl.'

Winterbourne looked along the path and saw a beautiful young lady advancing. 'American girls are the best girls,' he said, cheerfully, to his young companion.

'My sister ain't the best!' the child declared. 'She's always blowing at me.'

'I imagine that is your fault, not hers,' said Winterbourne. The young lady meanwhile had drawn near. She was dressed in white muslin, with a hundred frills and flounces, and knots of pale-coloured ribbon. She was bare-headed; but she balanced in her hand a large parasol, with a deep border of embroidery; and she was strikingly, admirably pretty. 'How pretty they are!' thought Winterbourne, straightening himself in his seat, as if he were prepared to rise.

The young lady paused in front of his bench, near the parapet of the garden, which overlooked the lake. The little boy had now converted his alpenstock into a vaulting-pole, by the aid of which he was springing about in the gravel, and kicking it up not a little.

'Randolph,' said the young lady, 'what *are* you doing?'

'I'm going up the Alps,' replied Randolph. 'This is the way!' And he gave another little jump, scattering the pebbles about Winterbourne's ears.

'That's the way they come down,' said Winterbourne.

'He's an American man!' cried Randolph, in his little hard voice.

The young lady gave no heed to this announcement, but looked straight at her brother. 'Well, I guess you had better be quiet,' she simply observed.

It seemed to Winterbourne that he had been in a manner

presented. He got up and stepped slowly towards the young girl, throwing away his cigarette. 'This little boy and I have made acquaintance,' he said, with great civility. In Geneva, as he had been perfectly aware, a young man was not at liberty to speak to a young unmarried lady except under certain rarely occurring conditions; but here, at Vevey, what conditions could be better than these? – a pretty American girl coming and standing in front of you in a garden. This pretty American girl, however, on hearing Winterbourne's observation, simply glanced at him; she then turned her head and looked over the parapet, at the lake and the opposite mountains. He wondered whether he had gone too far; but he decided that he must advance farther rather than retreat. While he was thinking of something else to say, the young lady turned to the little boy again.

'I should like to know where you got that pole,' she said.

'I bought it!' responded Randolph.

'You don't mean to say you're going to take it to Italy!'

'Yes, I am going to take it to Italy!' the child declared.

The young girl glanced over the front of her dress, and smoothed out a knot or two of ribbon. Then she rested her eyes upon the prospect again. 'Well, I guess you had better leave it somewhere,' she said, after a moment.

'Are you going to Italy?' Winterbourne inquired, in a tone of great respect.

The young lady glanced at him again. 'Yes, sir,' she replied. And she said nothing more.

'Are you – a – going over the Simplon?' Winterbourne pursued, a little embarrassed.

'I don't know,' she said. 'I suppose it's some mountain. Randolph, what mountain are we going over?'

'Going where?' the child demanded.

'To Italy,' Winterbourne explained.

'I don't know,' said Randolph. 'I don't want to go to Italy. I want to go to America.'

'Oh, Italy is a beautiful place!' rejoined the young man.

'Can you get candy there?' Randolph loudly inquired.

'I hope not,' said his sister. 'I guess you have had enough candy, and mother thinks so too.'

'I haven't had any for ever so long – for a hundred weeks!' cried the boy, still jumping about.

The young lady inspected her flounces and smoothed her ribbons again;, and Winterbourne presently risked an observation upon the beauty of the view. He was ceasing to be embarrassed, for he had begun to perceive that she was not in the least embarrassed herself. There had not been the slightest alteration in her charming complexion; she was evidently neither offended nor fluttered. If she looked another way when he spoke to her, and seemed not particularly to hear him, this was simply her habit, her manner. Yet, as he talked a little more, and pointed out some of the objects of interest in the view, with which she appeared quite unacquainted, she gradually gave him more of the benefit of her glance; and then he saw that this glance was perfectly direct and unshrinking. It was not, however, what would have been called an immodest glance, for the young girl's eyes were singularly honest and fresh. They were wonderfully pretty eyes; and, indeed, Winterbourne had not seen for a long time anything prettier than his fair countrywoman's various features – her complexion, her nose, her ears, her teeth. He had a great relish for feminine beauty; he was addicted to observing and analysing it; and as regards this young lady's face he made several observations. It was not at all insipid, but it was not exactly expressive; and though it was eminently delicate, Winterbourne mentally accused it – very forgivingly – of a want of finish. He thought it very possible that Master Randolph's sister was a coquette; he was sure she had a spirit of her own; but in her bright, sweet, superficial little visage there was no mockery, no irony. Before long it became obvious that she was much disposed towards conversation. She told him that they were going to Rome for the winter – she and her mother and Randolph. She asked him if he was a 'real American'; she wouldn't have taken him for one; he seemed more like a German – this was said after a little hesitation, especially when he spoke. Winterbourne, laughing, answered that he had met Germans who spoke like Americans; but that he had not, so far as he remembered, met an American who spoke like a German. Then he asked her if she would not be more comfortable in sitting upon the bench which he had just quitted. She answered that she liked standing up and walking about; but she presently sat down. She told him she was from New York State – 'if you know where that is'. Winterbourne learned more about her by catching hold of her small, slippery brother and making him stand a few minutes by his side.

'Tell me your name, my boy,' he said.

'Randolph C. Miller,' said the boy, sharply. 'And I'll tell you her name'; and he levelled his alpenstock at his sister.

'You had better wait till you are asked!' said this young lady, calmly.

'I should like very much to know your name,' said Winterbourne.

'Her name is Daisy Miller!' cried the child. 'But that isn't her real name; that isn't her name on her cards.'

'It's a pity you haven't got one of my cards!' said Miss Miller.

'Her real name is Annie P. Miller,' the boy went on.

'Ask him *his* name,' said his sister, indicating Winterbourne.

But on this point Randolph seemed perfectly indifferent; he continued to supply information with regard to his own family. 'My father's name is Ezra B. Miller,' he announced. 'My father ain't in Europe; my father's in a better place than Europe.'

Winterbourne imagined for a moment that this was the manner in which the child had been taught to intimate that Mr Miller had been removed to the sphere of celestial rewards. But Randolph immediately added, 'My father's in Schenectady. He's got a big business. My father's rich, you bet.'

'Well!' ejaculated Miss Miller, lowering her parasol and looking at the embroidered border. Winterbourne presently released the child, who departed, dragging his alpenstock along the path. 'He doesn't like Europe,' said the young girl. 'He wants to go back.'

'To Schenectady, you mean?'

'Yes; he wants to go right home. He hasn't got any boys here. There is one boy here, but he always goes round with a teacher; they won't let him play.'

'And your brother hasn't any teacher?' Winterbourne inquired.

'Mother thought of getting him one, to travel round with us.

There was a lady told her of a very good teacher; an American lady – perhaps you know her – Mrs Sanders. I think she came from Boston. She told her of this teacher, and we thought of getting him to travel round with us. But Randolph said he didn't want a teacher travelling round with us. He said he wouldn't have lessons when he was in the cars. And we *are* in the cars about half the time. There was an English lady we met in the cars – I think her name was Miss Featherstone; perhaps you know her. She wanted to know why I didn't give Randolph lessons – give him "instruction", she called it. I guess he could give me more instruction than I could give him. He's very smart.'

'Yes,' said Winterbourne; 'he seems very smart.'

'Mother's going to get a teacher for him as soon as we get to Italy. Can you get good teachers in Italy?'

'Very good, I should think,' said Winterbourne.

'Or else she's going to find some school. He ought to learn some more. He's only nine. He's going to college.' And in this way Miss Miller continued to converse upon the affairs of her family, and upon other topics. She sat there with her extremely pretty hands, ornamented with very brilliant rings, folded in her lap, and with her pretty eyes now resting upon those of Winterbourne, now wandering over the garden, the people who passed by, and the beautiful view. She talked to Winterbourne as if she had known him a long time. He found it very pleasant. It was many years since he had heard a young girl talk so much. It might have been said of this unknown young lady, who had come and sat down beside him upon a bench, that she chattered. She was very quiet, she sat in a charming tranquil attitude; but her lips and her eyes were constantly moving. She had a soft, slender, agreeable voice, and her tone was decidedly sociable. She gave Winterbourne a history of her movements and intentions, and those of her mother and brother, in Europe, and enumerated, in particular, the various hotels at which they had stopped. 'That English lady in the cars,' she said – 'Miss Featherstone – asked me if we didn't all live in hotels in America. I told her I had never been in so many hotels in my life as since I came to Europe. I have never seen so many – it's nothing but hotels.' But Miss Miller did not make this remark with a querulous accent;

she appeared to be in the best humour with everything. She declared that the hotels were very good, when once you got used to their ways, and that Europe was perfectly sweet. She was not disappointed – not a bit. Perhaps it was because she had heard so much about it before. She had ever so many intimate friends that had been there ever so many times. And then she had had ever so many dresses and things from Paris. Whenever she put on a Paris dress she felt as if she were in Europe.

'It was a kind of wishing-cap,' said Winterbourne.

'Yes,' said Miss Miller, without examining this analogy; 'it always made me wish I was here. But I needn't have done that for dresses. I am sure they send all the pretty ones to America; you see the most frightful things here. The only thing I don't like,' she proceeded, 'is the society. There isn't any society; or, if there is, I don't know where it keeps itself. Do you? I suppose there is some society somewhere, but I haven't seen anything of it. I'm very fond of society, and I have always had a great deal of it. I don't mean only in Schenectady, but in New York. I used to go to New York every winter. In New York I had lots of society. Last winter I had seventeen dinners given me; and three of them were by gentlemen,' added Daisy Miller. 'I have more friends in New York than in Schenectady – more gentlemen friends; and more young lady friends too,' she resumed in a moment. She paused again for an instant; she was looking at Winterbourne with all her prettiness in her lively eyes and in her light, slightly monotonous smile. 'I have always had,' she said, 'a great deal of gentlemen's society.'

Poor Winterbourne was amused, perplexed, and decidedly charmed. He had never yet heard a young girl express herself in just this fashion; never, at least, save in cases where to say such things seemed a kind of demonstrative evidence of a certain laxity of deportment. And yet was he to accuse Miss Daisy Miller of actual or potential *inconduite*, as they said at Geneva? He felt that he had lived at Geneva so long that he had lost a good deal; he had become dishabituated to the American tone. Never, indeed, since he had grown old enough to appreciate things, had he encountered a young American girl of so pronounced a type as this. Certainly she was very charming; but how deucedly

sociable! Was she simply a pretty girl from New York State –
were they all like that, the pretty girls who had a good deal of
gentlemen's society? Or was she also a designing, an audacious,
an unscrupulous young person? Winterbourne had lost his
instinct in this matter, and his reason could not help him. Miss
Daisy Miller looked extremely innocent. Some people had told
him that, after all, American girls were exceedingly innocent;
and others had told him that, after all, they were not. He was
inclined to think Miss Daisy Miller was a flirt – a pretty American
flirt. He had never, as yet, had any relations with young ladies of
this category. He had known, here in Europe, two or three
women – persons older than Miss Daisy Miller, and provided,
for respectability's sake, with husbands – who were great co-
quettes – dangerous, terrible women, with whom one's relations
were liable to take a serious turn. But this young girl was not a
coquette in that sense; she was very unsophisticated; she was
only a pretty American flirt. Winterbourne was almost grateful
for having found the formula that applied to Miss Daisy Miller.
He leaned back in his seat; he remarked to himself that she
had the most charming nose he had ever seen; he wondered
what were the regular conditions and limitations of one's intercourse with a pretty American flirt. It presently became apparent
that he was on the way to learn.

'Have you been to that old castle?' asked the young girl,
pointing with her parasol to the far-gleaming walls of the
Château de Chillon.

'Yes, formerly, more than once,' said Winterbourne. 'You too,
I suppose, have seen it?'

'No; we haven't been there. I want to go there dreadfully.
Of course I mean to go there. I wouldn't go away from here
without having seen that old castle.'

'It's a very pretty excursion,' said Winterbourne, 'and very
easy to make. You can drive, you know, or you can go by the
little steamer.'

'You can go in the cars,' said Miss Miller.

'Yes; you can go in the cars,' Winterbourne assented.

'Our courier says they take you right up to the castle,' the
young girl continued. 'We were going last week; but my mother

gave out. She suffers dreadfully from dyspepsia. She said she couldn't go. Randolph wouldn't go either; he says he doesn't think much of old castles. But I guess we'll go this week, if we can get Randolph.'

'Your brother is not interested in ancient monuments?' Winterbourne inquired, smiling.

'He says he don't care much about old castles. He's only nine. He wants to stay at the hotel. Mother's afraid to leave him alone, and the courier won't stay with him; so we haven't been to many places. But it will be too bad if we don't go up there.' And Miss Miller pointed again at the Château de Chillon.

'I should think it might be arranged,' said Winterbourne. 'Couldn't you get someone to stay – for the afternoon – with Randolph?'

Miss Miller looked at him a moment; and then, very placidly – 'I wish *you* would stay with him!' she said.

Winterbourne hesitated a moment. 'I would much rather go to Chillon with you.'

'With me?' asked the young girl, with the same placidity.

She didn't rise, blushing, as a young girl at Geneva would have done; and yet Winterbourne, conscious that he had been very bold, thought it possible she was offended. 'With your mother,' he answered very respectfully.

But it seemed that both his audacity and his respect were lost upon Miss Daisy Miller. 'I guess my mother won't go, after all,' she said. 'She don't like to ride round in the afternoon. But did you really mean what you said just now; that you would like to go up there?'

'Most earnestly,' Winterbourne declared.

'Then we may arrange it. If mother will stay with Randolph, I guess Eugenio will.'

'Eugenio?' the young man inquired.

'Eugenio's our courier. He doesn't like to stay with Randolph; he's the most fastidious man I ever saw. But he's a splendid courier. I guess he'll stay at home with Randolph if mother does, and then we can go to the castle.'

Winterbourne reflected for an instant as lucidly as possible – 'we' could only mean Miss Daisy Miller and himself. This programme seemed almost too agreeable for credence; he felt as if he ought to kiss the young lady's hand. Possibly he would have done so – and quite spoiled the project; but at this moment another person – presumably Eugenio – appeared. A tall, handsome man, with superb whiskers, wearing a velvet morning-coat and a brilliant watch-chain, approached Miss Miller, looking sharply at her companion. 'Oh, Eugenio!' said Miss Miller, with the friendliest accent.

Eugenio had looked at Winterbourne from head to foot, he now bowed gravely to the young lady. 'I have the honour to inform mademoiselle that luncheon is upon the table.'

Miss Miller slowly rose. 'See here, Eugenio,' she said. 'I'm going to that old castle, anyway.'

'To the Château de Chillon, mademoiselle?' the courier inquired. 'Mademoiselle has made arrangements?' he added, in a tone which struck Winterbourne as very impertinent.

Eugenio's tone apparently threw, even to Miss Miller's own apprehension, a slightly ironical light upon the young girl's situation. She turned to Winterbourne, blushing a little – a very little. 'You won't back out?' she said.

'I shall not be happy till we go!' he protested.

'And you are staying in this hotel?' she went on. 'And you are really an American?'

The courier stood looking at Winterbourne, offensively. The young man, at least, thought his manner of looking an offence to Miss Miller; it conveyed an imputation that she 'picked up' acquaintances. 'I shall have the honour of presenting to you a person who will tell you all about me,' he said smiling, and referring to his aunt.

'Oh well, we'll go some day,' said Miss Miller. And she gave him a smile and turned away. She put up her parasol and walked back to the inn beside Eugenio. Winterbourne stood looking after her; and as she moved away, drawing her muslin furbelows over the gravel, said to himself that she had the *tournure* of a princess.

2

He had, however, engaged to do more than proved feasible, in promising to present his aunt, Mrs Costello, to Miss Daisy Miller. As soon as the former lady had got better of her headache he waited upon her in her apartment; and, after the proper inquiries in regard to her health, he asked her if she had observed, in the hotel, an American family – a mamma, a daughter, and a little boy.

'And a courier?' said Mrs Costello. 'Oh, yes, I have observed them. Seen them – heard them – and kept out of their way.' Mrs Costello was a widow with a fortune; a person of much distinction, who frequently intimated that, if she were not so dreadfully liable to sick-headaches, she would probably have left a deeper impress upon her time. She had a long pale face, a high nose, and a great deal of very striking white hair, which she wore in large puffs and *rouleaux* over the top of her head. She had two sons married in New York, and another who was now in Europe. This young man was amusing himself at Homburg, and, though he was on his travels, was rarely perceived to visit any particular city at the moment selected by his mother for her own appearance there. Her nephew, who had come up to Vevey expressly to see her, was therefore more attentive than those who, as she said, were nearer to her. He had imbibed at Geneva the idea that one must always be attentive to one's aunt. Mrs Costello had not seen him for many years, and she was greatly pleased with him, manifesting her approbation by initiating him into many of the secrets of that social sway which, as she gave him to understand, she exerted in the American capital. She admitted that she was very exclusive; but, if he were acquainted with New York, he would see that one had to be. And her picture of the minutely hierarchical constitution of the society of that city, which she presented to him in many different lights, was, to Winterbourne's imagination, almost oppressively striking.

He immediately perceived, from her tone, that Miss Daisy

Miller's place in the social scale was low. 'I am afraid you don't approve of them,' he said.

'They are very common,' Mrs Costello declared. 'They are the sort of Americans that one does one's duty by not – not accepting.'

'Ah, you don't accept them?' said the young man.

'I can't, my dear Frederick. I would if I could, but I can't.'

'The young girl is very pretty,' said Winterbourne, in a moment.

'Of course she's pretty. But she is very common.'

'I see what you mean, of course,' said Winterbourne, after another pause.

'She has that charming look that they all have,' his aunt resumed. 'I can't think where they pick it up; and she dresses in perfection – no, you don't know how well she dresses. I can't think where they get their taste.'

'But, my dear aunt, she is not, after all, a Comanche savage.'

'She is a young lady,' said Mrs Costello, 'who has an intimacy with her mamma's courier?'

'An intimacy with the courier?' the young man demanded.

'Oh, the mother is just as bad! They treat the courier like a familiar friend – like a gentleman. I shouldn't wonder if he dines with them. Very likely they have never seen a man with such good manners, such fine clothes, so like a gentleman. He probably corresponds to the young lady's idea of a Count. He sits with them in the garden, in the evening. I think he smokes.'

Winterbourne listened with interest to these disclosures; they helped him to make up his mind about Miss Daisy. Evidently she was rather wild. 'Well,' he said, 'I am not a courier, and yet she was very charming to me.'

'You had better have said at first,' said Mrs Costello with dignity, 'that you had made her acquaintance.'

'We simply met in the garden, and we talked a bit.'

'*Tout bonnement!* And pray what did you say?'

'I said I should take the liberty of introducing her to my admirable aunt.'

'I am much obliged to you.'

'It was to guarantee my respectability,' said Winterbourne.

'And pray who is to guarantee hers?'

'Ah, you are cruel?' said the young man. 'She's a very nice girl.'

'You don't say that as if you believed it,' Mrs Costello observed.

'She is completely uncultivated,' Winterbourne went on. 'But she is wonderfully pretty, and, in short, she is very nice. To prove that I believe it, I am going to take her to the Château de Chillon.'

'You two are going off there together? I should say it proved just the contrary. How long had you known her, may I ask, when this interesting project was formed. You haven't been twenty-four hours in the house.'

'I had known her half an hour!' said Winterbourne, smiling.

'Dear me!' cried Mrs Costello. 'What a dreadful girl!'

Her nephew was silent for some moments. 'You really think, then,' he began earnestly, and with a desire for trustworthy information – 'you really think that – ' But he paused again.

'Think what, sir,' said his aunt.

'That she is the sort of young lady who expects a man – sooner or later – to carry her off?'

'I haven't the least idea what such young ladies expect a man to do. But I really think that you had better not meddle with little American girls that are uncultivated, as you call them. You have lived too long out of the country. You will be sure to make some great mistake. You are too innocent.'

'My dear aunt, I am not so innocent,' said Winterbourne, smiling and curling his moustache.

'You are too guilty, then?'

Winterbourne continued to curl his moustache, meditatively. 'You won't let the poor girl know you then?' he asked at last.

'Is it literally true that she is going to the Château de Chillon with you?'

'I think that she fully intends it.'

'Then, my dear Frederick,' said Mrs Costello, 'I must decline the honour of her acquaintance. I am an old woman, but I am not too old – thank Heaven – to be shocked!'

'But don't they all do these things – the young girls in America?' Winterbourne inquired.

Mrs Costello stared a moment. 'I should like to see my grand-daughters do them!' she declared, grimly.

This seemed to throw some light upon the matter, for Winter-bourne remembered to have heard that his pretty cousins in New York were 'tremendous flirts'. If, therefore, Miss Daisy Miller exceeded the liberal licence allowed to these young ladies, it was probable that anything might be expected of her. Winter-bourne was impatient to see her again, and he was vexed with himself that, by instinct, he should not appreciate her justly.

Though he was impatient to see her, he hardly knew what he should say to her about his aunt's refusal to become acquainted with her; but he discovered, promptly enough, that with Miss Daisy Miller there was no great need of walking on tiptoe. He found her that evening in the garden, wandering about in the warm starlight, like an indolent sylph, and swinging to and fro the largest fan he had ever beheld. It was ten o'clock. He had dined with his aunt, had been sitting with her since dinner, and had just taken leave of her till the morrow. Miss Daisy Miller seemed very glad to see him; she declared it was the longest evening she had ever passed.

'Have you been all alone?' he asked.

'I have been walking round with mother. But mother gets tired walking round,' she answered.

'Has she gone to bed?'

'No; she doesn't like to go to bed,' said the young girl. 'She doesn't sleep – not three hours. She says she doesn't know how she lives. She's dreadfully nervous. I guess she sleeps more than she thinks. She's gone somewhere after Randolph; she wants to try to get him to go to bed. He doesn't like to go to bed.'

'Let us hope she will persuade him,' observed Winterbourne.

'She will talk to him all she can; but he doesn't like her to talk to him,' said Miss Daisy, opening her fan. 'She's going to try to get Eugenio to talk to him. But he isn't afraid of Eugenio. Eugenio's a splendid courier, but he can't make much impression on Randolph! I don't believe he'll go to bed before eleven.' It appeared that Randolph's vigil was in fact triumphantly pro-. longed, for Winterbourne strolled about with the young girl for some time without meeting her mother. 'I have been looking round for that lady you want to introduce me to,' his companion resumed. 'She's your aunt.' Then, on Winterbourne's admitting the fact, and expressing some curiosity as to how she had learned it, she said she had heard all about Mrs Costello from the chambermaid. She was very quiet and very *comme il faut*; she wore white puffs; she spoke to no one, and she never dined at the *table d'hôte*. Every two days she had a headache. 'I think that's a lovely description, headache and all!' said Miss Daisy, chattering along in her thin, gay voice. 'I want to know her ever so much. I know just what *your* aunt would be; I know I should like her. She would be very exclusive. I like a lady to be exclusive; I'm dying to be exclusive myself. Well, we *are* exclusive, mother and I. We don't speak to everyone – or they don't speak to us. I suppose it's about the same thing. Anyway, I shall be ever so glad to know your aunt.'

Winterbourne was embarrassed. 'She would be most happy,' he said, 'but I am afraid those headaches will interfere.'

The young girl looked at him through the dusk. 'But I suppose she doesn't have a headache every day,' she said, sympathetically.

Winterbourne was silent a moment. 'She tells me she does,' he answered at last – not knowing what to say.

Miss Daisy Miller stopped and stood looking at him. Her prettiness was still visible in the darkness; she was opening and closing her enormous fan. 'She doesn't want to know me!' she said suddenly. 'Why don't you say so? You needn't be afraid. I'm not afraid!' And she gave a little laugh.

Winterbourne fancied there was a tremor in her voice; he was touched, shocked, mortified by it. 'My dear young lady,' he protested, 'she knows no one. It's her wretched health.'

The young girl walked on a few steps, laughing still. 'You needn't be afraid,' she repeated. 'Why should she want to know me?' Then she paused again; she was close to the parapet of the garden, and in front of her was the starlit lake. There was a vague sheen upon its surface, and in the distance were dimly seen mountain forms. Daisy Miller looked out upon the mysterious prospect, and then she gave another little laugh. 'Gracious! she *is* exclusive!' she said. Winterbourne wondered whether she was seriously wounded, and for a moment almost wished that her sense of injury might be such as to make it becoming in him to attempt to reassure and comfort her. He had a pleasant sense that she would be very approachable for consolatory purposes. He felt then, for the instant, quite ready to sacrifice his aunt, conversationally; to admit that she was a proud, rude woman, and to declare that they needn't mind her. But before he had time to commit himself to this perilous mixture of gallantry and impiety, the young lady, resuming her walk, gave an exclamation in quite another tone. 'Well; here's mother! I guess she hasn't got Randolph to go to bed.' The figure of a lady appeared, at a distance, very indistinct in the darkness, and advancing with a slow and wavering movement. Suddenly it seemed to pause.

'Are you sure it is your mother? Can you distinguish her in this thick dusk?' Winterbourne asked.

'Well!' cried Miss Daisy Miller, with a laugh, 'I guess I know my own mother. And when she has got on my shawl, too! She is always wearing my things.'

The lady in question, ceasing to advance, hovered vaguely about the spot at which she had checked her steps.

'I am afraid your mother doesn't see you,' said Winterbourne. 'Or perhaps,' he added – thinking, with Miss Miller, the joke permissible – 'perhaps she feels guilty about your shawl.'

'Oh, it's a fearful old thing!' the young girl replied, serenely. 'I told her she could wear it. She won't come here, because she sees you.'

'Ah, then,' said Winterbourne, 'I had better leave you.'

'Oh, no; come on!' urged Miss Daisy Miller.

'I'm afraid your mother doesn't approve of my walking with you.'

Miss Miller gave him a serious glance. 'It isn't for me; it's for you – that is, it's for *her*. Well; I don't know who it's for! But mother doesn't like any of my gentlemen friends. She's right down timid. She always makes a fuss if I introduce a gentleman. But I *do* introduce them – almost always. If I didn't introduce my gentlemen friends to mother,' the young girl added, in her little soft, flat monotone, 'I shouldn't think I was natural.'

'To introduce me,' said Winterbourne, 'you must know my name.' And he proceeded to pronounce it.

'Oh, dear; I can't say all that!' said his companion, with a laugh. But by this time they had come up to Mrs Miller, who, as they drew near, walked to the parapet of the garden and leaned upon it, looking intently at the lake and turning her back upon them. 'Mother!' said the young girl, in a tone of decision. Upon this the elder lady turned round. 'Mr Winterbourne,' said Miss Daisy Miller, introducing the young man very frankly and prettily. 'Common' she was, as Mrs Costello had pronounced her; yet it was a wonder to Winterbourne that, with her commonness, she had a singularly delicate grace.

Her mother was a small, spare, light person, with a wandering eye, a very exiguous nose, and a large forehead, decorated with a certain amount of thin, much-frizzled hair. Like her daughter, Mrs Miller was dressed with extreme elegance; she had enormous diamonds in her ears. So far as Winterbourne could observe, she gave him no greeting – she certainly was not looking at him. Daisy was near her, pulling her shawl straight. 'What are you doing, poking round here?' this young lady inquired; but by no means with that harshness of accent which her choice of words may imply.

'I don't know,' said her mother, turning towards the lake again.

'I shouldn't think you'd want that shawl!' Daisy exclaimed.

'Well – I do!' her mother answered, with a little laugh.

'Did you get Randolph to go to bed?' asked the young girl.

'No; I couldn't induce him,' said Mrs Miller, very gently. 'He wants to talk to the waiter. He likes to talk to that waiter.'

'I was telling Mr Winterbourne,' the young girl went on; and to the young man's ear her tone might have indicated that she had been uttering his name all her life.

'Oh, yes!' said Winterbourne; 'I have the pleasure of knowing your son.'

Randolph's mamma was silent; she turned her attention to the lake. But at last she spoke. 'Well, I don't see how he lives!'

'Anyhow, it isn't so bad as it was at Dover,' said Daisy Miller.

'And what occurred at Dover?' Winterbourne asked.

'He wouldn't go to bed at all. I guess he sat up all night – in the public parlour. He wasn't in bed at twelve o'clock: I know that.'

'It was half past twelve,' declared Mrs Miller, with mild emphasis.

'Does he sleep much during the day?' Winterbourne demanded.

'I guess he doesn't sleep much,' Daisy rejoined.

'I wish he would!' said her mother. 'It seems as if he couldn't.'

'I think he's real tiresome,' Daisy pursued.

Then, for some moments, there was silence. 'Well, Daisy Miller,' said the elder lady, presently, 'I shouldn't think you'd want to talk against your own brother!'

'Well, he *is* tiresome, mother,' said Daisy, quite without the asperity of a retort.

'He's only nine,' urged Mrs Miller.

'Well, he wouldn't go to that castle,' said the young girl. 'I'm going there with Mr Winterbourne.'

To this announcement, very placidly made, Daisy's mamma offered no response. Winterbourne took for granted that she deeply disapproved of the projected excursion; but he said to himself that she was a simple, easily managed person, and that a few deferential protestations would take the edge from her displeasure. 'Yes,' he began; 'your daughter has kindly allowed me the honour of being her guide.'

Mrs Miller's wandering eyes attached themselves, with a sort of appealing air, to Daisy, who, however, strolled a few steps farther, gently humming to herself. 'I presume you will go in the cars,' said her mother.

'Yes; or in the boat,' said Winterbourne.

'Well, of course, I don't know,' Mrs Miller rejoined. 'I have never been to that castle.'

'It is a pity you shouldn't go,' said Winterbourne, beginning to feel reassured as to her opposition. And yet he was quite prepared to find that, as a matter of course, she meant to accompany her daughter.

'We've been thinking ever so much about going,' she pursued; 'but it seems as if we couldn't. Of course Daisy – she wants to go round. But there's a lady here – I don't know her name – she says she shouldn't think we'd want to go to see castles *here*; she should think we'd want to wait till we got to Italy. It seems as if there would be so many there,' continued Mrs Miller, with an air of increasing confidence. 'Of course, we only want to see the principal ones. We visited several in England,' she presently added.

'Ah, yes! in England there are beautiful castles,' said Winterbourne. 'But Chillon, here, is very well worth seeing.'

'Well, if Daisy feels up to it – ,' said Mrs Miller, in a tone impregnated with a sense of the magnitude of the enterprise. 'It seems as if there was nothing she wouldn't undertake.'

'Oh, I think she'll enjoy it!' Winterbourne declared. And he desired more and more to make it a certainty that he was to have the privilege of a *tête-à-tête* with the young lady, who was still strolling along in front of them, softly vocalizing. 'You are not disposed, madam,' he inquired, 'to undertake it yourself?'

Daisy's mother looked at him, an instant, askance, and then walked forward in silence. Then – 'I guess she had better go alone,' she said, simply.

Winterbourne observed to himself that this was a very different type of maternity from that of the vigilant matrons who massed themselves in the forefront of social intercourse in the dark old city at the other end of the lake. But his meditations were interrupted by hearing his name very distinctly pronounced by Mrs Miller's unprotected daughter.

'Mr Winterbourne!' murmured Daisy.

'Mademoiselle!' said the young man.

'Don't you want to take me out in a boat?'

'At present?' he asked.

'Of course!' said Daisy.

'Well, Annie Miller!' exclaimed her mother.

'I beg you, madam, to let her go,' said Winterbourne, ardently; for he had never yet enjoyed the sensation of guiding through the summer starlight a skiff freighted with a fresh and beautiful young girl.

'I shouldn't think she'd want to,' said her mother. 'I should think she'd rather go indoors.'

'I'm sure Mr Winterbourne wants to take me,' Daisy declared. 'He's so awfully devoted!'

'I will row you over to Chillon, in the starlight.'

'I don't believe it!' said Daisy.

'Well!' ejaculated the elder lady again.

'You haven't spoken to me for half an hour,' her daughter went on.

'I have been having some very pleasant conversation with your mother,' said Winterbourne.

'Well; I want you to take me out in a boat!' Daisy repeated. They had all stopped, and she turned round and was looking at Winterbourne. Her face wore a charming smile, her pretty eyes were gleaming, she was swinging her great fan about. No; it's impossible to be prettier than that, thought Winterbourne.

'There are half a dozen boats moored at that landing-place,' he said, pointing to certain steps which descended from the garden to the lake. 'If you will do me the honour to accept my arm, we will go and select one of them.'

Daisy stood there smiling; she threw back her head and gave a little light laugh. 'I like a gentleman to be formal!' she declared.

'I assure you it's a formal offer.'

'I was bound I would make you say something,' Daisy went on.

'You see it's not very difficult,' said Winterbourne. 'But I am afraid you are chaffing me.'

'I think not, sir,' remarked Mrs Miller, very gently.

'Do, then, let me give you a row,' he said to the young girl.

'It's quite lovely, the way you say that!' cried Daisy.

'It will be still more lovely to do it.'

'Yes, it would be lovely!' said Daisy. But she made no movement to accompany him; she only stood there laughing.

'I should think you had better find out what time it is,' interposed her mother.

'It is eleven o'clock, madam,' said a voice, with a foreign accent, out of the neighbouring darkness; and Winterbourne, turning, perceived the florid personage who was in attendance upon the two ladies. He had apparently just approached.

'Oh, Eugenio,' said Daisy, 'I am going out in a boat!'

Eugenio bowed. 'At eleven o'clock, mademoiselle?'

'I am going with Mr Winterbourne. This very minute.'

'Do tell her she can't,' said Mrs Miller to the courier.

'I think you had better not go out in a boat, mademoiselle,' Eugenio declared.

Winterbourne wished to Heaven this pretty girl were not so familiar with her courier; but he said nothing.

'I suppose you don't think it's proper!' Daisy exclaimed, 'Eugenio doesn't think anything's proper.'

'I am at your service,' said Winterbourne.

'Does mademoiselle propose to go alone?' asked Eugenio of Mrs Miller.

'Oh, no; with this gentleman!' answered Daisy's mamma.

The courier looked for a moment at Winterbourne – the latter thought he was smiling – and then, solemnly, with a bow, 'As mademoiselle pleases!' he said.

'Oh, I hoped you would make a fuss!' said Daisy. 'I don't care to go now.'

'I myself shall make a fuss if you don't go,' said Winterbourne.

'That's all I want – a little fuss!' And the young girl began to laugh again.

'Mr Randolph has gone to bed!' the courier announced, frigidly.

'Oh, Daisy; now we can go!' said Mrs Miller.

Daisy turned away from Winterbourne, looking at him, smiling and fanning herself. 'Good night,' she said; 'I hope you are disappointed, or disgusted, or something!'

He looked at her, taking the hand she offered him. 'I am puzzled,' he answered.

'Well; I hope it won't keep you awake!' she said, very smartly; and, under the escort of the privileged Eugenio, the two ladies passed towards the house.

Winterbourne stood looking after them; he was indeed puzzled. He lingered beside the lake for a quarter of an hour, turning over the mystery of the young girl's sudden familiarities and caprices. But the only very definite conclusion he came to was that he should enjoy deucedly 'going off' with her somewhere.

Two days afterwards he went off with her to the Castle of Chillon. He waited for her in the large hall of the hotel, where the couriers, the servants, the foreign tourists were lounging about and staring. It was not the place he would have chosen, but she had appointed it. She came tripping downstairs, buttoning her long gloves, squeezing her folded parasol against her pretty figure, dressed in the perfection of a soberly elegant travelling-costume. Winterbourne was a man of imagination and, as our ancestors used to say, of sensibility; as he looked at her dress and, on the great staircase, her little rapid, confiding step, he felt as if there were something romantic going forward. He could have believed he was going to elope with her. He passed out with her among all the idle people that were assembled there; they were all looking at her very hard; she had begun to chatter as soon as she joined him. Winterbourne's preference had been that they should be conveyed to Chillon in a carriage; but she expressed a lively wish to go in the little steamer; she declared that she had a passion for steamboats. There was always such a lovely·breeze upon the water, and you saw such lots of people. The sail was not long, but Winterbourne's companion found time to say a great many things. To the young man himself their little excursion was so much of an escapade – an adventure – that, even allowing for her habitual sense of freedom, he had some expectation of seeing her regard it in the same way. But it must be confessed that, in this particular, he was disappointed. Daisy Miller was extremely animated, she was in charming spirits; but she was apparently not at all excited; she was not fluttered; she avoided neither his eyes nor those of anyone else; she blushed neither when she looked at him nor when she saw that people were looking at her. People continued to look at her a great deal, and Winterbourne took much satisfaction in his pretty companion's distinguished air. He had been a little afraid that she would talk loud, laugh overmuch, and even, perhaps, desire to move about the boat a good deal. But he quite forgot his fears; he sat smiling, with his eyes upon her face, while without moving from her place, she delivered herself of a great number of original reflections. It was the most charming garrulity he had ever heard. He had assented to the idea that she was 'common'; but was she so, after all, or was he simply getting used to her commonness? Her conversation was chiefly of what metaphysicians term the objective cast; but every now and then it took a subjective turn.

'What on *earth* are you so grave about?' she suddenly demanded, fixing her agreeable eyes upon Winterbourne's.

'Am I grave?' he asked. 'I had an idea I was grinning from ear to ear.'

'You look as if you were taking me to a funeral. If that's a grin, your ears are very near together.'

'Should you like me to dance a hornpipe on the deck?'

'Pray do, and I'll carry round your hat. It will pay the expenses of our journey.'

'I never was better pleased in my life,' murmured Winterbourne.

She looked at him a moment, and then burst into a little laugh. 'I like to make you say those things! You're a queer mixture!'

In the castle, after they had landed, the subjective element decidedly prevailed. Daisy tripped about the vaulted chambers, rustled her skirts in the corkscrew staircases, flirted back with a pretty little cry and a shudder from the edge of the *oubliettes*, and turned a singularly well-shaped ear to everything that Winterbourne told her about the place. But he saw that she cared very little for feudal antiquities, and that the dusky traditions of Chillon made but a slight impression upon her. They had the good fortune to have been able to walk about without other companionship than that of the custodian; and Winterbourne arranged with this functionary that they should not be hurried — that they should linger and pause wherever they chose. The custodian interpreted the bargain generously — Winterbourne, on his side, had been generous — and ended by leaving them quite to themselves. Miss Miller's observations were not remarkable for logical consistency; for anything she wanted to say she was sure to find a pretext. She found a great many pretexts in the rugged embrasures of Chillon for asking Winterbourne sudden questions about himself — his family, his previous history, his tastes, his habits, his intentions — and for supplying information upon corresponding points in her own personality. Of her own tastes, habits, and intentions Miss Miller was prepared to give the most definite, and indeed the most favourable, account.

'Well; I hope you know enough!' she said to her companion, after he had told her the history of the unhappy Bonivard. 'I never saw a man that knew so much!' The history of Bonivard had evidently, as they say, gone into one ear and out of the other. But Daisy went on to say that she wished Winterbourne would travel with them and 'go round' with them; they might know something, in that case. 'Don't you want to come and teach Randolph?' she asked. Winterbourne said that nothing could possibly please him so much; but that he had unfortunately other occupations. 'Other occupations? I don't believe it!' said Miss Daisy. 'What do you mean? You are not in business.' The young man admitted that he was not in business; but he had engagements which, even within a day or two, would force him to go back to Geneva. 'Oh, bother!' she said, 'I don't believe it!' and she began to talk about something else. But a few moments later, when he was pointing out to her the pretty design of an antique fireplace, she broke out irrelevantly, 'You don't mean to say you are going back to Geneva?'

'It is a melancholy fact that I shall have to return to Geneva tomorrow.'

'Well, Mr Winterbourne,' said Daisy; 'I think you're horrid!'

'Oh, don't say such dreadful things!' said Winterbourne, 'just at the last.'

'The last!' cried the young girl; 'I call it the first. I have half a mind to leave you here and go straight back to the hotel alone.' And for the next ten minutes she did nothing but call him horrid. Poor Winterbourne was fairly bewildered; no young lady had as yet done him the honour to be so agitated by the announcement of his movements. His companion, after this, ceased to pay any attention to the curiosities of Chillon or the beauties of the lake; she opened fire upon the mysterious charmer in Geneva, whom she appeared to have instantly taken it for granted that he was hurrying back to see. How did Miss Daisy Miller know that there was a charmer in Geneva? Winterbourne, who denied the existence of such a person, was quite unable to discover; and he was divided between amazement at the rapidity of her induction and amusement at the frankness of her *persiflage*. She seemed to him, in all this, an extraordinary mixture of innocence and crudity. 'Does she never allow you more than three days at a time?' asked Daisy, ironically. 'Doesn't she give you a vacation in summer? There's no one so hard worked but they can get leave to go off somewhere at this season. I suppose, if you stay another day, she'll come after you in the boat. Do wait over till Friday, and I will go down to the landing to see her arrive!' Winterbourne began to think he had been wrong to feel disappointed in the temper in which the young lady had embarked. If he had missed the personal accent, the personal accent was now making its appearance. It sounded very distinctly, at last, in her telling him she would stop 'teasing' him if he would promise her solemnly to come down to Rome in the winter.

'That's not a difficult promise to make,' said Winterbourne. 'My aunt has taken an apartment in Rome for the winter, and has already asked me to come and see her.'

'I don't want you to come for your aunt,' said Daisy; 'I want you to come for me.' And this was the only allusion that the young man was ever to hear her make to his invidious kinswoman. He declared that, at any rate, he would certainly come. After this Daisy stopped teasing. Winterbourne took a carriage, and they drove back to Vevey in the dusk; the young girl was very quiet.

In the evening Winterbourne mentioned to Mrs Costello that he had spent the afternoon at Chillon, with Miss Daisy Miller.

'The Americans – of the courier?' asked this lady.

'Ah, happily,' said Winterbourne, 'the courier stayed at home.'

'She went with you all alone?'

'All alone.'

Mrs Costello sniffed a little at her smelling-bottle. 'And that,' she exclaimed, 'is the young person you wanted me to know!'

3

Winterbourne, who had returned to Geneva the day after his excursion to Chillon, went to Rome towards the end of January. His aunt had been established there for several weeks, and he had received a couple of letters from her. 'Those people you were so devoted to last summer at Vevey have turned up here, courier and all,' she wrote. 'They seem to have made several acquaintances, but the courier continues to be the most *intime*. The young lady, however, is also very intimate with some third-rate Italians, with whom she rackets about in a way that makes much talk. Bring me that pretty novel of Cherbuliex's – *Paule Méré* – and don't come later than the 23rd.'

In the natural course of events, Winterbourne, on arriving in Rome, would presently have ascertained Mrs Miller's address at the American banker's and have gone to pay his compliments to Miss Daisy. 'After what happened at Vevey I certainly think I may call upon them,' he said to Mrs Costello.

'If, after what happens – at Vevey and everywhere – you desire to keep up the acquaintance, you are very welcome. Of course a man may know everyone. Men are welcome to the privilege!'

'Pray what is it that happens – here, for instance?' Winterbourne demanded.

'The girl goes about alone with her foreigners. As to what happens further, you must apply elsewhere for information. She has picked up half a dozen of the regular Roman fortune-hunters, and she takes them about to people's houses. When she comes to a party she brings with her a gentleman with a good deal of manner and a wonderful moustache.'

'And where is the mother?'

'I haven't the least idea. They are very dreadful people.'

Winterbourne meditated a moment. 'They are very ignorant – very innocent only. Depend upon it they are not bad.'

'They are hopelessly vulgar,' said Mrs Costello. 'Whether or no being hopelessly vulgar is being "bad" is a question for the metaphysicians. They are bad enough to dislike, at any rate; and for this short life that is quite enough.'

The news that Daisy Miller was surrounded by half a dozen wonderful moustaches checked Winterbourne's impulse to go straightway to see her. He had perhaps not definitely flattered himself that he had made an ineffaceable impression upon her heart, but he was annoyed at hearing of a state of affairs so little in harmony with an image that had lately flitted in and out of his

own meditations; the image of a very pretty girl looking out
of an old Roman window and asking herself urgently when Mr
Winterbourne would arrive. If, however, he determined to wait
a little before reminding Miss Miller of his claims to her consideration, he went very soon to call upon two or three other
friends. One of these friends was an American lady who had
spent several winters at Geneva, where she had placed her
children at school. She was a very accomplished woman and she
lived in the Via Gregoriana. Winterbourne found her in a little
crimson drawing-room, on a third floor; the room was filled
with southern sunshine. He had not been there ten minutes when
the servant came in, announcing 'Madame Mila!' This announcement was presently followed by the entrance of little Randolph
Miller, who stopped in the middle of the room and stood staring
at Winterbourne. An instant later his pretty sister crossed the
threshold; and then, after a considerable interval, Mrs Miller
slowly advanced.

'I know you!' said Randolph.

'I'm sure you know a great many things,' exclaimed Winterbourne, taking him by the hand. 'How is your education coming
on?'

Daisy was exchanging greetings very prettily with her hostess;
but when she heard Winterbourne's voice she quickly turned her
head. 'Well, I declare!' she said.

'I told you I should come, you know,' Winterbourne rejoined,
smiling.

'Well – I didn't believe it,' said Miss Daisy.

'I am much obliged to you,' laughed the young man.

'You might have come to see me!' said Daisy.

'I arrived only yesterday.'

'I don't believe that!' the young girl declared.

Winterbourne turned with a protesting smile to her mother;
but this lady evaded his glance, and seating herself, fixed her
eyes upon her son. 'We've got a bigger place than this,' said
Randolph. 'It's all gold on the walls.'

Mrs Miller turned uneasily in her chair. 'I told you if I were
to bring you, you would say something!' she murmured.

'I told *you*!' Randolph exclaimed. 'I tell *you*, sir!' he added jocosely, giving Winterbourne a thump on the knee. 'It *is* bigger, too!'

Daisy had entered upon a lively conversation with her hostess; Winterbourne judged it becoming to address a few words to her mother. 'I hope you have been well since we parted at Vevey,' he said.

Mrs Miller now certainly looked at him – at his chin. 'Not very well, sir,' she answered.

'She's got the dyspepsia,' said Randolph. 'I've got it too. Father's got it. I've got it worst!'

This announcement, instead of embarrassing Mrs Miller, seemed to relieve her. 'I suffer from the liver,' she said. 'I think it's this climate; it's less bracing than Schenectady, especially in the winter season. I don't know whether you know we reside at Schenectady. I was saying to Daisy that I certainly hadn't found anyone like Dr Davis, and I didn't believe I should. Oh, at Schenectady, he stands first; they think everything of him. He has so much to do, and yet there was nothing he wouldn't do for me. He said he never saw anything like my dyspepsia, but he was bound to cure it. I'm sure there was nothing he wouldn't try. He was just going to try something new when we came off. Mr Miller wanted Dasiy to see Europe for herself. But I wrote to Mr Miller that it seems as if I couldn't get on without Dr Davis. At Schenectady he stands at the very top; and there's a great deal of sickness there, too. It affects my sleep.'

Winterbourne had a good deal of pathological gossip with Dr Davis's patient, during which Daisy chattered unremittingly to her own companion. The young man asked Mrs Miller how she was pleased with Rome. 'Well, I must say I am disappointed,' she answered. 'We had heard so much about it; I suppose we had heard too much. But we couldn't help that. We had been led to expect something different.'

'Ah, wait a little, and you will become very fond of it,' said Winterbourne.

'I hate it worse and worse every day!' cried Randolph.

'You are like the infant Hannibal,' said Winterbourne.

'Nok I ain't!' Randolph declared, at a venture.

'You are not much like an infant,' said his mother. 'But we

have seen places,' she resumed, 'that I should put a long way
before Rome.' And in reply to Winterbourne's interrogation,
'There's Zürich,' she observed; 'I think Zürich is lovely; and
we hadn't heard half so much about it.'

'The best place we've seen is the *City of Richmond*!' said
Randolph.

'He means the ship,' his mother explained. 'We crossed in that
ship. Randolph had a good time on the *City of Richmond*.'

'It's the best place I've seen,' the child repeated. 'Only it was
turned the wrong way.'

'Well, we've got to turn the right way some time,' said Mrs
Miller, with a little laugh. Winterbourne expressed the hope that
her daughter at least found some gratification in Rome, and she
declared that Daisy was quite carried away. 'It's on account of
the society – the society's splendid. She goes round everywhere;
she has made a great number of acquaintances. Of course she
goes round more than I do. I must say they have been very
sociable; they have taken her right in. And then she knows a
great many gentlemen. Oh, she thinks there's nothing like Rome.
Of course, it's a great deal pleasanter for a young lady if she
knows plenty of gentlemen.'

By this time Daisy had turned her attention again to Winterbourne. 'I've been telling Mrs Walker how mean you were!'
the young girl announced.

'And what is the evidence you have offered?' asked Winterbourne, rather annoyed at Miss Miller's want of appreciation
of the zeal of an admirer who on his way down to Rome had
stopped neither at Bologna nor at Florence, simply because of a
certain sentimental impatience. He remembered that a cynical
compatriot had once told him that American women – the
pretty ones, and this gave a largeness to the axiom – were at
once the most exacting in the world and the least endowed with
a sense of indebtedness.

'Why, you were awfully mean at Vevey,' said Daisy. 'You
wouldn't do anything. You wouldn't stay there when I asked you.'

'My dearest young lady,' cried Winterbourne, with eloquence,
'have I come all the way to Rome to encounter your reproaches?'

'Just hear him say that!' said Daisy to her hostess, giving a twist to a bow on this lady's dress. 'Did you ever hear anything so quaint?'

'So quaint, my dear?' murmured Mrs Walker, in the tone of a partisan of Winterbourne.

'Well, I don't know,' said Daisy, fingering Mrs Walker's ribbons. 'Mrs Walker, I want to tell you something.'

'Motherr,' interposed Randolph, with his rough ends to his words, 'I tell you you've got to go. Eugenio'll raise something!'

'I'm not afraid of Eugenio,' said Daisy, with a toss of her head. 'Look here, Mrs Walker,' she went on, 'you know I'm coming to your party.'

'I am delighted to hear it.'

'I've got a lovely dress.'

'I am very sure of that.'

'But I want to ask a favour – permission to bring a friend.'

'I shall be happy to see any of your friends,' said Mrs Walker, turning with a smile to Mrs Miller.

'Oh, they are not my friends,' answered Daisy's mamma, smiling shyly, in her own fashion. 'I never spoke to them!'

'It's an intimate friend of mine – Mr Giovanelli,' said Daisy, without a tremor in her clear little voice or a shadow on her brilliant little face.

Mrs Walker was silent a moment, she gave a rapid glance at Winterbourne. 'I shall be glad to see Mr Giovanelli,' she then said.

'He's an Italian,' Daisy pursued, with the prettiest serenity. 'He's a great friend of mine – he's the handsomest man in the world – except Mr Winterbourne! He knows plenty of Italians, but he wants to know some Americans. He thinks ever so much of Americans. He's tremendously clever. He's perfectly lovely!'

It was settled that this brilliant personage should be brought to Mrs Walker's party, and then Mrs Miller prepared to take her leave. 'I guess we'll go back to the hotel,' she said.

'You may go back to the hotel, mother, but I'm going to take a walk,' said Daisy.

'She's going to walk with Mr Giovanelli,' Randolph proclaimed.

'I am going to the Pincio,' said Daisy, smiling.

'Alone, my dear – at this hour?' Mrs Walker asked. The after-noon was drawing to a close – it was the hour for the throng of carriages and of contemplative pedestrians. 'I don't think it's safe, my dear,' said Mrs Walker.

'Neither do I,' subjoined Mrs Miller. 'You'll get the fever as sure as you live. Remember what Dr Davis told you!'

'Give her some medicine before she goes,' said Randolph.

The company had risen to its feet; Daisy, still showing her pretty teeth, bent over and kissed her hostess. 'Mrs Walker, you are too perfect,' she said. 'I'm not going alone; I am going to meet a friend.'

'Your friend won't keep you from getting the fever,' Mrs Miller observed.

'Is it Mr Giovanelli?' asked the hostess.

Winterbourne was watching the young girl; at this question his attention quickened. She stood there smiling and smoothing her bonnet-ribbons; she glanced at Winterbourne. Then, while she glanced and smiled, she answered without a shade of hesi-tation, 'Mr Giovanelli – the beautiful Giovanelli.'

'My dear young friend,' said Mrs Walker, taking her hand, pleadingly, 'don't walk off to the Pincio at this hour to meet a beautiful Italian.'

'Well, he speaks English,' said Mrs Miller.

'Gracious me!' Daisy exclaimed, 'I don't want to do anything improper. There's an easy way to settle it.' She continued to glance at Winterbourne. 'The Pincio is only a hundred yards distant, and if Mr Winterbourne were as polite as he pretends he would offer to walk with me!'

Winterbourne's politeness hastened to affirm itself, and the young girl gave him gracious leave to accompany her. They passed downstairs before her mother, and at the door Winterbourne perceived Mrs Miller's carriage drawn up, with the ornamental courier whose acquaintance he had made at Vevey seated within. 'Good-bye, Eugenio!' cried Daisy, 'I'm going to take a walk.' The distance from the Via Gregoriana to the beautiful garden at the other end of the Pincian Hill is, in fact, rapidly traversed. As the day was splendid, however, and the concourse of vehicles, walkers, and loungers numerous, the young Americans found their progress much delayed. This fact was highly agreeable to Winterbourne, in spite of his consciousness of his singular situation. The slow-moving, idly gazing Roman crowd bestowed much attention upon the extremely pretty young foreign lady who was passing through it upon his arm; and he wondered what on earth had been in Daisy's mind when she proposed to expose herself, unattended, to its appreciation. His own mission, to her sense, apparently, was to consign her to the hands of Mr Giovanelli; but Winterbourne, at once annoyed and gratified, resolved that he would do no such thing.

'Why haven't you been to see me?' asked Daisy. 'You can't get out of that.'

'I have had the honour of telling you that I have only just stepped out of the train.'

'You must have stayed in the train a good while after it stopped!' cried the young girl, with her little laugh. 'I suppose you were asleep. You have had time to go to see Mrs Walker.'

'I knew Mrs Walker – ' Winterbourne began to explain.

'I knew where you knew her. You knew her at Geneva. She told me so. Well, you knew me at Vevey. That's just as good. So you ought to have come.' She asked him no other question than this; she began to prattle about her own affairs. 'We've got splendid rooms at the hotel; Eugenio says they're the best rooms in Rome. We are going to stay all winter – if we don't die of the fever; and I guess we'll stay then. It's a great deal nicer than I thought; I thought it would be fearfully quiet; I was sure it would be awfully poky. I was sure we should be going round all the time with one of those dreadful old men that explain about the pictures and things. But we only had about a week of that, and now I'm enjoying myself. I know ever so many people, and they are all so charming. The society's extremely select. There are all kinds – English, and Germans, and Italians. I think I like the English best. I like their style of conversation. But there are some lovely Americans. I never saw anything so hospitable. There's something or other every day. There's not much dancing; but I must say I never thought dancing was everything. I was always fond of conversation. I guess I shall have plenty at Mrs Walker's – her rooms are so small.' When they had passed the gate of the

Pincian Gardens, Miss Miller began to wonder where Mr Giovanelli might be. 'We had better go straight to that place in
front,' she said, 'where you look at the view.'

'I certainly shall not help you to find him,' Winterbourne
declared.

'Then I shall find him without you,' said Miss Daisy.

'You certainly won't leave me!' cried Winterbourne.

She burst into her little laugh. 'Are you afraid you'll get lost –
or run over? But there's Giovanelli, leaning against that tree.
He's staring at the women in the carriages: did you ever see
anything so cool?'

Winterbourne perceived at some distance a little man standing
with folded arms, nursing his cane. He had a handsome face,
an artfully poised hat, a glass in one eye, and a nosegay in his
button-hole. Winterbourne looked at him a moment and then
said, 'Do you mean to speak to that man?'

'Do I mean to speak to him? Why, you don't suppose I mean
to communicate by signs?'

'Pray understand, then,' said Winterbourne, 'that I intend to
remain with you.'

Daisy stopped and looked at him, without a sign of troubled
consciousness in her face; with nothing but the presence of her
charming eyes and her happy dimples. 'Well, she's a cool one!'
thought the young man.

'I don't like the way you say that,' said Daisy. 'It's too
imperious.'

'I beg your pardon if I say it wrong. The main point is to give
you an idea of my meaning.'

The young girl looked at him more gravely, but with eyes that
were prettier than ever. 'I have never allowed a gentleman to
dictate to me, or to interfere with anything I do.'

'I think you have made a mistake,' said Winterbourne. 'You
should sometimes listen to a gentleman – the right one?'

Daisy began to laugh again, 'I do nothing but listen to gentlemen!' she exclaimed. 'Tell me if Mr Giovanelli is the right one?'

The gentleman with the nosegay in his bosom had now perceived our two friends, and was approaching the young girl with
obsequious rapidity. He bowed to Winterbourne as well as to

the latter's companion; he had a brilliant smile, an intelligent eye; Winterbourne thought him not a bad-looking fellow. But he nevertheless said to Daisy – 'No, he's not the right one.'

Daisy evidently had a natural talent for performing introductions; she mentioned the name of each of her companions to the other. She strolled along with one of them on each side of her; Mr Giovanelli, who spoke English very cleverly – Winterbourne afterwards learned that he had practised the idiom upon a great many American heiresses – addressed her a great deal of very polite nonsense; he was extremely urbane, and the young American, who said nothing, reflected upon that profundity of Italian cleverness which enables people to appear more gracious in proportion as they are more acutely disappointed. Giovanelli, of course, had counted upon something more intimate; he had not bargained for a party of three. But he kept his temper in a manner which suggested far-stretching intentions. Winterbourne flattered himself that he had taken his measure. 'He is not a gentleman,' said the young American; 'he is only a clever imitation of one. He is a music-master, or a penny-a-liner, or a third-rate artist. Damn his good looks!' Mr Giovanelli had certainly a very pretty face; but Winterbourne felt a superior indignation at his own lovely fellow-countrywoman's not knowing the difference between a spurious gentleman and a real one. Giovanelli chattered and jested and made himself wonderfully agreeable. It was true that if he was an imitation the imitation was very skilful. 'Nevertheless,' Winterbourne said to himself, 'a nice girl ought to know!' And then he came back to the question whether this was in fact a nice girl. Would a nice girl – even allowing for her being a little American flirt – make a rendezvous with a presumably low-lived foreigner? The rendezvous in this case, indeed, had been in broad daylight, and in the most crowded corner of Rome; but was it not impossible to regard the choice of these circumstances as a proof of extreme cynicism? Singular though it may seem, Winterbourne was vexed that the young girl, in joining her *amoroso*, should not appear more impatient of his own company, and he was vexed because of his inclination. It was impossible to regard her as a perfectly well-conducted young lady; she was wanting in a certain indispensable delicacy. It would therefore simplify matters greatly to be able to treat her as the object of one of those sentiments which are called by romancers 'lawless passions'. That she should seem to wish to get rid of him would help him to think more lightly of her, and to be able to think more lightly of her would make her much less perplexing. But Daisy, on this occasion, continued to present herself as an inscrutable combination of audacity and innocence.

She had been walking some quarter of an hour, attended by her two cavaliers, and responding in a tone of very childish gaiety, as it seemed to Winterbourne, to the pretty speeches of Mr Giovanelli, when a carriage that had detached itself from the revolving train drew up beside the path. At the same moment Winterbourne perceived that his friend Mrs Walker – the lady whose house he had lately left – was seated in the vehicle and was beckoning to him. Leaving Miss Miller's side, he hastened to obey her summons. Mrs Walker was flushed; she wore an excited air. 'It is really too dreadful,' she said. 'That girl must not do this sort of thing. She must not walk here with you two men. Fifty people have noticed her.'

Winterbourne raised his eyebrows. 'I think it's a pity to make too much fuss about it.'

'It's a pity to let the girl ruin herself!'

'She is very innocent,' said Winterbourne.

'She's very crazy!' cried Mrs Walker. 'Did you ever see anything so imbecile as her mother? After you had all left me, just now, I could not sit still for thinking of it. It seemed too pitiful, not even to attempt to save her. I ordered the carriage and put on my bonnet, and came here as quickly as possible. Thank heaven I have found you!'

'What do you propose to do with us?' asked Winterbourne, smiling.

'To ask her to get in, to drive her about here for half an hour, so that the world may see she is not running absolutely wild, and then to take her safely home.'

'I don't think it's a very happy thought,' said Winterbourne; 'but you can try.'

Mrs Walker tried. The young man went in pursuit of Miss Miller, who had simply nodded and smiled at his interlocutrix

in the carriage and had gone her way with her own companion.
Daisy, on learning that Mrs Walker wished to speak to her,
retraced her steps with a perfect good grace and with Mr Giovanelli at her side. She declared that she was delighted to have a
chance to present this gentleman to Mrs Walker. She immediately
achieved the introduction, and declared that she had never in
her life seen anything so lovely as Mrs Walker's carriage-rug.

'I am glad you admire it,' said this lady, smiling sweetly.
'Will you get in and let me put it over you?'

'Oh, no, thank you,' said Daisy. 'I shall admire it much more
as I see you driving round with it.'

'Do get in and drive with me,' said Mrs Walker.

'That would be charming, but it's so enchanting just as I am!'
and Daisy gave a brilliant glance at the gentlemen on either side
of her.

'It may be enchanting, dear child, but it is not the custom here,'
urged Mrs Walker, leaning forward in her victoria with her hands
devoutly clasped.

'Well, it ought to be, then!' said Daisy. 'If I didn't walk I
should expire.'

'You should walk with your mother, dear,' cried the lady
from Geneva, losing patience.

'With my mother dear!' exclaimed the young girl. Winterbourne saw that she scented interference. 'My mother never
walked ten steps in her life. And then, you know,' she added with
a laugh, 'I am more than five years old.'

'You are old enough to be more reasonable. You are old
enough, dear Miss Miller, to be talked about.'

Daisy looked at Mrs Walker, smiling intensely. 'Talked
about? What do you mean!'

'Come into my carriage and I will tell you.'

Daisy turned her quickened glance again from one of the
gentlemen beside her to the other. Mr Giovanelli was bowing
to and fro, rubbing down his gloves and laughing very agree-
ably; Winterbourne thought it a most unpleasant scene. 'I don't
think I want to know what you mean,' said Daisy presently.
'I don't think I should like it.'

Winterbourne wished that Mrs Walker would tuck in her

carriage-rug and drive away; but this lady did not enjoy being defied, as she afterwards told him. 'Should you prefer being thought a very reckless girl?' she demanded.

'Gracious me!' exclaimed Daisy. She looked again at Mr Giovanelli, then she turned to Winterbourne. There was a little pink flush in her check; she was tremendously pretty. 'Does Mr Winterbourne think,' she asked slowly, smiling, throwing back her head and glancing at him from head to foot, 'that – to save my reputation – I ought to get into the carriage?'

Winterbourne coloured; for an instant he hesitated greatly. It seemed so strange to hear her speak that way of her 'reputation'. But he himself, in fact, must speak in accordance with gallantry. The finest gallantry, here, was simply to tell her the truth; and the truth, for Winterbourne, as the few indications I have been able to give have made him known to the reader, was that Daisy Miller should take Mrs Walker's advice. He looked at her exquisite prettiness; and then he said very gently, 'I think you should get into the carriage'.

Daisy gave a violent laugh. 'I never heard anything so stiff! If this is improper, Mrs Walker,' she pursued, 'then I am all improper, and you must give me up. Good-bye; I hope you'll have a lovely ride!' and, with Mr Giovanelli, who made a triumphantly obsequious salute, she turned away.

Mrs Walker sat looking after her, and there were tears in Mrs Walker's eyes. 'Get in here, sir,' she said to Winterbourne, indicating the place beside her. The young man answered that he felt bound to accompany Miss Miller; whereupon Mrs Walker declared that if he refused her this favour she would never speak to him again. She was evidently in earnest. Winterbourne overtook Daisy and her companion and, offering the young girl his hand, told her that Mrs Walker had made an imperious claim upon his society. He expected that in answer she would say something rather free, something to commit herself still farther to that 'recklessness' from which Mrs Walker had so charitably endeavoured to dissuade her. But she only shook his hand, hardly looking at him, while Mr Giovanelli bade him farewell with a too emphatic flourish of the hat.

Winterbourne was not in the best possible humour as he took

his seat in Mrs Walker's victoria. 'That was not clever of you,' he said candidly, while the vehicle mingled again with the throng of carriages.

'In such a case,' his companion answered, 'I don't wish to be clever, I wish to be *earnest*!'

'Well, your earnestness has only offended her and put her off.'

'It has happened very well,' said Mrs Walker. 'If she is so perfectly determined to compromise herself, the sooner one knows it the better; one can act accordingly.'

'I suspect she meant no harm,' Winterbourne rejoined.

'So I thought a month ago. But she has been going too far.'

'What has she been doing?'

'Everything that is not done here. Flirting with any man she could pick up; sitting in corners with mysterious Italians; dancing all the evening with the same partners; receiving visits at eleven o'clock at night. Her mother goes away when visitors come.'

'But her brother,' said Winterbourne, laughing, 'sits up till midnight.'

'He must be edified by what he sees. I'm told that at their hotel everyone is talking about her, and that a smile goes round among the servants when a gentleman comes and asks for Miss Miller.'

'The servants be hanged!' said Winterbourne angrily. 'The poor girl's only fault,' he presently added, 'is that she is very uncultivated.'

'She is naturally indelicate,' Mrs Walker declared. 'Take that example this morning. How long had you known her at Vevey?'

'A couple of days.'

'Fancy, then, her making it a personal matter that you should have left the place!'

Winterbourne was silent for some moments; then he said, 'I suspect, Mrs Walker, that you and I have lived too long at Geneva!' And he added a request that she should inform him with what particular design she had made him enter her carriage.

'I wished to beg you to cease your relations with Miss Miller – not to flirt with her – to give her no further opportunity to expose herself – to let her alone, in short.'

'I'm afraid I can't do that,' said Winterbourne. 'I like her extremely.'

'All the more reason that you shouldn't help her to make a scandal.'

'There shall be nothing scandalous in my attentions to her.'

'There certainly will be in the way she takes them. But I have said what I had on my conscience,' Mrs Walker pursued. 'If you wish to rejoin the young lady I will put you down. Here, by the way, you have a chance.'

The carriage was traversing that part of the Pincian Garden which overhangs the wall of Rome and overlooks the beautiful Villa Borghese. It is bordered by a large parapet, near which there are several seats. One of the seats, at a distance, was occupied by a gentleman and a lady, towards whom Mrs Walker gave a toss of her head. At the same moment these persons rose and walked towards the parapet. Winterbourne had asked the coachman to stop; he now descended from the carriage. His companion looked at him a moment in silence; then, while he raised his hat, she drove majestically away. Winterbourne stood there; he had turned his eyes towards Daisy and her cavalier. They evidently saw no one; they were too deeply occupied with each other. When they reached the low garden-wall they stood a moment looking off at the great flat-topped pine-clusters of the Villa Borghese; then Giovanelli seated himself familiarly upon the broad ledge of the wall. The western sun in the opposite sky sent out a brilliant shaft through a couple of cloud-bars; whereupon Daisy's companion took her parasol out of her hands and opened it. She came a little nearer and he held the parasol over her; then, still holding it, he let it rest upon her shoulder, so that both their heads were hidden from Winterbourne. This young man lingered a moment, then he began to walk. But he walked – not towards the couple with the parasol; towards the residence of his aunt, Mrs Costello.

4

He flattered himself on the following day that there was no smiling among the servants when he, at least, asked for Mrs

Miller at her hotel. This lady and her daughter, however, were not at home; and on the next day, after repeating his visit, Winterbourne again had the misfortune not to find them. Mrs Walker's party took place on the evening of the third day, and in spite of the frigidity of his last interview with the hostess, Winterbourne was among the guests. Mrs Walker was one of those American ladies who, while residing abroad, make a point, in their own phrase, of studying European society; and she had on this occasion collected several specimens of her diversely born fellow-mortals to serve, as it were, as text-books. When Winterbourne arrived Daisy Miller was not there; but in a few moments he saw her mother come in alone, very shyly and ruefully. Mrs Miller's hair, above her exposed-looking temples, was more frizzled than ever. As she approached Mrs Walker, Winterbourne also drew near.

'You see I've come all alone,' said poor Mrs Miller. 'I'm so frightened; I don't know what to do; it's the first time I've ever been to a party alone – especially in this country. I wanted to bring Randolph or Eugenio, or someone, but Daisy just pushed me off by myself. I ain't used to going round alone.'

'And does not your daughter intend to favour us with her society?' demanded Mrs Walker, impressively.

'Well, Daisy's all dressed,' said Mrs Miller, with that accent of the dispassionate, if not of the philosophic, historian with which she always recorded the current incidents of her daughter's career. 'She's got dressed on purpose before dinner. But she's got a friend of hers there; that gentleman – the Italian – that she wanted to bring. They've got going at the piano; it seems as if they couldn't leave off. Mr Giovanelli sings splendidly. But I guess they'll come before very long,' concluded Mrs Miller hopefully.

'I'm sorry she should come – in that way,' said Mrs Walker.

'Well, I told her that there was no use in her getting dressed before dinner if she was going to wait three hours,' responded Daisy's mamma. 'I didn't see the use of her putting on such a dress as that to sit round with Mr Giovanelli.'

'This is most horrible!' said Mrs Walker, turning away and addressing herself to Winterbourne. '*Elle s'affiche.* It's her revenge for my having ventured to remonstrate with her. When she comes I shall not speak to her.'

Daisy came after eleven o'clock, but she was not, on such an occasion, a young lady to wait to be spoken to. She rustled forward in radiant loveliness, smiling and chattering, carrying a large bouquet and attended by Mr Giovanelli. Everyone stopped talking and turned and looked at her. She came straight to Mrs Walker. 'I'm afraid you thought I never was coming, so I sent mother off to tell you. I wanted to make Mr Giovanelli practise some things before he came; you know he sings beautifully, and I want you to ask him to sing. This is Mr Giovanelli; you know I introduced him to you; he's got the most lovely voice and he knows the most charming set of songs. I made him go over them this evening, on purpose; we had the greatest time at the hotel.' Of all this Daisy delivered herself with the sweetest, brightest audibleness, looking now at her hostess and now round the room, while she gave a series of little pats, round her shoulders, to the edges of her dress. 'Is there anyone I know?' she asked.

'I think everyone knows you!' said Mrs Walker pregnantly, and she gave a very cursory greeting to Mr Giovanelli. This gentleman bore himself gallantly. He smiled and bowed and showed his white teeth, he curled his moustaches and rolled his eyes, and performed all the proper functions of a handsome Italian at an evening party. He sang, very prettily, half a dozen songs, though Mrs Walker afterwards declared that she had been quite unable to find out who asked him. It was apparently not Daisy who had given him his orders. Daisy sat at a distance from the piano, and though she had publicly, as it were, professed a high admiration for his singing, talked, not inaudibly, while it was going on.

'It's a pity these rooms are so small; we can't dance,' she said to Winterbourne, as if she had seen him five minutes before.

'I am not sorry we can't dance,' Winterbourne answered; 'I don't dance.'

'Of course you don't dance; you're too stiff,' said Miss Daisy. 'I hope you enjoyed your drive with Mrs Walker.'

'No I didn't enjoy it; I preferred walking with you.'

'We paired off, that was much better,' said Daisy. 'But did you ever hear anything so cool as Mrs Walker's wanting me to get into her carriage and drop poor Mr Giovanelli; and under the pretext that it was proper? People have different ideas! It would have been most unkind; he had been talking about that walk for ten days.'

'He should not have talked about it at all,' said Winterbourne; 'he would never have proposed to a young lady of this country to walk about the streets with him.'

'About the streets?' cried Daisy, with her pretty stare. 'Where then would he have proposed to her to walk? The Pincio is not the streets, either; and I, thank goodness, am not a young lady of this country. The young ladies of this country have a dreadfully poky time of it, so far as I can learn; I don't see why I should change my habits for *them*.'

'I am afraid your habits are those of a flirt,' said Winterbourne gravely.

'Of course they are,' she cried, giving him her little smiling stare again. 'I'm a fearful, frightful flirt! Did you ever hear of a nice girl that was not? But I suppose you will tell me now that I am not a nice girl.'

'You're a very nice girl, but I wish you would flirt with me, and me only,' said Winterbourne.

'Ah! thank you, thank you very much; you are the last man I should think of flirting with. As I have had the pleasure of informing you, you are too stiff.'

'You say that too often,' said Winterbourne.

Daisy gave a delighted laugh. 'If I could have the sweet hope of making you angry, I would say it again.'

'Don't do that; when I am angry I'm stiffer than ever. But if you won't flirt with me, do cease at least to flirt with your friend at the piano; they don't understand that sort of thing here.'

'I thought they understood nothing else!' exclaimed Daisy.

'Not in young unmarried women.'

'It seems to me much more proper in young unmarried women than in old married ones,' Daisy declared.

'Well,' said Winterbourne, 'when you deal with natives you

must go by the custom of the place. Flirting is a purely American custom; it doesn't exist here. So when you show yourself in public with Mr Giovanelli and without your mother – '

'Gracious! Poor mother!' interposed Daisy.

'Though you may be flirting, Mr Giovanelli is not; he means something else.'

'He isn't preaching, at any rate,' said Daisy with vivacity. 'And if you want very much to know, we are neither of us flirting; we are too good friends for that; we are very intimate friends.'

'Ah,' rejoined Winterbourne, 'if you are in love with each other it is another affair.'

She had allowed him up to this point to talk so frankly that he had no expectation of shocking her by this ejaculation; but she immediately got up, blushing visibly, and leaving him to exclaim mentally that little American flirts were the queerest creatures in the world. 'Mr Giovanelli, at least,' she said, giving her interlocutor a single glance, 'never says such very disagreeable things to me.'

Winterbourne was bewildered; he stood staring. Mr Giovanelli had finished singing; he left the piano and came over to Daisy. 'Won't you come into the other room and have some tea?' he asked, bending before her with his decorative smile.

Daisy turned to Winterbourne, beginning to smile again. He was still more perplexed, for this inconsequent smile made nothing clear, though it seemed to prove, indeed, that she had a sweetness and softness that reverted instinctively to the pardon of offences. 'It has never occurred to Mr Winterbourne to offer me any tea,' she said, with her little tormenting manner.

'I have offered you advice,' Winterbourne rejoined.

'I prefer weak tea!' cried Daisy, and she went off with the brilliant Giovanelli. She sat with him in the adjoining room, in the embrasure of the window, for the rest of the evening. There was an interesting performance at the piano, but neither of these young people gave heed to it. When Daisy came to take leave of Mrs Walker, this lady conscientiously repaired the weakness of which she had been guilty at the moment of the young girl's arrival. She turned her back straight upon Miss Miller and left her to depart with what grace she might. Winterbourne was standing near the door; he saw it all. Daisy turned very pale and looked at her mother, but Mrs Miller was humbly unconscious of any violation of the usual social forms. She appeared, indeed, to have felt an incongruous impulse to draw attention to her own striking observance of them. 'Goodnight, Mrs Walker,' she said; 'we've had a beautiful evening. You see if I let Daisy come to parties without me, I don't want her to go away without me.' Daisy turned away, looking with a pale, grave face at the circle near the door; Winterbourne saw that, for the first moment, she was too much shocked and puzzled even for indignation. He on his side was greatly touched.

'That was very cruel,' he said to Mrs Walker.

'She never enters my drawing-room again,' replied his hostess.

Since Winterbourne was not to meet her in Mrs Walker's drawing-room, he went as often as possible to Mrs Miller's hotel. The ladies were rarely at home, but when he found them the devoted Giovanelli was always present. Very often the polished little Roman was in the drawing-room with Daisy alone, Mrs Miller being apparently constantly of the opinion that discretion is the better part of surveillance. Winterbourne noted, at first with surprise, that Daisy on these occasions was never embarrassed or annoyed by his own entrance; but he very presently began to feel that she had no more surprises for him; the unexpected in her behaviour was the only thing to expect. She showed no displeasure at her *tête-à-tête* with Giovanelli being interrupted; she could chatter as freshly and freely with two gentlemen as with one; there was always, in her conversation, the same odd mixture of audacity and puerility. Winterbourne remarked to himself that if she was seriously interested in Giovanelli it was very singular that she should not take more trouble to preserve the sanctity of their interviews, and he liked her the more for her innocent-looking indifference and her apparently inexhaustible good humour. He could hardly have said why, but she seemed to him a girl who would never be jealous. At the risk of exciting a somewhat derisive smile on the reader's part, I may affirm that with regard to the women who had hitherto interested him it very often seemed to Winterbourne among the possibilities that, given certain contingencies, he should be afraid – literally afraid – of these ladies. He had a pleasant sense that he should never be afraid of Daisy Miller. It must be added that this sentiment was not altogether flattering to Daisy; it was part of his conviction, or rather of his apprehension, that she would prove a very light young person.

But she was evidently very much interested in Giovanelli. She looked at him whenever he spoke; she was perpetually telling him to do this and to do that; she was constantly 'chaffing' and abusing him. She appeared completely to have forgotten that Winterbourne had said anything to displease her at Mrs Walker's little party. One Sunday afternoon, having gone to St Peter's with his aunt, Winterbourne perceived Daisy strolling about the great church in company with the inevitable Giovanelli. Presently he pointed out the young girl and her cavalier to Mrs Costello. This lady looked at them a moment through·her eyeglass, and then she said:

'That's what makes you so pensive in these days, eh?'

'I had not the least idea I was pensive,' said the young man.

'You are very much preoccupied, you are thinking of something.'

'And what is it,' he asked, 'that you accuse me of thinking of?'

'Of that young lady's, Miss Baker's, Miss Chandler's – what's her name? – Miss Miller's intrigue with that little barber's block.'

'Do you call it an intrigue,' Winterbourne asked – 'an affair that goes on with such peculiar publicity?'

'That's their folly,' said Mrs Costello, 'it's not their merit.'

'No,' rejoined Winterbourne, with something of that pensiveness to which his aunt had alluded. 'I don't believe that there is anything to be called an intrigue.'

'I have heard a dozen people speak of it; they say she is quite carried away by him.'

'They are certainly very intimate,' said Winterbourne.

Mrs Costello inspected the young couple again with her optical instrument. 'He is very handsome. One easily sees how it is. She thinks him the most elegant man in the world, the finest gentleman. She has never seen anything like him; he is better even than the courier. It was the courier probably who introduced him, and if he succeeds in marrying the young lady, the courier will come in for a magnificent commission.'

'I don't believe she thinks of marrying him,' said Winterbourne, 'and I don't believe he hopes to marry her.'

'You may be very sure she thinks of nothing. She goes on from day to day, from hour to hour, as they did in the Golden Age. I can imagine nothing more vulgar. And at the same time,' added Mrs Costello, 'depend upon it that she may tell you any moment that she is "engaged".'

'I think that is more than Giovanelli expects,' said Winterbourne.

'Who is Giovanelli?'

'The little Italian. I have asked questions about him and learned something. He is apparently a perfectly respectable little man. I believe he is in a small way a *cavaliere avvocato*. But he doesn't move in what are called the first circles. I think it is really not absolutely impossible that the courier introduced him. He is evidently immensely charmed with Miss Miller. If she thinks him the finest gentleman in the world, he, on his side, has never found himself in personal contact with such splendour, such opulence, such expensiveness, as this young lady's. And then she must seem to him wonderfully pretty and interesting. I rather doubt whether he dreams of marrying her. That must appear to him too impossible a piece of luck. He has nothing but his handsome face to offer, and there is a substantial Mr Miller in that mysterious land of dollars. Giovanelli knows that he hasn't a title to offer. If he were only a count or a *marchese*! He must wonder at his luck at the way they have taken him up.'

'He accounts for it by his handsome face, and thinks Miss Miller a young lady *qui se passe ses fantaisies*!' said Mrs Costello.

'It is very true,' Winterbourne pursued, 'that Daisy and her mamma have not yet risen to that stage of – what shall I call it? – of culture, at which the idea of catching a count or a *marchese* begins. I believe that they are intellectually incapable of that conception.'

'Ah! but the *cavaliere* can't believe it,' said Mrs Costello.

Of the observation excited by Daisy's 'intrigue', Winterbourne
gathered that day at St Peter's sufficient evidence. A dozen of
the American colonists in Rome came to talk with Mrs Costello,
who sat on a little portable stool at the base of one of the great
pilasters. The vesper-service was going forward in splendid
chants and organ-tones in the adjacent choir, and meanwhile,
between Mrs Costello and her friends, there was a great deal
said about poor little Miss Miller's going really 'too far'.
Winterbourne was not pleased with what he heard; but when,
coming out upon the great steps of the church, he saw Daisy,
who had emerged before him, get into an open cab with her
accomplice and roll away through the cynical streets of Rome,
he could not deny to himself that she was going very far indeed.
He felt very sorry for her – not exactly that he believed that she
had completely lost her head, but because it was painful to
hear so much that was pretty and undefended and natural
assigned to a vulgar place among the categories of disorder.
He made an attempt after this to give a hint to Mrs Miller. He
met one day in the Corso a friend – a tourist like himself – who
had just come out of the Doria Palace, where he had been walking
through the beautiful gallery. His friend talked for a moment
about the superb portrait of Innocent X by Velazquez, which
hangs in one of the cabinets of the palace, and then said, 'And
in the same cabinet, by the way, I had the pleasure of contemplating a picture of a different kind – that pretty American girl
whom you pointed out to me last week.' In answer to Winterbourne's inquiries, his friend narrated that the pretty American
girl – prettier than ever – was seated with a companion in the
secluded nook in which the great papal portrait is enshrined.

'Who was her companion?' asked Winterbourne.

'A little Italian with a bouquet in his buttonhole. The girl is
delightfully pretty, but I thought I understood from you the
other day that she was a young lady *du meilleur monde*.'

'So she is!' answered Winterbourne; and having assured
himself that his informant had seen Daisy and her companion
but five minutes before, he jumped into a cab and went to call on
Mrs Miller. She was at home; but she apologized to him for
receiving him in Daisy's absence.

'She's gone out somewhere with Mr Giovanelli,' said Mrs Miller. 'She's always going round with Mr Giovanelli.'

'I have noticed that they are very intimate,' Winterbourne observed.

'Oh! it seems as if they couldn't live without each other!' said Mrs Miller. 'Well, he's a real gentleman, anyhow. I keep telling Daisy she's engaged!'

'And what does Daisy say?'

'Oh, she says she isn't engaged. But she might as well be!' this impartial parent resumed. 'She goes on as if she was. But I've made Mr Giovanelli promise to tell me, if *she* doesn't. I should want to write to Mr Miller about it – shouldn't you?'

Winterbourne replied that he certainly should; and the state of mind of Daisy's mamma struck him as so unprecedented in the annals of parental vigilance that he gave up as utterly irrelevant the attempt to place her upon her guard.

After this Daisy was never at home, and Winterbourne ceased to meet her at the houses of their common acquaintances, because, as he perceived, these shrewd people had quite made up their minds that she was going too far. They ceased to invite her, and they intimated that they desired to express to observant Europeans the great truth that, though Miss Daisy Miller was a young American lady, her behaviour was not representative – was regarded by her compatriots as abnormal. Winterbourne wondered how she felt about all the cold shoulders that were turned towards her, and sometimes it annoyed him to suspect that she did not feel at all. He said to himself that she was too light and childish, too uncultivated and unreasoning, too provincial, to have reflected upon her ostracism or even to have perceived it. Then at other moments he believed that she carried about in her elegant and irresponsible little organism a defiant, passionate, perfectly observant consciousness of the impression she produced. He asked himself whether Daisy's defiance came from the consciousness of innocence or from her being, essentially, a young person of the reckless class. It must be admitted that holding oneself to a belief in Daisy's 'innocence' came to seem to Winterbourne more and more a matter of fine-spun gallantry. As I have already had occasion to relate, he was angry at finding himself reduced to chopping logic about this young lady; he was vexed at his want of instinctive certitude as to how far her eccentricities were generic, national, and how far they were personal. From either view of them he had somehow missed her, and now it was too late. She was 'carried away' by Mr Giovanelli.

A few days after his brief interview with her mother, he encountered her in that beautiful abode of flowering desolation known as the Palace of the Caesars. The early Roman spring had filled the air with bloom and perfume, and the rugged surface of the Palatine was muffled with tender verdure. Daisy was strolling along the top of one of those great mounds of ruin that are embanked with mossy marble and paved with monumental inscriptions. It seemed to him that Rome had never been so lovely as just then. He stood looking off at the enchanting harmony of line and colour that remotely encircles the city, inhaling the softly humid odours and feeling the freshness of the year and the antiquity of the place reaffirm themselves in mysterious interfusion. It seemed to him also that Daisy had never looked so pretty; but this had been an observation of his whenever he met her. Giovanelli was at her side, and Giovanelli, too, wore an aspect of even unwonted brilliancy.

'Well,' said Daisy, 'I should think you would be lonesome!'

'I onesome?' asked Winterbourne.

'You are always going round by yourself. Can't you get anyone to walk with you?'

'I am not so fortunate,' said Winterbourne, 'as your companion.'

Giovanelli, from the first, had treated Winterbourne with distinguished politeness; he listened with a deferential air to his remarks; he laughed, punctiliously, at his pleasantries; he seemed disposed to testify to his belief that Winterbourne was a superior young man. He carried himself in no degree like a jealous wooer; he had obviously a great deal of tact; he had no objection to your expecting a little humility of him. It even seemed to Winterbourne at times that Giovanelli would find a certain mental relief in being able to have a private understanding with him – to say to him, as an intelligent man, that, bless you, *he* knew how extraordinary was this young lady, and didn't flatter himself with delusive – or at least *too* delusive – hopes of matrimony and dollars. On this occasion he strolled away from his companion to pluck a sprig of almond blossom, which he carefully arranged in his buttonhole.

'I know why you say that,' said Daisy, watching Giovanelli. 'Because you think I go round too much with *him*!' And she nodded at her attendant.

'Everyone thinks so – if you care to know,' said Winterbourne.

'Of course I care to know!' Daisy exclaimed seriously. 'But I don't believe it. They are only pretending to be shocked. They don't really care a straw what I do. Besides, I don't go round so much.'

'I think you will find they do care. They will show it – disagreeably.'

Daisy looked at him a moment. 'How – disagreeably?'

'Haven't you noticed anything?' Winterbourne asked.

'I have noticed you. But I noticed you were as stiff as an umbrella the first time I saw you.'

'You will find I am not so stiff as several others,' said Winterbourne, smiling.

'How shall I find it?'

'By going to see the others.'

'What will they do to me?'

'They will give you the cold shoulder. Do you know what that means?'

Daisy was looking at him intently; she began to colour. 'Do you mean as Mrs Walker did the other night?'

'Exactly!' said Winterbourne.

She looked away at Giovanelli, who was decorating himself with his almond blossom. Then looking back at Winterbourne – 'I shouldn't think you would let people be so unkind!' she said.

'How can I help it?' he asked.

'I should think you would say something.'

'I do say something'; and he paused a moment. 'I say that your mother tells me that she believes you are engaged.'

'Well, she does,' said Daisy very simply.

Winterbourne began to laugh. 'And does Randolph believe it?' he asked.

'I guess Randolph doesn't believe anything,' said Daisy. Randolph's scepticism excited Winterbourne to further hilarity, and he observed that Giovanelli was coming back to them. Daisy, observing it too, addressed herself to her countryman. 'Since you have mentioned it,' she said, 'I *am* engaged.' ... Winterbourne looked at her; he had stopped laughing. 'You don't believe it!' she added.

He was silent a moment; and then, 'Yes, I believe it!' he said.

'Oh, no, you don't,' she answered. 'Well, then – I am not!'

The young girl and her cicerone were on their way to the gate of the enclosure, so that Winterbourne, who had but lately entered, presently took leave of them. A week afterwards he went to dine at a beautiful villa on the Caelian Hill, and, on arriving, dismissed his hired vehicle. The evening was charming, and he promised himself the satisfaction of walking home beneath the Arch of Constantine and past the vaguely lighted monuments of the Forum. There was a waning moon in the sky, and her radiance was not brilliant, but she was veiled in a thin cloud-curtain which seemed to diffuse and equalize it. When, on his return from the villa (it was eleven o'clock), Winterbourne approached the dusky circle of the Colosseum, it occurred to him, as a lover of the picturesque, that the interior, in the pale moonshine, would be well worth a glance. He turned aside and walked to one of the empty arches, near which, as he observed, an open carriage – one of the little Roman street-cabs – was stationed. Then he passed in among the cavernous shadows of the great structure, and emerged upon the clear and silent arena. The place had never seemed to him more impressive. One half of the gigantic circus was in deep shade; the other was sleeping in the luminous dusk. As he stood there he began to murmur Byron's famous lines, out of *Manfred*; but before he had finished his quotation he remembered that if nocturnal meditations in the Colosseum are recommended by the poets, they are deprecated by the doctors. The historic atmosphere was there, certainly; but the historic atmosphere, scientifically considered, was no better than a villainous miasma. Winterbourne walked to the middle of the arena, to take a more general glance, intending thereafter to make a hasty retreat. The great cross in the centre was covered with shadow; it was only as he drew near it that he made it out distinctly. Then he saw that two persons were stationed upon the low steps which formed its base. One of these was a woman, seated; her companion was standing in front of her.

Presently the sound of the woman's voice came to him distinctly in the warm night air. 'Well, he looks at us as one of the old lions or tigers may have looked at the Christian martyrs!' These were the words he heard, in the familiar accent of Miss Daisy Miller.

'Let us hope he is not very hungry,' responded the ingenious Giovanelli. 'He will have to take me first; you will serve for dessert!'

Winterbourne stopped, with a sort of horror; and, it must be added, with a sort of relief. It was as if a sudden illumination had been flashed upon the ambiguity of Daisy's behaviour and the riddle had become easy to read. She was a young lady whom a gentleman need no longer be at pains to respect. He stood there looking at her – looking at her companion, and not reflecting that though he saw them vaguely, he himself must have been more brightly visible. He felt angry with himself that he had bothered so much about the right way of regarding Miss Daisy Miller. Then, as he was going to advance again, he checked himself; not from the fear that he was doing her injustice, but from a sense of the danger of appearing unbecomingly exhilarated by this sudden revulsion from cautious criticism. He turned away towards the entrance of the place; but as he did so he heard Daisy speak again.

'Why, it was Mr Winterbourne! He saw me – and he cuts me!'

What a clever little reprobate she was, and how smartly she played an injured innocence! But he wouldn't cut her. Winterbourne came forward again, and went towards the great cross. Daisy had got up; Giovanelli lifted his hat. Winterbourne had now begun to think simply of the craziness, from a sanitary point of view, of a delicate young girl lounging away the evening in this nest of malaria. What if she *were* a clever little reprobate?

That was no reason for her dying of the *perniciosa*. 'How long have you been here?' he asked, almost brutally.

Daisy, lovely in the flattering moonlight, looked at him a moment. Then – 'All the evening,' she answered gently. . . . 'I never saw anything so pretty.'

'I am afraid,' said Winterbourne, 'that you will not think Roman fever very pretty. This is the way people catch it. I wonder,' he added, turning to Giovanelli, 'that you, a native Roman, should countenance such a terrible indiscretion.'

'Ah,' said the handsome native, 'for myself, I am not afraid.'

'Neither am I – for you! I am speaking for this young lady.'

Giovanelli lifted his well-shaped eyebrows and showed his brilliant teeth. But he took Winterbourne's rebuke with docility. 'I told the Signorina it was a grave indiscretion; but when was the Signorina ever prudent?'

'I never was sick, and I don't mean to be!' the Signorina declared. 'I don't look like much, but I'm healthy! I was bound to see the Colosseum by moonlight; I shouldn't have wanted to go home without that; and we have had the most beautiful time, haven't we, Mr Giovanelli! If there has been any danger, Eugenio can give me some pills. He has got some splendid pills.'

'I should advise you,' said Winterbourne, 'to drive home as fast as possible and take one!'

'What you say is very wise,' Giovanelli rejoined. 'I will go and make sure the carriage is at hand.' And he went forward rapidly.

Daisy followed with Winterbourne. He kept looking at her; she seemed not in the least embarrassed. Winterbourne said nothing; Daisy chattered about the beauty of the place. 'Well, I *have* seen the Colosseum by moonlight!' she exclaimed. 'That's one good thing.' Then, noticing Winterbourne's silence, she asked him why he didn't speak. He made no answer; he only began to laugh. They passed under one of the dark archways; Giovanelli was in front with the carriage. Here Daisy stopped a moment, looking at the young American. '*Did* you believe I was engaged the other day?' she asked.

'It doesn't matter what I believed the other day,' said Winterbourne, still laughing.

'Well, what do you believe now?'

'I believe that it makes very little difference whether you are engaged or not!'

He felt the young girl's pretty eyes fixed upon him through the thick gloom of the archway; she was apparently going to answer. But Giovanelli hurried her forward. 'Quick, quick,' he said; 'if we get in by midnight we are quite safe.'

Daisy took her seat in the carriage, and the fortunate Italian placed himself beside her. 'Don't forget Eugenio's pills!' said Winterbourne, as he lifted his hat.

'I don't care,' said Daisy, in a little strange tone, 'whether I have Roman fever or not!' Upon this the cab-driver cracked his whip, and they rolled away over the desultory patches of the antique pavement.

Winterbourne – to do him justice, as it were – mentioned to no one that he had encountered Miss Miller, at midnight, in the Colosseum with a gentleman; but nevertheless, a couple of days later, the fact of her having been there under these circumstances was known to every member of the little American circle, and commented accordingly. Winterbourne reflected that they had of course known it at the hotel, and that, after Daisy's return, there had been an exchange of jokes between the porter and the cab-driver. But the young man was conscious at the same moment that it had ceased to be a matter of serious regret to him that the little American flirt should be 'talked about' by low-minded menials. These people, a day or two later, had serious information to give: the little American flirt was alarmingly ill. Winter-bourne, when the rumour came to him, immediately went to the hotel for more news. He found that two or three charitable friends had preceded him, and that they were being entertained in Mrs Miller's salon by Randolph.

'It's going round at night,' said Randolph – 'that's what made her sick. She's always going round at night. I shouldn't think she'd want to – it's so plaguey dark. You can't see anything here at night, except when there's a moon. In America there's always a moon!' Mrs Miller was invisible; she was now, at least, giving her daughter the advantage of her society. It was evident that Daisy was dangerously ill.

Winterbourne went often to ask for news of her, and once he

saw Mrs Miller, who, though deeply alarmed, was – rather to his surprise – perfectly composed, and, as it appeared, a most efficient and judicious nurse. She talked a good deal about Dr Davis, but Winterbourne paid her the compliment of saying to himself that she was not, after all, such a monstrous goose. 'Daisy spoke of you the other day,' she said to him. 'Half the time she doesn't know what she's saying, but that time I think she did. She gave me a message; she told me to tell you. She told me to tell you that she never was engaged to that handsome Italian. I am sure I am very glad; Mr Giovanelli hasn't been near us since she was taken ill. I thought he was so much of a gentleman; but I don't call that very polite! A lady told me that he was afraid I was angry with him for taking Daisy round at night. Well, so I am; but I suppose he knows I'm a lady. I would scorn to scold him. Anyway, she says she's not engaged. I don't know why she wanted you to know; but she said to me three times – "Mind you tell Mr Winterbourne." And then she told me to ask if you remembered the time you went to that castle, in Switzerland. But I said I wouldn't give any such messages as that. Only, if she is not engaged, I'm sure I'm glad to know it.'

But, as Winterbourne had said, it mattered very little. A week after this the poor girl died; it had been a terrible case of the fever. Daisy's grave was in the little Protestant cemetery, in an angle of the wall of imperial Rome, beneath the cypresses and the thick spring flowers. Winterbourne stood there beside it, with a number of other mourners; a number larger than the scandal excited by the young lady's career would have led you to expect. Near him stood Giovanelli, who came nearer still before Winterbourne turned away. Giovanelli was very pale; on this occasion he had no flower in his buttonhole; he seemed to wish to say something. At last he said, 'She was the most beautiful young lady I ever saw, and the most amiable.' And then he added in a moment, 'And she was the most innocent.'

Winterbourne looked at him, and presently repeated his words, 'And the most innocent?'

'The most innocent!'

Winterbourne felt sore and angry. 'Why the devil,' he asked, 'did you take her to that fatal place?'

Mr Giovanelli's urbanity was apparently imperturbable. He looked on the ground a moment, and then he said, 'For myself, I had no fear; and she wanted to go.'

'That was no reason!' Winterbourne declared.

The subtle Roman again dropped his eyes. 'If she had lived, I should have got nothing. She would never have married me, I am sure.'

'She would never have married you?'

'For a moment I hoped so. But no, I am sure.'

Winterbourne listened to him; he stood staring at the raw protuberance among the April daisies. When he turned away again Mr Giovanelli, with his light slow step, had retired.

Winterbourne almost immediately left Rome; but the following summer he again met his aunt, Mrs Costello, at Vevey. Mrs Costello was fond of Vevey. In the interval Winterbourne had often thought of Daisy Miller and her mystifying manners. One day he spoke of her to his aunt – said it was on his conscience that he had done her injustice.

'I am sure I don't know,' said Mrs Costello. 'How did your injustice affect her?'

'She sent me a message before her death which I didn't understand at the time. But I have understood it since. She would have appreciated one's esteem.'

'Is that a modest way,' asked Mrs Costello, 'of saying that she would have reciprocated one's affection?'

Winterbourne offered no answer to this question; but he presently said, 'You were right in that remark that you made last summer. I was booked to make a mistake. I have lived too long in foreign parts.'

Nevertheless, he went back to live at Geneva, whence there continue to come the most contradictory accounts of his motives of sojourn: a report that he is 'studying' hard – an intimation that he is much interested in a very clever foreign lady.